Renée Vivien
&
Hélène de Zuylen de Nyevelt

FAUSTINA

AND OTHER STORIES

Translated and with an Introduction by

Brian Stableford

THIS IS A SNUGGLY BOOK

ISBN: 978-1-943813-85-8

Contents

Introduction

THIS is the second of three volumes translating prose works by Pauline Mary Tarn (1877-1909); the first, *Lilith's Legacy: Prose Poems and Short Stories,* contains all the shorter prose works signed with her best-known pseudonym, originally "R. Vivien" and subsequently "Renée Vivien." This second volume contains stories that were published in *Netsuké* (Alphonse Lemerre 1904), signed "Paule Riversdale"—a pseudonym used jointly by Pauline Tarn and Baroness Héléne van Zuylen van Nijevelt van de Haar (née Hélène de Rothschild, 1863-1947)—and stories published in *Copeaux* (Lemerre, dated 1904 but probably actually published in 1905), bearing the signature Hélène de Zuylen de Nyevelt, the version of her name used for publication by the Baroness. The third volume will contain the two works entitled *Une Femme m'apparut* that Tarn published as Renée Vivien in 1904 and 1905 respectively, which are too dissimilar to be considered merely as a single work that underwent revision between editions.

Although *Netsuké* was published before *Copeaux,* as was the collection of short fiction *La Dame à la louve* (tr. as "The She-Wolf Lady" in *Lilith's Legacy*), also published in 1904 by Lemerre, bearing the signature Renée Vivien, the work contained in the three collections had probably been accumulated over time and was sorted thematically rather than chronologically, so I felt free to place the stories in the later collection first in the present volume, as that seemed to produce a more esthetically-satisfactory arrangement. It also seems probable, with the aid of hindsight, that the reason the three collections bear three different signatures might have more to do with the decision to avoid an apparent glut of publications under a single signature than to distinguish their authorship precisely. Although Hélène de Zuylen surely made some contribution to the collection bearing her name, and to the Paule Riversdale volume, it was probably minor in both cases, stylistic and thematic analysis suggesting strongly that the bulk of the material, even in *Copeaux*, was Pauline Tarn's.

The introduction to *Lilith's Legacy* contains a brief overview of Pauline Tarn's life and career, which there is no need to repeat here in full. It is, however, crucial to an understanding of the work in this volume that Tarn had had a close relationship with the American socialite Natalie Barney in 1899-1901, which she broke off when she transferred her affection to Hélène de Zuylen; throughout her relationship with Zuylen, Barney tried frequently to win her back, and Tarn appears to have felt torn between them, unable to decide how to move forward in her love life, until she finally decided to break with both of them in 1906—a decision that did not put an end to the contest, or to her confusion.

That confusion was further compounded by the fact that Tarn felt compelled to keep her lesbianism secret, at least from her mother and sister—who lived in London—and although Natalie Barney made no secret of the fact that she was a lesbian, the married Zuylen would not acknowledge her own lesbianism publicly, so her affair with Tarn was conducted clandestinely. Thus, although the work published under the names "Paule Riversdale" and "Renée Vivien" often featured explicitly lesbian themes, the stories in *Copeaux* do not, although reading between the lines suggests that some of the items have significant subtexts— blatantly obvious ones in such stories as "La Princesse captive" (tr. as "The Captive Princess")—and that several of them are surely reflections on the problematic relationship that existed between the two authors.

Pauline Tarn's sexuality eventually became common knowledge in Paris society, along with the knowledge that she was "Renée Vivien," although she does seem to have protected her family from London gossip. She went so far as to publish a selection from her earlier works, carefully eliminating all lesbian themes, under the signature "Pauline M. Tarn," which she seems to have done specifically with her family in mind. Tarn's biographer, Jean Goujon, observes with regret that it was impossible for him to determine how much, or exactly what, the Baroness' family might have known about her secrets, because all her papers were lost when—along with the rest of the Rothschild family, into which she had been born—she fled Paris in a hurry during the German invasion of 1940.

Although one more short story collection and two novels appeared under the signature Hélène de Zuylen de Nyevelt after *Copeaux*, and it was also attached to five plays, Zuylen published very little after Tarn's death, and nothing at all after the outbreak of the Great War. Her Dutch husband was the president of the Automobile Club de France, and she involved herself in motor racing from the very beginning of the sport; motoring and the careful refurbishment of her husband's family home in Utrecht seem to have been her principal occupations, alongside which her sexual relationships and writing only occupied a relatively small segment of her activity. She did, however, found the Renée Vivien Prize in 1935, in order to give annual encouragement to French female poets, and the short story collection *L'Inoubliée* [The Unforgotten] (1910) is a manifest, if somewhat disguised, tribute to Tarn. The novels *La Dernière étreinte* [The Last Embrace] (1912) and *L'Enjoleuse* [The Cajoler, or The Tease] (1914) might also be regarded as masked tributes. If it were not for Pauline Tarn's involvement in it, therefore, Hélène de Zuylen's literary work would be of relatively little interest, and it is that involvement which recommends the stories in the present volume for attention.

At first glance, the stories in *Copeaux* seem markedly different in manner and theme from the two volumes of prose poems that had been published under the Vivien pseudonym in 1902 and 1903, although some of them—notably "Paroles des Saisons" (tr. as "What the Seasons Say")—are, in fact, prose poems. Even in the longer items, however, there are sufficient links, thematically and methodically, to those earlier works to provide strong evidence of connection and evolution. There are similar strong connections between the Orientalia in *Copeaux* and the more narrowly focused Orientalia that fills the whole of *Netsuké*. There are also links between some of the items in *Copeaux* and the highly distinctive exercises in misandry that make up the bulk of *La Dame à la louve*, although the misandry of *Copeaux* is considerably more subtle and less aggressive, as in the wry comedy "Invraisemblable histoire de Prosper Prouvost" (tr. as "The Improbable Story of Prosper Prouvost").

In spite of the careful moderation of its misandry, the tacitly female narrative viewpoint gives an extra cutting edge to all the stories in *Copeaux* that feature male protagonists, especially sharp in the sardonic and sarcastic *femme fatale* story "Faustina." Although, as previously noted, there is nothing in *Copeaux* that resembles the items of fervent lesbian propaganda that feature in the concluding sections of both *La Dame à la louve* and *Nesuké*, let alone the ardent advocacy of *Une Femme m'apparut*, it is worth noting that some of the stories hinge on problematic confrontations between two female characters, which are simultaneously affectionate and adversarial—or, to use one of Tarn's favorite oxymoronic pairings, sweet and bitter. Although that kind of staging is by no means obsessive, it does crop up frequently enough to be considered something of a preoccupation. Far more frequent, however, perhaps sufficiently to qualify as an obsession, is a preoccupation and fascination with death, constant in almost all of Pauline Tarn's work

The more extravagant exercises in symbolism included in *Copeaux*, including "Paroles des Saisons," not only have strong thematic affinities with the prose poems in the Vivien collection *Du Vert au Violet* (1903; tr. as "From Green to Violet") but also share the same highly distinctive quality that isolates them from other Symbolist works using a similar lexicon of symbols. Even the doyenne of female Decadent Symbolists, Rachilde, never matched the flamboyance or the ferocity of the cited portmanteau's disillusionment, and Tarn's work in the pure Symbolist vein, even the fraction of it possibly wrought in collaboration with Hélène de Zuylen, represents a uniquely acute facet of the Decadent polyhedron.

The first section of stories in *Netsuké* mostly consists of straightforward recyclings of traditional Japanese tales, not collected from source—Tarn had not yet visited Japan in 1904—but from previous popularizations in French and English. The second section, bearing the subtitle "Contes Chinois" [Chinese Tales], is similar, although the improvisations and transfigurations are a little more ambitious, but the third section, "Après le Japonais" [In the Japanese Style] includes some wholly original stories, which are more striking, and perhaps more revealing, thus comprising an appropriate conclusion to the present volume.

As noted in the introduction to the first volume of the trio, it is as much by virtue of her idiosyncrasies as because of her considerable, if somewhat inconsistent, artistry that Pauline Tarn was, and still remains, a fascinating writer. The items in *Netsuké* and *Copeaux* appear to have been deliberately separated out, in the first case in order to concentrate, and in the second to eliminate, certain aspects of her work, but in alliance they nevertheless provide a significant testament to her versatility and artistry. The present volume therefore provides a highly significant supplement to *Lilith's Legacy* in illustrating the magnitude of Pauline Tarn's literary achievement and the uncommonly broad spectrum of her interests. This volume and its predecessor, in combination, offer a panoramic overview of her shorter prose endeavors.

The translations of the stories from *Copeaux* were made from a copy of the Lemerre edition. The translations of the stories from *Netsuké* were made from a copy of the 2014 reprint of the collection published by ErosOnyx in the Collection Classiques series, under the signature Renée Vivien. I have omitted some material from *Copeaux,* including a long poem allegedly translated from an Indian source (although I have retained a shorter item of the same sort) and five brief stories, some of which are anecdotal items of a trivial nature and one a straightforward dramatization of a brief passage in the Old Testament. I have omitted one poem from the final section of *Netsuké.*

—Brian Stableford.

FAUSTINA

AND OTHER STORIES

WOODCHIPS

The Son of the Seven Blind Ranis
A Hindu Tale

A very powerful Rajah was the husband of seven Ranis who were all equally beautiful and equally beloved, but all of whom remained sterile.

The Rajah was a passionate hunter. He took pleasure in vast deployments of his beaters in the jungle, and struggles with furious tigers. One day, as he was getting ready to mount a sumptuously-caparisoned elephant, the seven Ranis each sent him an anxious and desolate message. All of them begged him not to turn his steps northwards, because they had been tormented by a bad dream. A peril would take the Rajah by surprise if he headed northwards, they said.

The Rajah listened in silence to the seven messengers of the seven Ranis. Then he accorded the seven Ranis his formidable oath not to turn his steps northwards that day.

The seven messengers of the seven Ranis returned, their souls reassured, to their mistresses. But the youngest Rani continued weeping, in spite of the formidable oath made by the Rajah before his departure for the hunt. The youngest Rani wept, and could not be consoled.

For a long time, the Rajah wandered in the jungle. He headed eastwards, without finding any royal game. Then he turned westwards and southwards, also in vain. Then, exasperated by the futile pursuit, the Rajah, as passionate a hunter as he was an amorous husband, forgot the oath he had made to the seven Ranis and turned his steps toward the north.

So, the Rajah turned northwards. At that moment he saw a white gazelle with golden horns and silver hooves fleeing through the lianas, like a flash of lightning in the green darkness of the jungle. His heart rejoicing at that royal prey, the Rajah ordered his servants to corner the white gazelle with the silver hooves and the golden horns; but the gazelle, eluding their cunning, ran through the lianas and fled toward a familiar mountain.

The Rajah pursued the royal game until dusk. Carried away by the ardor of the hunt, he left the crowd of his servants behind. Alone, he was obstinate in the pursuit of the white gazelle with the golden horns and the silver hooves. For seven days and seven nights he pursued the mysterious beast without respite. He pursued it all the way to the highest peak of the neighboring country, and saw it enter, with a single bound, a miserable hut at the top of the mountain.

The hunter followed it, intoxicated by his cruel triumph.

Having crossed the threshold he stopped, struck by amazement.

An old woman was crouching before a pot of rice that was simmering in the hearth. The red flames lit up her face, similar to that of the Demoness who serves Kali, the goddess of murder and death. The weight of the years curbed her shoulders and bent her back. She was almost venerable in her ancient ferocity.

Approaching the old woman, the Rajah interrogated her about the inexplicable flight of the gazelle with the golden horns. The old woman muttered a few words in an unknown language.

Suddenly, the darkness of the hut was illuminated, and was filled by harmony and strange perfumes, and the Rajah saw a virgin surge forth before him, whiter than the snows of Gwashbrari, the mountain of the luminous glaciers. Having only seen and loved the amber flesh of the seven Ranis, the Rajah was dazzled by an ecstatic astonishment. The hair of the unknown woman was fluid gold, and her feet were silvery, like the moon.

Before that magical and sovereign beauty, the Rajah forgot the world. He did not realize that the woman who had put on the form of a white gazelle in order to lure him, and then the appearance of a radiant virgin, was a very powerful and exceedingly cruel dayan.[1] Prostrating himself at her feet, he, a redoubted and redoubtable Rajah, begged her to share his bed.

The unknown woman refused, smiling, and said to him: "O Rajah, you are the husband of seven wives, and I want a husband to love me who will only cherish my image uniquely."

The Rajah having begged her again, however, she finally replied: "Bring me as a wedding present the eyes of the seven Ranis, your wives."

Mad with desire and amour, the Rajah returned to his palace. He had the eyes of the seven Ranis, his wives, plucked out; and on his orders, the seven blind Ranis were thrown into a dungeon where impious women had once died of starvation.

---

1 Author's note: "A witch."

The Rajah brought the dayan the eyes of the seven Ranis, his wives, as a wedding present; and the woman who had put on the form of a white gazelle with golden horns and silver hooves uttered an evil laugh on receiving the necklace of dark eyes. Having received the necklace from the Rajah's hands, she put it around the wrinkled neck of her mother, the old kutni,[1] who wore it proudly, like a necklace of black diamonds.

Then, getting to her feet, the virgin with the silver feet and golden hair went with the Rajah to the palace of the seven Ranis. She sparkled with the jewels and crowns of the seven Ranis and became the Rajah's unique Rani.

The seven blind Ranis languished in the funereal dungeon where impious women had once died of starvation. Days without sunlight and nights without stars went by. The youngest of the seven Ranis, who had been pregnant when she was thrown into the funereal dungeon, gave birth to a vigorous and handsome son there.

The seven Ranis, fearing for the life of the child, who had come to illuminate their long darkness with his laughter and his voice, concealed his birth from the jailers, and the seven Ranis surrounded him with an equally fervent tenderness.

When the child, the son of the seven blind Ranis, had grown for five or six years in the darkness of the funereal dungeon, the Rajah gave the order to allow the seven royal prisoners to die of starvation, and the horrors of hunger tortured the seven blind Ranis.

In their despair, they conceived a very simple ruse. Their bloody fingernails hollowed out a passage through the wall of dried mud, large enough for the little body of a child

____

1 Author: "A witch of inferior rank."

8

to pass through, but too small to attract the suspicious attention of the jailers. Before dawn, the unique son of the seven blind Ranis slid through the wall of dried mud.

He went to beg in the plains and in the streets. In order to make passers-by sympathetic, he sang the plaintive songs that he had been taught in the funereal dungeon by his seven blind mothers; and the songs were so ingenuously sad and tender that the passers-by took pity on him and lavished the little beggar with rice cakes, pieces of sugar cane, mangoes and maize. And when night fell, the unique son of the seven blind Ranis slid through the wall of dried mud and brought his seven mothers the obliging offerings that he had collected for them.

The seven blind Ranis ate and rejoiced. Every day from then on, before dawn, their unique son slid through the wall of dried mud and, having obtained rice cakes and mangoes by begging, brought them back at nightfall.

The seven Ranis spent several tenebrous years in that fashion. When the child reached adolescence, he stopped begging. Having inherited from his father a love of fine hunts, he went to track game in the jungle. When night fell, he brought the produce of his hunting to his blind mothers.

One day, proud of his bow and quiver, he went past the palace where the seven dethroned Ranis had once been resplendent in their glory. At that moment, the dayan was triumphant there in her cruel joy. The unique son of the seven blind Ranis passed insouciantly in front of the palace of his seven dethroned mothers.

Seeing a flock of blue and mauve silky pigeons circling around the windows, the adolescent took aim at one of them and brought it down adroitly with a light arrow.

Now, the white Rani—the white Rani with the golden hair and the silver feet, the Rani who, in the form of a gazelle, had lured the Rajah to the hut where she had revealed herself in her splendor as a woman—had chanced to raise the blind at her window. She saw the dead pigeon fall at the feet of the adolescent; and, possessing all the secrets of magic, she recognized in the adolescent hunter the son of the Rajah, the unique son whose birth had been concealed by the seven blind mothers.

Simultaneously angry and fearful, divining in that adolescent a future avenger, the dayan resolved to make him perish. She therefore leaned out and appeared to him, all white beneath her heavy golden hair. Having sent a messenger to the son of the seven blind mothers, she had him enter her royal audience chamber, among cushions of silk and Cashmere, musical instruments and odorous vapors escaping from cassolettes.

As white as the moon, she proposed to the adolescent to buy the pigeon he had just killed from him; but the son of the seven dethroned Ranis replied with a polite refusal, for, he said, he had to take the pigeon back to his seven blind mothers, whom he nourished with the produce of his bow.

The royal dayan listened patiently. Then, getting to her feet, all white and golden, she told him that she had the power to render to the seven blind mothers the living eyes that had once been plucked out on the cruel order of the Rajah. And the adolescent, seeing that white and golden woman, so different from the brown women of his homeland, understood that the stranger possessed marvelous secrets and unknown talismans. He accepted the proposal that she made him, that he should give her the pigeon in exchange for the eyes of his seven blind mothers, joyfully.

The royal dayan commanded the adolescent to search for the hut where she had appeared to the Rajah, white beneath her long golden hair. "Find a solitary cabin," she said to him, "at the summit of the highest mountain of the neighboring country. There you will find an old woman crouching before a pot of fuming rice. She is wearing a necklace of living eyes around her neck, the eyes of your seven blind mothers. Hand the old woman this shard of pottery, on which I have traced bizarre characters. She will immediately return to you the necklace of living eyes that she wears around her neck, the eyes of your seven blind mothers."

The adolescent considered, without understanding them, the bizarre characters that the white and golden Rani had traced with her milky fingers. Now, those characters had a terrible meaning. The dayan ordered her old mother, whose visage was similar to the visage of the servant of Kali, to kill the person who brought her that message.

The unique son of the seven Ranis immediately set forth in search of the seven pairs of living eyes that the terrible old woman wore around her neck in the guise of a necklace.

While traversing the capital of the neighboring land, he saw that its entire population was lamenting desperately. When he interrogated the passers-by that he encountered about the cause of the universal mourning, they replied that, the daughter of the Rajah having refused to take a husband, the sacred race was going to die out.

The lineage that was about to disappear thus was simultaneously merciful to the humble and terrible to oppressors, and the people, who loved the Ranis and Rajahs of that noble race, lamented seeing it disappear forever. The only daughter of the Rajah had sworn before the altar of Kali only to marry the unique son of seven mothers.

The adolescent also learned that the unique daughter of the Rajah was as chaste as the lotuses of the seven sacred pools in the gardens of the goddesses. As well as being as chaste as the sacred lotuses, she was knowledgeable in the precious art of supernatural things. She had knowledge of the times to come and the worlds beyond the terrestrial world. She was familiar with the spirits of light and darkness.

The adolescent presented himself before the Rajah's daughter. He revealed to her that, being the unique son of seven mothers, he was the husband marked out for her by fate. The daughter of the Rajah, very knowledgeable and very wise, understood that the stranger was telling the truth, and that he was indeed the husband sent to her by destiny.

The Rajah's daughter was as radiant as a brown sun with all the splendor of her amber body. Her eyes were lakes of darkness. As beautiful as the night, she appeared to him, ardently perfumed; and the Rajah's daughter held out her hand to the stranger. She took him by the hand and they both went through the city. Dazzled, they walked hand in hand without hearing the clamors of delight that greeted them and without seeing the happy multitude that enveloped them in tender gazes.

They walked thus, radiant and proud of loving one another. And toward evening, sitting under the magnolias, the future husband of the Rajah's daughter told her the story of his mysterious existence and the misfortune of the seven blind Ranis, his dolorously passionate mothers.

The Rajah's daughter listened to the young man with a pensive mildness. Having the compassionate soul of a woman in love, she commanded the unique son of the seven blind Ranis to recover the living eyes of his mothers before espousing her in front of the people.

Confident in the wisdom of his royal fiancée, the young man showed her the fragment of pottery on which was inscribed, in bizarre characters, the white Rani's order. And the very knowledgeable and very wise fiancée understood the murderous inscription. On a fragment of pottery exactly similar to the first, she wrote a contrary order in the same bizarre characters: *Act in accordance with the desire of this young man, for he is my servant and my envoy.*

Knowing that men are inconsiderate and talkative, however, the Rajah's daughter did not reveal the subterfuge to her future husband.

When the unique son of the seven blind Ranis went into the hut, he saw the old mother of the royal dayan crouching before the fuming pot of rice. After having examined the bizarre characters traced on the shard of pottery for a long time, she asked him what he desired; and, on his response, she detached the necklace of living eyes that ornamented her neck, cursing.

The unique son of the seven blind Ranis saw, sadly, that the necklace was composed of thirteen eyes and no longer fourteen, for the old women with a demonic face had devoured one of the eyes. A bitterness was mingled with his delight, and he understood, in his heroic and joyful young soul, that no felicity is pure of new desires or regrets.

When he returned to the funeral dungeon he rendered their living eyes to the first six Ranis. To the youngest Rani he returned one unique eye, weeping. He promised to take the place of the vanished eye, by means of his vigilance and his clairvoyant tenderness.

The adolescent quit the seven Ranis in order to rejoin his very knowledgeable and very wise future wife. As he was passing the palace of the white Rani, however, he saw for a second time the flock of blue and mauve pigeons circling in the sunlight. And, taking aim at a silky pigeon with a light arrow, he brought it down . . .

The Rani with the golden hair and silver feet heard a great flutter of wings at her window; she raised the blind, and the young man she had sent to his death appeared, triumphant. The royal dayan conceived a jealous dolor in consequence. She sent one of her servants to the young man.

He found himself once again in the presence of the mysterious woman, strangely white beneath her golden hair; and as he had the candid soul of a hero, he told the ingenuous story of his fortunate adventures, without malice.

When the white Rani learned that the adolescent had returned their living eyes to her seven rivals, she burned with an anger more vehement than amour. Then she traced, with a feverish hand, the same bizarre characters on a shard of pottery. Those bizarre characters composed a cruel order to kill the messenger and spread his young fuming blood like water.

Having traced the murderous order she turned to the son of the seven Ranis and begged him to give her the pigeon that he had just killed. She promised him in exchange the miraculous Cow of the Joghi, the Cow whose inexhaustible milk is so abundant that it forms a lake as large as a kingdom. Her mother, she said, would render the adolescent the possessor of the miraculous Cow, when he had brought her the fragment of pottery.

Having the candid soul of a hero, the adolescent listened without suspicion to the royal dayan. Before returning to the old woman with the demonic visage, however, he traversed the kingdom of his future wife; and the adolescent was drawn by amour to the Rajah's daughter, who was waiting for him, brown and perfumed, and burning beneath her golden veils. The two of them exchanged long speeches and long silences beneath the magnolias.

Having read the murderous order of the white Rani, the very knowledgeable and very wise fiancée chose another fragment of pottery, identical to the first, and traced, in the same bizarre characters, a contrary order: *Act in accordance with the desire of this young man, for he is my servant and my envoy.*

Knowing that men are inconsiderate and talkative, however, the Rajah's daughter did not reveal the subterfuge to her future husband.

When the adolescent entered the hut where the old woman with the demonic visage was crouching, the latter read the order inscribed on the shard of pottery with an astonished fury. And having read it, she showed him the mysterious route that leads to the sacred pasture where the miraculous Cow of the Joghi browses placidly. She told him the words that he had to pronounce when the Joghi interrogated him.

Having followed the mysterious route through the water and the mountains, the adolescent reached the sacred plain. The Cow, jealously guarded by eighteen thousand djinn, was grazing serenely among strange flowers and unknown perfumes. She was browsing blue grass, and her horned head disappeared in the clouds. The sacred milk ran from her udders like white rain, and formed an opaque and luminous river.

Seeing a mortal in the celestial pasture, the Joghi interrogated him in a grim tone. The adolescent replied, in accordance with the recommendations of the prescient kutni, that he was the envoy of King Indra; for King Indra, who accords the rain, is the lord of the Marouts, savage and demonic winds, the Joghis and the Djinn.

On hearing the name of the lord of the Marouts, the Joghi trembled in all his thin limbs. The adolescent also told the Joghi that King Indra had sent him to him in order to take his desiccated skin, for King Indra wanted that skin, expertly prepared, for the sacred drums that humans call thunder.

The Joghi, prostrate at the adolescent's feet, begged him to spare him, promising to give him the miraculous Cow whose horned head disappeared in the clouds. The son of seven mothers pretended to consent to that exchange, and took away the miraculous Cow.

The seven Ranis welcomed their returned son and the divine Beast that had followed him faithfully with joy. The inexhaustible milk made them richer than the Rajah himself, for they sold that milk not only to the inhabitants of the kingdom, but to all the habitants of the neighboring kingdoms.

The adolescent, his heart light, then set forth to return to the Rajah's daughter, his future wife. But as he was passing the palace of the white Rani, he saw for the third time, circling around the scintillating roof, the flock of mauve and blue pigeons. For the third time, he launched an arrow, which hit one of the birds. And for the third time, the white Rani, hearing a great flutter of wings, raised the blind. White beneath her golden hair, she sent one of her servants to the adolescent.

When he was in her presence, she interrogated him. Having the candid soul of a hero, the adolescent narrated his fortunate adventures without malice.

Then the white Rani, in her jealous fury, traced bizarre characters on a shard of pottery again; and, handing them to the young man, she promised him, in exchange for the pigeon he had just killed, the miraculous Rice that grows in a single azure night and covers three kingdoms with its quivering ears. The adolescent was not at all astonished by that prodigious exchange, having the simple and candid soul of a hero.

The Rajah's daughter was waiting for him with an intoxicated anguish under the magnolias; and when the unique son of the seven mothers had shown her the fragment of pottery she changed the deadly inscription and traced the words: *Obey my servant's orders as you would obey my own.* And without dread, the Rajah's daughter sent her future husband to the kutni with the demonic visage.

Crouching before the fuming pot, the old woman welcomed her daughter's messenger with a muted anger, but she was so basely fearful of the terrible dayan who had once emerged from her womb that she obeyed the order inscribed on the fragment of broken pottery. She showed the adolescent the mysterious route that leads to the field of the miraculous Rice.

She recommended him to have no fear of the eighteen million Marouts and Djinn that guard the Rice. He had to traverse the field without terror, and pluck without terror the tallest ear, which grew in the exact center of the sacred field; but in carrying his marvelous trophy away, he must not turn round.

Thus, the adolescent having attained his goal, found himself in the field guarded by eighteen million Marouts and Djinn. While he traversed the sacred field, the contrary winds fell silent and the Djinn floated silently over his passage like uncertain shadows.

Without terror, he plucked the tallest ear, which rose up in the exact center of the sacred field. Gloriously, he was carrying away his trophy when he heard the melodious appeal of feminine voices behind him. With a poignant softness, those voices begged him: "Pluck us too, O valiant one!"

The hero remembered the advice of the old woman, and he did not turn round; but one voice softer than all the others rose above them, musically tender: "Pluck me as you have plucked the sacred ear, O valiant one!" And that voice was the voice of the Rajah's daughter, the promised spouse.

Forgetful of everything except his vivacious amour, the hero turned round, believing that he would see behind him the brown and perfumed image of the promised spouse . . . but the laughter of breezes and the clamors of wind rose up, and the hero fell, thunderstruck. Only a few sparse ashes marked the place where he had passed, joyful and young and triumphant.

Thus the unique son of the seven Ranis died, on the threshold of his desire. He took away the best Victory of all: the first red intoxication that precedes disgust. And he took away the sweetest amour of all: the first desire that precedes lassitude. The Rajah's daughter, his promised wife, understood and was glad to retain in her heart an amour that was eternal, being unsated . . .

Faustina

PUBLIUS AVIDIUS FLACCUS was a poor poet who was worth neither more nor less than the majority of men; for those who place poets above the multitude are strangely mistaken. The soul of a poet only differs from common souls by virtue of a keener faculty of suffering.

Avidius was wandering through the sunlit streets of Rome. He had just finished some rather bad verses, imitations of Virgil. An inhabitant of cities, he celebrated bucolic splendors. Avidius was not a good poet; his mind was too ingenuously passionate to triumph over complicated and subtle rhythms. Avidius was very young. He was neither handsomer nor uglier than the majority of men—which is to say that he possessed a mediocre face, except that the bright laughter of his youth animated his mouth and illuminated his eyes.

On a day of indolence, Publius Avidius Flaccus was wandering the streets of Rome without darting a glance at the prostitutes who passed beside him. Their heavy tresses, the color of dark wine, did not attract his uncertain pupils. Their loose robes did not draw him into their perfumed wake. Avidius disdained the welcoming beauty of prostitutes, for Avidius was in love. Better and worse than that, he was in love with a name.

Faustina!

That sovereign name hovered over all lips. It sang there like an insidious music. It quivered there like a perfidious confession.

Faustina!

Rome entire vibrated with the echoes of that soft and sonorous name. Faustina, the sumptuous wife of Antoninus Pius, whom the army and the plebs had recognized as Caesar Augustus, had just received the title of Augusta.[1] She bore it with pride and grace, like an adornment. In speaking of her, the crowds translated their scornful amour. She was said to be very beautiful and imperiously voluptuous. Avidius knew that men had desired her to the extent of murder and the point of death.

Gradually, the ardor of the dream had slid into his veins. Avidius wanted to contemplate, with his dazzled eyes, the image evoked with so much fervor. Knowing that the Empress was to take her place beside the Caesar for the circus games, he resolved to go there. Faustina loved the fumes of blood and the glorious gasps of wounded gladiators. Avidius, although he was an amorous, pastoral and pacific poet, rejoiced in the thought of that festival of massacre.

Faustina!

---

1 Annia Galeria Faustina, sometimes known as Faustina I (100-140 A.D.) died not long after her husband, Antoninus Pius, was proclaimed emperor in 138, but she retained a quasi-legendary status, continuing to play an important symbolic role in his reign, as a deity, to whom the Temple of Faustina was erected in the Forum and in whose name a charity for the support of female orphans was established. Antoninus and Faustina were frequently cited thereafter as exemplars of conjugal harmony.

The musical name mingled with the sonority of clarions and the glorious gasps of wounded gladiators, Rome entire clamored it, howled it and sang it with scorn, with terror and with passion.

Faustina!

The scarlet dawn finally rose on the scarlet day. Avidius, his heart disordered, joined the multitude that was hurrying toward the arenas. The sun caused the stones to vibrate with a dormant and lukewarm life. Smiling women were selling bunches of flowers that put a silent beauty into the agitated streets. The sky was impassively blue. Everything exhaled a glad indifference. While walking, Avidius respired a cruel felicity, universally spread.

The sun sang over the city. The sun sang over the arenas. Hastily, Avidius climbed the steps and sat down, in a tumultuous internal joy.

The people were waiting. The Empress and the Emperor had not yet come to take their places among the spectators, above the combatants. The people were waiting. A murmur quivered, and was exacerbated.

Faustina!

It was her to whom the people appealed mutedly, desired and adored with scorn. She was the one who would smile triumphantly at the death of men. It was toward her that the fumes of blood and the glorious gasps of wounded gladiators would shortly rise up

The people repeated the terrible and dear name: "Faustina!"

Suddenly, Avidius tottered and went pale. Anoninus Pius' cortege entered and unfurled slowly.

The universe was sparkling before his dazzled gaze. The universe was buzzing in his ears. Vaguely, Avidius perceived the sumptuousness of colors, the pomp of perfumes, and the magnificence of music. Finally, his vision cleared. He saw Faustina, rhythmic and triumphant.

Her heavy curly tresses hung down like grapes swollen with black blood. Her forehead was made to bear with disdain the weight of diadems. Her eyelids seemed heavy with sleep and her eyes drunk on dreams. Oh, the eyes of Faustina, in which an imperial ennui was dormant! They harbored all amorous and warm darkness. And those lips, burning and burned by innumerable kisses!

Faustina had sat down, enveloped in imperial purple, like the goddess of the setting sun with violet clouds. Amethysts shone profoundly on her fingers and in her hair. Her imperious and soft hands were limp. Her perfumes rose up like flames.

Avidius contemplated her. Under the poet's troubled gaze, the games unfurled. The defeated fell. Victors died of their victory. The wounded implored the uncertain favor of life. Others, in their red dolor, appealed for the suavity of death, more tender than balms. But Avidius only saw Faustina's eyes. He only saw her nostrils flaring like happy petals. He only saw the splendid neck, oppressed by ecstatic sighs. All of that perverse beauty seemed to be offering itself and delivering itself to carnage. The fumes of blood, precious and rare, were exhaled toward her. The gladiators killed one another before her voluptuous gaze. They fought and died for that splendid woman who only cherished the wounds and the death of men.

She was so beautiful thus that the people, forgetful of their carnivorous joys, acclaimed her, the dying praised her with their last breath, and even the Vestals kissed the hem of her robe studded with amethysts. She was so beautiful thus that the mediocre poet Avidius discovered a heroic soul within himself.

Freely, he resolved to die in his turn under the voluptuous gaze of Faustina.

Thus, Avidius, the amorous, pastoral and pacific cantor, learned the bloody métier of the gladiator. And the day came round again of the games in which the imperial and cruel soul of Faustina took pleasure.

As if in a dream, Avidius saw her enveloped in purple, like the goddess of the setting sun in violet clouds. As if in a dream he saw her slowly picking apart vine-branches and roses with bored fingers. As if in a dream, he contemplated the heavy clusters of her hair and the warm darkness of her pupils. He saw her thus, beautiful in all her implacable beauty of an Empress and courtesan, seemingly offering herself and delivering herself to the carnage.

Detaching himself from his companions, the gladiators consecrated like him to death, he approached in such a fashion as to be heard by the Empress and was the first to utter the heroic cry: "*Ave Faustina, morituri le salutant . . .*"

And his companions, the gladiators consecrated like him to death, took up and prolonged the fine clamor: "*Ave Faustina, morituri le salutant . . .*"

She heard, and her imperial and cruel lips smiled. She heard and smiled. And Avidius, the mediocre poet and hero, was glad to die; for he was dying in the glare of that gaze, in the light of that smile . . .

He fought with an obstinate courage, for he knew that the bitterness of the struggle sharpens the final joy of seeing a valorous combatant fall. He fought with an obstinate courage, in order to render his death more beautiful and more desirable. Faustina would covet that death like a royal jewel for her sovereign brow. She would rejoice in that beautiful end of a beautiful combat.

Avidius, the mediocre poet, understood that he was redeeming by his noble defeat the paltry poverty of his verses. His death would be a unique poem. His demise would equal in splendor the quivering strophes that he had not been able to transcribe for the future admiration of mortals.

And Faustina smiled at the bloody arena.

Eventually, Avidius, the mediocre poet and hero, succumbed. He saw again, in a supreme red flash, the Dionysiac clusters of the loosened hair. He saw again the drunken pupils and the voluptuous nostrils that were inhaling the fumes of blood. Finally, he saw again the lips laughing at the massacre.

Avidius, the hero and the poet of his own death, collapsed slowly on the crimson sand. His agonizing eyes were still searching for the imperial and cruel visage. And the multitude uttered an immense clamor of fear, scorn and amour.

Faustina! Faustina! Faustina!

The Sin Against the Roses

ROSAMUND,[1] *sitting alone, amid the roses*: "Since King Henry has quit me to go make war in France, I'm bored in the midst of my flowers. I'm sated with their hues and have had enough of their perfumes. I'm weary of lilies. I'm weary of clematis. I'm weary of bluebells and foxgloves. I'm even weary of roses. And I'm bored . . . and I'm bored . . . (*Distractedly, she pulls the petals off a red rose.*) How I wept when I saw him leave, white on a black warhorse. His armor sparkled in the sunlight. I followed with my eyes the distant gleam of his helmet. And a great inexplicable dolor tormented me mysteriously. I sobbed like a child, saying to myself aloud: 'I shall not see him again . . . I shall not see him again . . .' And he left. I have remained solitary, amid all my roses." (*She sings:*)

---

1 Rosamund Clifford, nicknamed "the Rose of the World," was the mistress of the twelfth-century English King Henry II. The legend claims that he conducted his affair in the middle of a maze in the grounds of his house at Woodstock in order to conceal it from his wife Eleanor of Aquitaine, but the latter found the heart of the maze and offered her a choice between being stabbed to death or drinking poison, although later versions embellished the story in various ways; it gave rise to many other literary versions, including an opera by Donizetti and a poem by Guillaume Apollinaire.

The weight of satiety
Weighs down my closed eyelids . . .
O gardens say to summer:
"Rosamund is weary of roses . . ."

Say, O violet gaze
Of morning, say: "Rosamund
Is even weary of the reflection
Of her bright face in the water."

The weight of satiety
Weighs down my closed eyelids . . .
O gardens say to summer:
"Rosamund is weary of roses . . ."

(An old knight appears, holding the guiding thread of the labyrinth in his hand. Rosamund gets up and runs to him.)

Rosamund: "O Knight, Knight, Knight, you have come! I'm happy to see you. In truth, I'm happy to see your long gray beard and your gray head, your forehead burned by so many old suns. O Knight, you're very old and very austere, and I'm very young and very insouciant, but I'm glad to see you. You do not know how heavy solitude is . . . even solitude among the roses."

The Old Knight: "O Rosamund, how young you are!"

Rosamund: "It's sad to be young, is it not, Knight? It's sad to be young, is it not? One wishes for so many unrealizable things, when one is young. One desires them so passionately. And one believes that it is possible to attain them one day. It's sad to believe that everything is possible and to fear, in spite of everything, something unknown and obscure. One hopes for and one fears everything, because one is young and does not know life. O Knight, Knight, Knight, when I'm old, very old, as old as you are, will I no longer hope for anything and no longer fear anything?"

The Old Knight: "You will no longer hope for anything but the night, and that is all that you will fear."

Rosamund: "I would like to be old already. I am weary of my youth. You have a gaze so placid, Knight, I would like to possess a heart as serene as yours. Tell me, Knight, tell me, do you no longer love anyone?"

The Old Knight, *smiling*: "No, Rosamund I no longer love. I am too old for love."

Rosamund: "I would like to be old, I would like to be old! (*Changing her tone.*) What have you brought me, Knight, under your ample cloak?"

The Old Knight, *handing her a bunch of red roses*: "Roses."

Rosamund: "I'm weary of roses! I'm weary of roses! (*She shreds the roses and tramples them underfoot.*) I'm bad, because I'm bored; I'm cruel, because I'm bored; I'm bored, because I'm young. If I were your age Knight, it would appear to me quite natural to be alone among flowers. I wouldn't be saddened at all by being solitary. Feeling chilly, I'd warm myself in the sun. I'd respire the beneficent perfumes of the earth and moist roses. I'd amuse myself watching the shadow rotate around the sundial. It would seem quite simple to me and very good to be alone in this beautiful garden. Tell me, Knight, if I wait with great patience, will I be old later? Tell me, truly, whether I'll be old one day. Youth is so long, so long, you see . . ."

The Old Knight, *reading the motto around the sundial:* "All things have an end."

Rosamund: "All things have an end, I know. That motto is boring and banal. Knight, what are you holding so tightly in your iron-gloved hand?"

The Old Knight: "I'm holding the guiding thread of this flowery labyrinth, where the King, who loves you, keeps you enclosed for your safety."

Rosamind: "Give me that guiding thread, Knight. Give me that thread and let me go out, for a few minutes, of this eternal garden where I'm so passionately bored. I won't do any harm, Knight. I'll wander in a path bordered by mulberries or eglantines. I'll go into a naïve meadow where clover perfumes the bindweed. I'll go along laughing, across a field of quivering oats. Oats are so beautiful when the wind curbs them as it passes. They flow back and forth like a little sea. It's like a tide of ears. O Knight, let me run through the glaucous oats!"

The Old Knight: "You know that's impossible for me, Rosamund. Queen Eleanor, who is vindictive and jealous, hates you because her husband loves you. She is trying to kill you. If she discovers the secret of your flowery refuge, she will have you killed."

Rosamund: "She'll have me killed?"

The Old Knight: "She only desires one thing on earth: your death."

Rosamund: "O my flowers, you are silently soft, you are silently beautiful, and I prefer your familiar beauty to the unknown and peril! (*To the Old Knight:*) And what if Queen Eleanor has me killed anyway?"

The Old Knight: "Think of the dolor the King, who loves you, would feel then."

Rosamund: "If he loved me, he wouldn't leave me here, sitting sad and solitary among the roses."

The Old Knight: "He has confided the care of watching over your safety to me. I am the guardian of your security and your existence. Your fragile life depends on my untiring solicitude. You will not leave here, Rosamund, while I am alive."

Rosamund: "Will I not leave this eternal labyrinth and this eternal garden, Knight?"

The Old Knight: "No, Rosamund, you will not leave here while I am alive."

Rosamund (*very quietly*): "I was wrong to speak to you as I just did, Knight. I know that you are the faithful servant of the King, and my faithful and devoted servant. See, Knight, how beautiful my roses are. I have been ingrate toward my roses. I repent of my ingratitude. May my roses be as beautiful as the sun! Knight, pick a few roses for me. I won't complain any more, I won't be impatient or bad any more. Pick a few roses for me, in order that I can weave them into a nice crown."

(The Old Knight leans over to pick the roses. He drops the guiding thread. Rosamund seizes it and throws the tangled thread over the hedge of the enclosure.)

Rosamund, *smiling*: "Greetings to the first passer-by, to the first passer-by to whom that thread reveals the secret path of the labyrinth! Greetings to the first human being who will break the monotony of my happy days! Greetings to the first terror, the first suffering!"

The Old Knight: "O Rosamund, Rosamund, what have you done!"

Rosamund, *triumphant*: "I can hear a sound of footsteps. The footsteps are approaching. One might think they were the footsteps of armed men. Can you hear the clink of bucklers and lances?"

The Old Knight: "Someone was lying in wait for us. You've doomed us, Rosamund." (*He draws away into the labyrinth.*)

Rosamund: "O my roses! (*She leans toward them.*) I was wrong, I was certainly wrong. But I was so weary of solitude, and the monotonous little music of that fountain, and all of you, my roses! (*She sniffs them.*) One is sated with happiness so promptly. Only wearies of peace so rapidly. Out there, there is hazard and adventure. There's life and death. (*She listens to the clash of swords.*) "Death . . . perhaps . . . Death . . . what is death, my roses, my roses who shed your petals so rapidly?"

(*Queen Eleanor appears, with a vial of poison
in one hand and a dagger in the other.*)

Rosamund: "Greetings, O first passer-by to whom the guiding thread revealed the secret of the labyrinth."

Eleanor: "I am Queen Eleanor."

Rosamund: "You're very beautiful. You're terribly beautiful."

Eleanor: "Less beautiful than you, Rosamund, since King Henry has forsaken me for you."

(*A silence.*)

The Knight, *agonizing outside*: "Rosamund! Rosamund!"

Rosamund: "My knight has been killed. Why have you killed him?"

Eleanor: "Because, with him alive. I would not have been able to accomplish my design."

Rosamund: "You hate me, Madame the Queen. My lady and my mistress, the Queen, you hate me mortally."

Eleanor: "I hate you as only queens can hate. I despise you, I disdain you, and I want your death."

Rosamund: "You want my death, O my mistress the Queen!"

Eleanor: "I want your death, Rosamund. That is why I have come here among your roses."

Rosamund: "O my roses! O my roses! O my roses!"

Eleanor: "Are you ready to die, Rosamund?"

Rosamund: "I knew full well, I said it just a little while ago: I am too young. I am too young to live happily, and too young to die. My mistress the Queen, I am too young to die. Think that I have not tasted the full savor of life. I have not been able to respire all of it. I have not contemplated all the colors of the dawn. I have not seen all the appearances of dusk. Let me live, at least until the roses in my garden have shed their petals."

Eleanor: "You have lived too long, Rosamund, since I order you to die."

Rosamund: "I would die without regret and without terrors, if I were old. But I cannot die, my mistress the Queen. I have not had time to think about it. In truth, my mistress the Queen, I have not had time to think about it."

Eleanor: "Think about it now, Rosamund."

Rosamund: "Death . . . that great black thing . . . I can't understand it. I've never thought about it before today.

And now that great black thing is looming up before me. O my mistress the Queen, do not make me die!"

Eleanor: "Here is a vial of poison, Rosamund, and here is a dagger. If you do not consent to drink the poison, I will kill you with the dagger. Choose."

Rosamund: "Oh, how the blade shines! I'll drink the poison, but don't make the blade of that dagger shine in my eyes. (*She takes the vial from the Queen's hand.*) Death is terrible for those who die young, for dying young is not a natural end. There is such a revolt of all the flesh that that revolt must be prolonged into the next world. One must not sleep in peace in the tomb when one dies young. And all the life, all the life that I have not known! All that I don't yet know! All that I would have been able to learn and feel! I regret all of life; I regret its dolors as much as its joys, for I don't know either one. Inflict no matter what torture on me, O my mistress the Queen! Tear out my fingernails, teeth and hair. To suffer would be to live. At least it would be living. It's impossible for me not to live regardless. My mistress the Queen, I can't die."

Eleanor, *raising the dagger*: "In a few moments, you will be dead, Rosamund."

Roasamund: "Yes . . . yes . . . I'll drink the poison. But don't make the blade of that dagger shine . . . Dead . . . dead . . . dead . . . O my roses, who loved me! O my roses, to which I have been so ingrate . . . O my roses . . ." (*She drinks the poison, and falls among the shredded roses.*)

Merciful Hope

IN a distant chimerical country lived a little cripple with limpid eyes. Everyone loved her because she had a soft and deep voice, and because her eyes laughed in her dolorous face. Lona lived in a cottage, the flowery roof of which formed a wild, delicately perfumed garden. An odor of grass and moss warmed up there in the sunlight. The little cripple dreamed there for long hours, with her eyes closed. She loved to sense the penetrating warmth of summer through her dazzled eyelids. Large red, yellow and violet patches fluttered in the darkness.

Lona loved marvelous stories, but, as she lived in almost constant solitude, she had to make them up herself in order to appease her hunger for the unreal. She resembled those women who, weary of weeping, console themselves with the aid of their own music.

The land where Lona lived was a northern country. Beautiful fir trees grew there, the dark green of which stood out boldly from the shining blue-tinted snow. They were both vigorous and slender. Like Vikings, they stood up proudly in their heroic grace. Solemn lakes were hollowed out in the mountains. They seemed to be sleeping an enchanted slumber. The vesperal breezes scarcely troubled the stagnant reflections of their opaque mirrors. Others were strangely limpid and resembled gulfs of light. Alongside the paths were tangled bushes bearing meager roses with frail perfumes.

A Queen governed the chimerical realm wisely. She lived inaccessibly in a gray palace built on a crag overhanging an abyss. She never showed herself to the gaze of her subjects. Her invisible hand weighed gently upon the land, but her woman's gaze never illuminated the crowd on any feast day. All that the people knew, without ever have contemplated her, was that she was very beautiful. All that the people knew, without having heard her, that she was very wise and very melodious. And they also knew that she was very augustly good.

Lona often evoked the mysterious beauty of that Queen, whom the multitude loved without knowing her.

One morning of warm hopes and young verdure, a stranger came to the land. Her violet eyes were darkened by the tenebrous reflection of her hair, as evening is darkened by the reflection of the imminent night. A thick line of bistre ringed the purple of her eyes. The Queen had words of welcome addressed to her, for no stranger had ever come to that distant and somewhat savage land before.

All the inhabitants of the country received her joyfully. The young women brought her the most radiant flowers from their gardens, the adolescents the most flavorsome fruits from their orchards. The old women spun the flax of their patient distaffs for her. And they all crowded around her with anxious lips and attentive eyes, in order to interrogate her and listen to her by turns. The stranger told them magical tales. She enabled them to see in thought the countries that extended on the far side of the luminous seas.

She sang them songs in her unknown language. Without understanding the words, they loved those bizarre and sad chants.

Going past Lona's cottage one day, the stranger felt sorry for the solitary little cripple. She felt sorry for her, for not being able to dance in the sunlight, shaking the pleats of her dress in order to make the radiance and the belated perfumes fall. She felt sorry for her, for not being able to wander over the mountains at dusk. She also felt sorry for her, for not being able to pick flowers in the meadows, laughing with young companions.

For the first time, an immense sadness descended into Lona's soul. She understood that a dream is only the image of happiness and not its essence. She glimpsed magnificent palpable realities. And suddenly, she felt desperately alone and poor, by virtue of having lived until then in a land of shadows populated by phantoms.

"Queens and kings possess the divine power of curing," the stranger said to her one day. "Let the Queen place her sacred hand on your forehead, for the royal touch dissipates all ills. God has wanted it thus, in placing his monarchs above other men. Kings are destined for graver joys and higher dolors than the crowd of mortals. God himself has ornamented their foreheads with the sovereign crown. He has put power and wisdom into them. They are his messengers and his elect. That is why the royal touch dissipates all ills."

Lona listened to the stranger, not only with her ears but with her eyes and all of her emaciated face.

"Is not the Queen very good and very beautiful?" asked the little cripple.

"She is so beautiful," replied the stranger, "that she never puts on the crown and never ornaments herself with any jewel. Gazes, which are only distracted by the vulgar glare of crowns and gems, are dazzled by the sole magnificence of the royal beauty. The Queen is divinely blonde. Her hair is a pale flame, and her eyes are a brighter blue than the glaciers. Her beauty ensures that she is as good as the sunlight and the snow, and all beautiful things."

Lona meditated on those words for a long time.

The days went by, and the little cripple felt weaker and wearier from one hour to the next. She even lost the strength to dream. More often than not she remained devoid of thought, her eyelids closed over a dolorous interior night.

Seven heralds came, in accordance with the ceremony, to announce the passage of the Queen through the little village. She was finally going to reveal herself to her subjects, who loved her without knowing her. She would come without any other magnificence than her royal beauty, without a crown over her hair and without jewels on her dress.

In a fever of belated joy, Lona seemed to be reanimated. Her cheeks reddened slightly, and her eyes reflected the sunlight again.

The unprecedented day dawned. It was an august and clement day. The sun lavished its light sumptuously. The air was mild. The royal cortege filed though the pomp of roses, the splendor of green bushes and the solemnity of tall trees.

When the Queen, divinely beautiful under the royal awning, was within sight of the village, the seven heralds who were preceding her by a hundred paces, announced her glorious arrival. There were eddies in the crowds, cries and tears of delight. Women and sick children extended their supplicant hands toward the Queen. The poor uncovered their wounds, imploring the balm of the royal touch.

Hearing those clamors of joy and anxiety, Lona raised herself up weakly. In her turn, she wanted to hold out her supplicant hands, imploring the balm of the royal touch . . .

Her exhausted body fell back . . .

Her eyelids closed on an interior void.

Lona died without seeing the distant face of the Queen. But the stranger did not feel sorry for her, for the dead child had only known the aerial charm of life: Hope, the daughter of Illusion, and Anticipation, the daughter of Dream.

The Piety of Rajah Karan

RAJAH KARAN was pious, severe and prodigal in giving alms. Scorning vain terrestrial riches, he only coveted the treasures of the soul. In order to possess infinite bliss, he made a religious oath before the altar of the sovereign Indra who accords the rain. He swore only to break his fast every day after having distributed to the poor of his realm a bag of gold weighing as much as an elephant. In truth, Karan was a pious Rajah prodigal in giving alms.

To the great wonder of the neighboring Rajahs and his entire people, Rajah Karan kept his religious oath without ever emptying his royal coffers.

Now, the incomprehensible abundance of Rajah Karan's wealth came from a supernatural source.

In his zeal to obtain the mysterious treasures of the soul, Karan had gone to a venerable Fakir. Everyone knows that Fakirs are terrible and sacred. They command visible and invisible things. They resuscitate the dead. They cure leprosy and the plague. They appease Kali, the Goddess of Smallpox, by means of their incantations and prayers. The Marouts, wild winds, obey them like submissive slaves. The Djinn are their docile servants. The Fakirs, beloved by the Gods, sometimes nourish themselves on human flesh, before subsequently giving their own bodies as fodder to their disciples.

In his immense zeal, Rajah Karan made a pact with a venerable Fakir. Every day, before dawn, he came to offer his flesh to the cannibal Fakir. Every day, before dawn, he consented to a horrible death; for the Fakir plunged him alive into a cauldron of boiling oil. Having devoured him, he gave him in recompense a bag of gold weighing as much as an elephant. Shaking his ragged cloak, the Fakir made the large bag of gold weighing as much as an elephant fall out of it.

Every day, before dawn, Rajah Karan died and was re-born thus, for the joy and the prosperity of the poor. Every day, before dawn, he offered himself in a poignant sacrifice in order to obtain the mysterious treasures of the soul.

In truth, Karan was a pious Rajah prodigal in giving alms; but Karan did not know that simple love is better than all endeavors and all religious sacrifices.

Toward the seventh year of Karan's reign, a great disturbance agitated the shores of Lake Mansarobar. Lake Mansarobar is as deep as the sea. Its waters bathe the Realm of the Dead. That is why its waters are more motionless and more silent than the surface of a limpid glacier. Lake Mansarobar is the abode of the Wild Swans that only nourish themselves on unpierced pearls. That is why the feathers of the Wild Swans are whiter than the snows and the snow. But in the seventh year of Karan's reign a great shortage of pearls afflicted the shores of Lake Mansarobar.

A couple of famished swans abandoned the holy waters and took flight for a more hospitable land. They flew away sadly and finally stopped in Ujjayin. Whiter than smoke, they came down, dying, in the garden of Rajah Bikramajit.

Rajah Bikramajit was a merciful and tender soul. He loved simple and impenetrable creatures simply. Without being pious, he was good. And because he loved fraternal beasts fraternally, he understood their simple and impenetrable language. The two dying swans had come down in Bikramajit's garden among the mango trees and the date palms. The steward of the gardens, on seeing the strange beauty of the birds, threw them the most delicate seeds, but in vain. The swans refused that vulgar nourishment, proud in their expiring whiteness.

The steward of the gardens, perplexed and sensing a sacred mystery, prostrated himself before Bikramajit, and told him that two swans, whiter than the foam of the sea, were dying of hunger outside the palace, and refusing all nourishment.

Bikramajit hastened to the two dying swans and, speaking to them in their simple and mysterious language, he interrogated them.

The swans replied to him that unpierced pearls were their quotidian fodder and that any other nourishment was foreign and deadly to them.

And Bikramajit, moved to compassion on seeing the two swans dying, chose, in order to appease their hunger, the most luminously rare unpierced pearls in his royal treasury.

When Bikramajit had exhausted the pearls of his treasury in order to nourish the exiled swans every day, he sent messengers throughout the realm. Those messengers had orders to bring back unpierced pearls, at any price. Bikramajit also commanded divers to search the sea bed, in order to collect the pearls indispensable to the divine life of the swans.

One day, however, the messengers and the divers presented themselves empty-handed before the desolate Rajah. There were no more pearls in the realm or in the sea.

Then the two swans opened their snowy wings very wide, and slowly, solemnly, they took off and abandoned Bikramajit's garden. While flying above the palace and the foliage they sang the praises of the hospitable and generous Rajah divinely.

Then the two swans, singing Bikramajiit's praises, traversed Karan's realm. Karan, who died and was resurrected before dawn every morning for the good of his people, was struck by amazement on hearing them sing. Gripped by a great jealous dolor, he murmured:

"Who is this unknown man that the birds are praising? Every day I condemn myself to an atrocious death and I am born again before dawn, in order to pay with my own flesh for the gold that I distribute to my people. Nevertheless, no bird in the sky sings my praises."

He ordered his bird-catchers to lure and trap the two wild swans, but the bird-catchers were unable to impede the majestic flight of the free and pure birds. Toward evening, however, weary and dying of hunger, the two swans alighted on the Rajah's terrace, and Karan, rejoicing, spread gilded grains before the mysterious birds.

But the swans refused all nourishment. In faint voices they sang: "Glory to Bikramajit! When we were perishing of hunger, he gave us for food the most beautiful pearls in his kingdom."

Karan, having understood the hymn of the divine birds, thanks to his piety, threw before them all the pearls that his profound coffers contained. Because one of the pearls was pierced, however, the haughty swans refused to eat and sang obstinately, in a fainter voice: "Glory to Bikramajit! Glory to Bikramajit!"

In vain, Karan lavished the most beautiful pearls of his treasure upon the indifferent swans; they persisted in their aristocratic scorn. And Karan, irritated by their disdain, summoned the most skillful bird-catcher in his realm, who finally trapped the swans and imprisoned them in a golden cage.

Then the female swan said to Karan, in a clear voice: "Rajahs ought not to imprison a feminine being. Bikramajit never imprisoned a feminine being like this, for Bikramajit was just as well as generous, and you, Karan, in spite of your piety, are neither generous nor just."

On hearing the bird's reproach, Karan did not want to be deemed less generous and less just than his rival Bikramajit. He set the captive free, and the captive fled with a great flutter of wings. She took off and fled southwards, all the way to Bikramajit's gardens. And, landing with a great flutter of wings at Bikramajit's feet, she told him about her dolorous adventure and the captivity of her companion.

Bikramajit, being a compassionate soul, wanted to liberate the solitary swan, and he quit his realm clad in the rags of a pauper in order to liberate a bird. Under the name of Bikrou, he wandered through abandoned plains and hostile cities.

On an indecisive evening, he stopped in front of the palace of the pious Karan, and, joining the servants of the pious Karan, he helped them to distribute abundant gold to the poor.

Bikramajit resolved to discover the secret origin of those inexhaustible riches; and the patient Bikramajit, the most generous of Rajahs, spied on Karan for a long time. He spied for a long time, and saw him crossing the Fakir's threshold before dawn.

Having raised the window-blind, he saw him go into the cauldron of boiling oil alive. He saw him devoured by the Fakir and resurrected by the Fakir's incantations.

In order to liberate the swan imprisoned by the pious Karan, Bikramajit resigned himself nobly to an even more atrocious sacrifice. He slashed his flesh with his royal sword. Into the raw wounds he introduced vehement pepper, bitter salt and spices, crushed pomegranate seeds and gram flour.

Thus prepared, he crossed the Fakir's threshold. The Fakir was still asleep, in a religious and solemn slumber; and the generous Bikramajit went into the boiling oil alive.

Woken up by the odor and the sound of the flavorsome cooking, the Fakir, as was his custom, devoured the flesh of the victim. The taste of the pepper, the salt, the pomegranate seeds and the gram flour flattered his palate, while the odor of the spices dilated his nostrils; and the Fakir, grateful and rejoicing, resuscitated Rajah Bikramajit by means of his incantations. He promised to accord him whatever he asked of him.

Bikramajit, as wise as he was generous, asked the Fakir for his ragged mantle, from which the inexhaustible gold poured. Having promised, the Fakir kept his promise, and handed Bikramajit his venerable cloak.

When Karan came into the Fakir's abode in his turn he found the Fakir asleep and sated, and when he requested the salary of his unaccomplished torture, the Fakir replied that the prodigious garment was no longer in his possession.

Karan understood then that he would die of hunger, for, being a pious Rajah, he could not break his religious oath. In order to prolong his uncertain existence for one more day, however, he emptied his royal treasure into the hands of the people, who besieged the palace every morning.

The next day, at the time of the quotidian alms, the Rajah's treasurers prostrated themselves before him, lamenting; the royal treasury was exhausted.

Then Karan turned away and, retiring to the most obscure chamber in his palace, he prepared to die of starvation.

On the second day, the generous Bikramajit appeared to him under the name and in the garments of the servant Bikrou and offered him, in exchange for the captive swan, the mantle from which the inexhaustible gold poured.

In exchange for the prodigious mantle, Karan set the solitary swan free.

The liberated swan opened its broad wings, whiter than the foam of the sea, and, flying above Karan's palace it sang, divinely: "Glory to Bikramajit! Glory to Bikramajit! Glory to Bikramajit!"

Hearing the praises of his rival, Karan bowed his head. He realized that Bikramajit was better than him. For, although he had consented to an atrocious torture for the good of a people, Bikramajit had subjected himself to an even greater torture in order to render liberty to a bird.

In the violet air of the evening, the melodious swan drew away like a fleeting cloud, and, as it drew away, it sang in a divine voice: "Glory to Bikramajit! Glory to Bikramajit! Glory to Bikramajit!"

The Starless Air

Here, sighs, plaints and great pains
Resonated in the starless air;
That is why I wept for the first time.
In various languages, horrible words,
Words of dolor, in the angry tones,
Of shrill and hoarse voices, and the sound of clapping
Make a turbulent tumult,
In the air that is no longer nuanced by weather.
Like the sand when it swirls in spirals.[1]

FRA ANIELLO was the youngest of the Fraticelli of a pious convent huddled on the side of a mountain. He guarded the doors of the monastery. Having lived on the blue summits since his earliest years, near the limpid azure, he possessed the ingenuous heart of a child. He had confidence in God and in men. No doubt or suspicion had ever obscured his naïve eyes.

Being happy is very simple, he often thought. *To be happy, it's sufficient to be without sin and not to nourish any wicked ambition.*

---

1 These lines are retranslated from a French translation—which, inevitably, does not rhyme or scan—of a passage from Canto III of Dante's *Inferno*.

And, seeing the distant earth so beautiful, he sensed divine approval floating over the universe. He divined the eternal smile gilding the immaculate mountains. In truth, Fra Aniello possessed the ingenuous heart of a child.

He had once listened, with a curious astonishment, to the story of the rebellion of the Archangels. For, ignorant of doubt and suspicion, he was also unaware of revolt and hatred.

Fra Aniello took pleasure in seeing the renewed miracle of the dawn. It did not bring him any anguish, or any uncertainty regarding the future. On his knees, the young monk greeted the puerile rosy tints of first light, and the dawn appeared to him to be glorious and beneficent, like a nativity.

Fra Aniello loved the earth and the sky without mistrust. Even death did not frighten him; it was only the peaceful sleep before the dawn, only the obscure threshold on which one pauses momentarily before entering into the radiant life, into the divine life.

The young monk often thought about the Paradise that awaited him, where he would join the multitude of the elect. On high, souls were like the sparkling grains of dust that swirl in common light. Every soul was an exalted sound in the universal music . . .

Fra Aniello closed his eyes. He entered with a reverential dread into the house of the Virgin. She was sitting in a bare room, in which her presence was the only splendor. Behind her, the open window cut out a distant blue landscape. The mountains visible therein appeared very slight, a terrestrial blue beneath the immaterial blue of the sky. A river, as slender as a snake, meandered between azure meadows. But the Virgin was not contemplating the unreal landscape. Her eyes were lowered in an immutable dream. An angel with a juvenile round face, an angel whose deployed wings formed a double rainbow, was standing to her right. Retained on his shoulder was an ample red robe. A second angel, with a virginal face, was standing to her left. He was clad in an orange robe and was carrying an amber vase. A third angel was kneeling at the Madonna's feet. Only the short infantile curls of his bowed head were visible, and the flight of vast green pleats that uncovered a bare heel.

The Virgin's eyelids were not raised upon the three angels who were observing her. Her eyelids were luminous with her interior gaze. The rectangular neckline of her straight robe revealed the frail emergence of her long Florentine neck, for she adopted for each soul the particular beauty of its terrestrial homeland. Thus, Fra Aniello found in her the spiritualized grace of the women of his natal city. The tapering chin gave the radiant visage an expression of celestial melancholy.

Then Fra Aniello found himself on the terrace of Saint Agnes. Lilies were flourishing there, blue and incarnate in sunlit pots. An angel with upright and pointed wings was watering them carefully. A bench was set against the wall, in an agreeable shade. Through the open window, Fra Aniello saw billowing curtains of a beautiful deep and soft red color. The floor-tiles extended a delicate black and yellow mosaic artfully. It was the hour when the saint came on to the terrace for the morning meditation . . .

But the convent bell sounded matins or vespers, and Fra Aniello woke up on an earth that was certainly very beautiful and very good, but less good and less beautiful than his celestial imaginations.

Often, therefore, Fra Aniello thought about Paradise. The mysterious Inferno did not trouble his heart at all. When his thoughts wandered, fugitively, toward the place of damnation, he evoked black imps, ugly and horned, with comical grimaces, pursuing souls shamefully deprived of all garments.

They were exposed to gazes in their ridiculous nudity. Fra Aniello considered, with pity, their bulging bellies and their excessively thin arms, which formed a pleasant contrast with their improbably puffy thighs. The demons ran after the reproved with pitchforks, in order to precipitate them into the bottom of cauldrons where pitch and oil were burning. The grotesquery of those infernal apparitions, however, attenuated their horror.

Fra Aniello avoided meditating on the Inferno. That was too redoubtable an enigma for his ingenuous mind. He preferred not to make use of his own reason in that matter, and to refer it to the great goodness of God. God had judged eternal punishments necessary; doubtless he concealed excellent and merciful motives. In any case, he, Fra Aniello, was not damned. He possessed the modest but firm certainty of that.

One evening, however, he was troubled by strange thoughts. A tempestuous wind was blowing over the mountains. The darkness was opaque and hot, like bitumen and pitch. The lightning cast red flames of pyres and tortures. An inexpressible terror traversed things. The thunder was as formidable as a divine sentence, and the wind unleashed its cries and its moans. It was the vain appeal of the Chastised. It was the sobbing of futile remorse. It was the continuous plaint of irreparable punishments.

Fra Aniello, huddled in a corner of his cell, with a half-told rosary in his trembling fingers, thought with gravity about the Inferno. He heard the cries of the tormented souls and the howls of the demonic torturers. The strident clamors of the storm-wind made him shiver, chilled by an unknown dread.

And suddenly, Fra Aniello shuddered in all his limbs. A voice mingled with the sound of the wind, and that voice was more terrible than the sound of the wind itself, so much frightful despair was rebelling within it. With its wild anguish, it drowned out the appeals of the tortured souls. All of human rebellion and dolor was protesting therein, heart-rending and cruel, and a hatred as formidable as the hatred of the accursed archangels was dully menacing therein.

Fra Aniello made the sign of the cross while reciting an *Ave*, but the voice was still imploring and menacing. And the young monk, requesting the protection of God and the Virgin, went down the narrow stairway that led to the gate of the monastery, with his bunch of keys in his hand.

The wind was insulting the darkness with its impotent anger. It struck the young monk in the face. Fra Aniello shivered in the perfidious obscurity. A gust extinguished the candle he was carrying.

Fra Aniello finally opened the convent door. Fear stifled a cry that was frozen on his lips.

A form was outlined by the light of a smoky torch coming from a cell.

The robe of the stranger was straight, with pleats as severe as a monk's habit. The hood, thrown back, allowed the sight of a bitter face ravaged by terrible wrinkles. The black eyes were burning. They were the eyes of the accursed archangel, cruel and sad.

Fra Aniello recoiled before the apparition. An emphatic prayer gave him an unanticipated bravery.

"Who are you?" he asked, making a broad sign of the cross.

The voice finally replied to him; it appeared to emerge from the darkness.

"I am Dante the exile."

The haggard monk considered him.

"What are you seeking in our convent?" he asked, again.

"Peace . . ."

Fra Aniello went pale. The gulf of human despair was hollowed out before his terrified eyes. He wanted to respond, to offer the wanderer the peaceful shelter of the monastery . . . but the wind, as if increasing its fury, slammed the partly-opened gate shut.

When Fra Aniello opened it again, the exile had disappeared.

For the first time, Fra Aniello sensed and understood all the terror and all the horror of suffering, and the abomination of it appeared to him, gripped him, and finally imposed itself on his puerile heart.

Fra Aniello knew doubt. The spirit of rebellion entered into him, imperious and poignant. A momentarily-stammered prayer died on his lips.

He had lost the softness of his faith. Revolt dried up his tears. He understood that he could no longer enter the infantile and charming heaven of the Elect of simple hearts, because the dolorous and grim stranger had opened a crack in the red doors of the Inferno for him.

The Improbable Story of
Prosper Prouvost

PROSPER PROUVOST was reposing beneath a florid arbor in his garden. The wisteria cast a mauve shadow over his face. Frogs were singing strangely on the edge of the nearby pond, and their concert dominated the shrill chant of the cicadas. The evening air was very mild and very sad.

Prosper Prouvost was interesting himself in the meanders and frail spirals designed by the blue smoke of his cigarette, and savoring artfully a liqueur in which the warm perfume of sunlit oranges persisted. In the vesperal silence, someone rang the bell at the gate. Prosper Prouvost was getting to his feet, cursing, when he saw, with surprise, that the unknown person had just opened the closed gate without any invitation.

And Prosper Prouvost was equally surprised to see that the unknown person was himself.

His other self, identical in every feature, advanced toward him. Except that the second self was dressed in black. It was a ceremonious mourning dress, such as one wears when making visits of condolence. Nothing was lacking: neither the severely cut jacket, nor the dark cravat, nor the falsely contrite expression.

"How distressed I am to learn, and to inform you at the same time, of the sad news of your demise," said the second Prosper Prouvost to the first Prosper Prouvost, sitting down facing himself, with a decent emotion. "You were such a good son, such a devoted parent, such a loyal friend, such an excellent comrade. All those who approached you had granted you the warmest affection and the most profound esteem, for the rectitude and goodness of your character, and you have left behind you inconsolable regrets."

While speaking, the second Prosper Prouvost wiped away a tear.

"What augments the grief of those who cherished you even more, is the suddenness of the accident that struck you down. To have seen you, this very morning, joyful and healthy, and to be weeping over your cadaver this evening! Oh, Monsieur, what an anguishing thought—and how small we are before fatalities!"

Decidedly, thought Prosper Prouvost, *I'm ignobly banal and banally ignoble. And there's not a word of sincere emotion in all that I just said. My pretentious hypocrisy sickens me. I'd like to give myself a couple of slaps. I really am displaying too somber a cretinism.*

But his second self continued the funeral oration placidly.

"What a gallant and charming man we have just lost in your person! Noble hearts are becoming rarer from day to day. I won't mention the truly highly developed intelligence of the dear departed . . ."

He bowed.

Prosper Prouvost considered himself with a malevolent interest. For the first time, he noticed the vulgarity of certain of his features, the coarseness of his plebeian nose and the inanity of his smile. For the first time, he saw himself as he was, pharisaic and pompous, and he detested himself sincerely.

"Believe me, my dear friend, no words can translate my profound dolor. My desolation is boundless. And be persuaded that I will conserve your memory throughout my existence. I shall never forget the fraternal hours that we spent together."

He took out of his pocket a black-bordered handkerchief marked with his own initials.

"We have traversed the best years of life side by side: the years of youth. Those are the ones that in the future one remembers with the greatest tenderness."

"But I'm stupid, I'm stupid, frightfully stupid!" cried Prosper Prouvost, finally, beside himself. "Is it possible that I've never perceived it before this evening? I'm a complete idiot. How have I been able to endure my own imbecility throughout my existence? How have I been able to hear myself speaking without weeping with shame and disgust? How have I been able to be myself without having recourse to beneficent suicide? My God! My God! My God!"

"I don't want to be indiscreet, or to prolong this painful visit, my dear friend, but I wanted to bring you personally the expression of my sympathy and regret."

And Prosper Prouvost quit himself, with a cordial handshake.

He died a few hours later, serene and satisfied to be rid of himself.

Obscure Royalty

ON one of the torrid nights of the Cape, Alcine Percheron, the wife of a French consul, sought in vain to retain fugitive sleep. Darkness was consuming her, as well as somber flames. Fever, with shining eyes, was prowling around her bed. It seemed to Madame Percheron that a red-hot iron weight was crushing her breast. She turned over and over like a torture victim on a bed of coals.

The hours weighed upon her. An anxious torpor gradually descended upon the brain of the feverish woman. She became half-drowsy, tortured and weary of her tortures.

The disk of the moon was obscured, but the light of the stars diffused in a crepuscular ambiguity. Tangles of stars were flamboyant against a backcloth of tropical azure, and mortal perfumes were exhaled by poisonous flowers.

Through the open window a freshness rose from the nearby river where crocodiles were dreaming under the lotuses. In her drowsiness, the sleeper felt the wellbeing of those light gusts, like the fumes of the water. She slid smoothly into a velvety forgetfulness. The felted footsteps of Slumber were in the room. It wandered, familiar and mysterious, and its gaze penetrated the mesh of the mosquito-net, like a gigantic cobweb.

Alcine's hair was coiled up like clusters of grapes. Alcine's hair was the color of dark red grapes, tinted with heavy blues. It hung down, more heavily than clusters of ripe grapes, on the raw whiteness of the pillow. Moths were fluttering, beating their nocturnal wings quietly.

Suddenly, the sleeper shuddered at a furtive sound. It was like the effort of a man who was hoisting himself up to the window with the aid of tenacious creepers. She listened vaguely. Then, the notion of things becoming clearer in her brain, still confused by the vapors of sleep, she raised her head. A furious terror was muffled within her, a mad terror that chilled her with a mortuary sweat.

Someone really was hoisting himself up to her window. And, convulsively sitting up, Alcine waited. An obscure form was confusedly outlined by the starlight, a masculine form, alert and well-built. It was a young man, to judge by the athletic flexibility of his movements . . .

He came in . . .

An inexpressible horror was strangled in the young woman's throat. Like a mute, she made hoarse efforts to articulate a scream, but no sound emerged from her dry throat. She fell back, half-fainting.

Through an abominable stupor, she felt herself carried away in powerful arms. She felt herself carried away, like a small child, in those arms, the strength of which made itself tender in order not to hurt her. She felt herself tightly clasped to a hairy chest, the chest of a robust man. She could not see any of the features of the man who was hold-ing her in such a fervent embrace. His head was profiled like a dark patch upon the starlight.

Alcine had the impression of an irresistible flight across the rolling plains and the fields of rice. Then there was the odorous darkness of a forest. Gusts of slumber emanated from the plants. The nocturnal breath of leaves rose and fell, a living and regular respiration. The young woman entered into the muted life, the formidable life of the trees . . .

Feebly, she opened her agonized eyes slightly. The starlight was shining very distantly, filtered by the dense foliage.

Finally, the man stopped. He deposited her on the nocturnal ground with great delicacy, very gently.

Bewildered to the point of unconsciousness, Alcine saw that she was in the midst of a grave and dignified assembly. Seated in the same fashion as venerable senators, all the men seemed to be deliberating silently. They were staying up late in order to ward off a peril, or to make a patriotic resolution. The young woman admired the nobility of their attitudes . . .

They all turned their obscure visages toward her. They all appeared to be collecting themselves in order to admire her. And the one that had carried her all the way there in his Herculean arms bowed down and kissed the hem of her robe. Then he straightened up, dominating the august council with his imposing stature.

Solemnly, the entire mute crowd bowed to her; and in the inclination of all those severe brows, Alcine saw a submissive deference. The one whose captive she was stood tall, like a king in the midst of his people. It was a strong and beautiful race, a race of free men. And now, taking her by the hand, the one who reigned over the multitude led the young woman to a throne of latanier leaves, and put a bamboo scepter into her fingers. Then he crowned her with a royal headband of red daturas; and, with a gesture full of authority and amour, he sat her down by his side, like a queen beside a king, on the emerald throne.

She considered him by the confused light of the distant star. She glimpsed him, powerful and muscular, hairy, like vigorous men. In the indistinct clarity, she found a great resemblance between him and her husband, the consul Percheron, one of the handsomest men in the French colony. In spite of her terror, she felt vaguely proud of being the elect of that truly regal man, that majestic man, free among all men.

She was a queen. She was the mistress of the obscure people whose virile stature and male visages she divined. She drew herself up to her full height, with an instinctive pride.

The disk of the moon emerged from an accumulation of nocturnal clouds. The disk of the moon emerged from between the clouds and from the darkness. And, paler than a resuscitated corpse, Alcine saw around her a mute assembly of gorillas. A gorilla was regally seated by her side, the gorilla that had carried her away into the mysteriously odorous forest.

Gradually, the young woman became accustomed to her strange royalty.

Human notions of the world are, in sum, only an accumulation of prejudices. Alcine perceived very rapidly that the fraternal and gentle gorillas were worth no less than the men among whom she had spent her youth.

Her subjects sometimes showed themselves ferociously avaricious and bellicose when they fought over a ripe fruit, but their cupidity and their ferocity brought them closer then to human beings, whose interested quarrels she remembered. They jabbered in a circle, sitting on their long tails.[1] But are not men more loquacious than the noisiest congress of apes? Have they not instituted meetings, conferences, clubs and official speeches in order to satisfy their innate amour for chatter?

And on moonlit nights, religious and contrite, the gorillas raised the visages of ecstatic devotees toward the heavens illuminated by angelic gleams. They meditated, as if in profound prayer. Their pious brows were bathed with pure light, and tears of mystical adoration flowed from their eyes, lost in the beyond . . .

Alcine loved her submissive people, more united and more peaceful, in sum, than a nation of human beings. She had given the king who had chosen her to share his throne the name of her husband, Édouard. She baptized his court similarly with the names of her relatives, friends and all those with whom she had previously had relationships.

She loved the female gorillas most of all, for their highly developed maternal tenderness. All of them enveloped their progeny with the most enlightened solicitude and the most vigilant love. The sentiment of the family was as powerful among the gorillas as it was in the most respectable bourgeoisie of France; and as for their morality, it only different from that of humans by virtue of an admirable lack of cynical hypocrisy.

Alcine learned the expressive and simple language of her people without great difficulty. The absence of gram-

---

1 Gorillas were still almost legendary creatures in nineteenth-century France, and it is understandable that the author seems to be under the misapprehension that they have long tails; many other writers of the era made similar mistakes in building fanciful literary images of the great apes.

mar simplified the task singularly. The sole need to which that language did not respond was calumny: a manifest inferiority, to tell the truth, to human speech. Thanks to the wisdom of her government and the charm of her white youth, Alcine quickly conquered the love and esteem of her people.

Her happy reign was, however, brutally interrupted by the invasion of a human tribe. They dispersed Alcine's subjects pitilessly. In the depths of the odorous forest there were strange clamors of massacres, the gasps of murdered gorillas, howls and plaints. Blood spattered and splashed the lianas. The implacable combat was furious. Moans of agony died away into a mortal silence. Then the cries rose up again, the long cries of the wounded and the hoarse cries of the dying . . .

And the young woman woke up, still trembling, in the matinal bedroom, where the rosy rays of sunlight were playing among the curtains.

The little black maidservant with the polite eyes and the tumultuous hair came in, gravely carrying the morning meal of fresh bananas, golden red guavas and majestic pineapples, with a cup of palm wine.

Esau's Repentance

THE man of the fields, Esau, returned from hunting. His soul was oppressed by the fall of night, for he had sold his birthright.

Wandering freely here and there, he shook off his brother's yoke, which weighed upon his neck; but the sadness remained within him. He had immolated to his immediate hunger the impalpable and splendid birthright. He had sacrificed the dream to the reality, and now he was discovering that reality has a life less intense than the dream.

The dolorous cry of old rose again to his lips: "Since I am going to die, what use is my birthright?"

Overwhelmed by fatigue on returning from the fields, he had sobbed those words of human cowardice. Now, because the peril was averted, because he was standing up in his youth and his strength, he understood that it would have been better to die than to sell his birthright.

Certainly, he would have done better to die in his pride and in his loyalty; but he had come back, overwhelmed by fatigue, to the tents where his brother was having a dish of lentils cooked, and the beast in him had cried out, imperious and ferocious. It had howled with distress and hunger. Vanquished, devoid of will before the need of the present moment, Esau had scorned his birthright.

How vain the sacred promise had appeared to him when he succumbed to lassitude and hunger!

> *God will give you the dew of heaven*
> *And the fat of the land,*
> *Wheat and wine in abundance,*
> *The peoples will submit to you*
> *And nations will bow down before you.*
> *You will be the masters of your brothers*
> *And your mother's sons will bow to you.*
> *Accursed will be whoever curses you*
> *And blessed whoever blesses you.*

The sun had set. Esau arrived in a desert place. He picked up a stone, with which he made his pillow. But God did not appear to Esau to say to him: "I am the Eternal, the God of Abraham, your father, and the God of Isaac. The earth on which you lie down, I will give to you, to you and your posterity. Your posterity will be like the dust of the earth; you will extend from the west to the east, from the north and the south, and all the races of the earth will be blessed in you and your posterity."

No divine dream radiated over the stone bed-head of the wanderer; for, dying of hunger, he had scorned his birthright.

He evoked his lamentable life. Neither the light laughter of the daughters of Heth nor their barbaric jewels, nor their loosened hair over their bare shoulders, had lightened his unquiet spirit. He thought of the benediction that his brother Jacob had stolen from him; and, thinking about the benediction with which Isaac had blessed Jacob, he conceived a hatred against his brother. The sad words of

Isaac resounded again in his ears: "What can I do for you, my son?"

The heat devoured him during the day and the cold during the night, and sleep fled his eyes. In order to comfort him, he had neither gracious and glorious visions nor the echo of divine words. And in his heart he repented of not having preferred death to the abandonment of his sacred right.

Night fell over his repentance. The irreparable was consummated. The Eternal had turned away from him. The Eternal would not heap him with benefits. The Eternal would not render him his posterity similar to the sand of the sea, so abundant that no one would be able to count its grains.

The oriental night was the color of an obscure emerald. The green darkness was perfumed by all the lilies of the fields. But Esau was not contemplating the beauty of the night, for he was vainly sobbing his vain repentance.

He was sobbing, like all of those who yield to necessity, like all of those who, being privileged, are unable to be heroic to the point of death in order to safeguard their divine privileges. He ought to have died. And he understood that, too late. He had vanquished himself.

Night fell over the stones. Night fell in Esau's soul. He divined confusedly that, in the distant future, other souls would be racked in the same fashion. They would know the same repentance too late, for having, like him, scorned their birthright . . .

Esau humiliated his brow. And, as before, he raised his voice and wept.

The Lassitude of the Road

A PILGRIM wandered for seven years in the Punjab, in the hope of one day discovering the secret of terrestrial felicity. Through his fatigues and his tears, indomitably, he sought perfect serenity. On his route he saw Fakirs and Joghis plunged in their meditations. He interrogated them, having respect or their wisdom; for Fakirs are endowed with supernatural faculties. They can metamorphose gardens desiccated by heat into a vast blossoming of verdure and daturas. They can ripen the fruits of autumn in spring and cause the flowers of spring to bloom in autumn. Water into which they plunge their hands is transmuted into blood. Fresh and pure sugar is changed, in accordance with their whim, into gray ashes. And the gray ashes become, under their incantations, fresh and pure sugar. They possess marvelous powers of healing and can cause severed feet and hands to grow again. And if the body of a Fakir is eaten by his disciples, they possess his magical attributions in their turn.

In spite of their profound wisdom, however, the Fakirs were unable to inform the pilgrim of the means of possessing terrestrial felicity.

He searched in vain, in spite of his prayers to Indra, the beneficent god who accords the rain, Indra, who keeps the sacred Cow whose possession ensures the accomplishment of all desires.

One evening, when he was going along a river bank, he saw a serpent with emerald scales under the lotuses. The beast was asleep, scintillating and coiled up. The pilgrim had learned from the Fakirs and the Joghis that divine wisdom is often contained in the sacred bodies of animals. He waited for the serpent to wake up, and when the serpent dragged itself on to the road, the old man followed it, more attentive and more silent than a shadow.

The serpent crawled toward the palace of the Begum. The Begum's daughter was about to marry a very powerful Rajah. The serpent hid in the shiny foliage of a mango tree, among the mangoes. The Begum's servants came into the gardens in order to pick the most beautiful fruits there.

The serpent, hidden in the shiny foliage, was brought to the young bride in a basket gemmed with moonstones. Having eaten the most beautiful fruits from the royal garden, she went to sleep in happy idleness; and the serpent, hidden beneath the shiny foliage among the mangoes, bit her between her breasts.

The tiny, invisible wound caused the virginal daughter of the Begum to die in a few moments, and the serpent, satisfied, crawled along the road again.

The entire region mourned that royal death, and the old man, weary of the road, followed in the tracks of the serpent, more attentive and more silent than a shadow.

The serpent now crawled toward a bungalow where two women of the people were offering one another white veils as a sign of amity. The serpent hid under the white veils and bit the younger of the two women on the wrist. The younger of the two women died suddenly. And, weary of the road, the old man followed in the tracks of the serpent, more attentive and more silent than a shadow.

The serpent crawled toward a field of sorghum, where it took on the form of a beautiful woman with a gilded moon on her forehead and a red star on her amber chin. Her hair was bushy and tenebrously odorous, like a jungle. Her eyes had the perfidy of a nocturnal river. And the pariahs and the coolies went toward the woman who had a red star on her chin and a gilded moon on her forehead. The woman was fatal; all those who knew her amour died. And, weary of the road, the old man followed in the tracks of the serpent, more attentive and more silent than a shadow.

The serpent crawled toward pious solitudes, and took on the form of a venerable Joghi. He seemed to be plunged in the meditation of prayer. All the invalids and all the poor people of the region came to him in procession: the blind, to beg him to open their eyes to the light; the wounded in order that he might cure their wounds; the lepers, in order that he might render their flesh healthy; and the sorrowful, in order that he might dry their tears. While returning to their dwellings, cured and joyful, however, the recipients of the miracle all died on the road. And, weary of the road, the old man followed in the tracks of the serpent, more attentive and more silent than a shadow.

Finally, the serpent shed its luminously green scales and appeared in its veritable form: that of a very august old man with a long beard as white as fresh snow. And the very august old man smiled at the pilgrim weary of the road.

The latter, encouraged by the fraternal sight of an old man as grave and sage as himself, seized the unknown man by his long solemn beard.

"Who are you?" the pilgrim weary of the road dared to ask.

"I am the Lord of the Dead," the old man replied. "I am the Envoy who brings humans consoling demise. My two sacred names are Malak-ul-Maut and Kala Bhairava."[1]

"I've followed you for long hot days along the rude roads," said the pilgrim then, "and I'm weary of the road. My body is devoid of vigor and yielding under the burden of the years. I have no more hope in my eyes. I have followed you beneath heavy noons and desolate sunsets. The ash of twilights extinguished my beautiful expectations a long time ago and evening has invaded my soul. Now, I have followed you patiently and dolorously, and I'm weary of the road. Grant my peace and repose, O Lord of the Dead."

"Your hour has not yet come," replied the implacable old man. "Every man is accompanied by his death. It follows in his footsteps with the appearance of a dwarf with black skin and scarlet lips. The dwarf carries a black wand with which he continually describes circles in the air. He is attached to the man he follows by a black chain, each link of which represents a year. And the man only perceived his death, which remains invisible until then, when the black chain that attaches it to him breaks, on my order, and, free and in control instead of being a slave, it drags him despotically into the darkness. Now, the chain that binds you to death has ninety links. The dwarf with the scarlet lips has only broken sixty. You must accomplish another thirty years of terrestrial existence."

---

1 Malak-ul-maut is the Islamic angel of death; Kala Bhairava is a Hindu deity also revered by Buddhists, who is the ruler of time.

The feverish and bleak evening was approaching, containing in its uncertain soul the dread of darkness.

"O Master of the Dead," implored the pilgrim, "deign to listen to my sobs. I am weary of the road, for I have followed you dolorously and patiently. I have followed you for long days over rude paths. Dusk is falling. Deign now, to accord my fatigue your peace and repose . . ."

But the Lord of the Dead pushed him away, and disappeared around a bend in the road.

Éliane's Funeral Lilies

IN the distant time when people liked verses, a humble minstrel was wandering along the water's edge celebrating the royal amours of Lancelot and Guinevere and the magical amours of Merlin and Viviane. But the harp did not support the ardent violence of his impetuous hands well. The high notes quavered and the low notes groaned, discordantly.

Throughout a long day of fasting, from the dappled dawn to the ocher evening, the minstrel had wandered in the villages. He had sung songs of celebration in one main square, but the passers-by had turned away with tears and sobs because the most beautiful girl in the village had just died, and her relatives had laid her to rest that very morning in a rustic coffin garlanded with honeysuckle and marigolds.

Later, further on, saddened by the sadness of others, the minstrel had sung songs of mourning, but the passers-by had fled with loud bursts of laughter, for they were commemorating a benevolent saint, and all the inhabitants of the village had put on their best clothes in order to honor that pleasant and clement memory.

The minstrel sensed then that his thoughts were not in harmony with the thoughts of other men. He was afflicted by that, being a tender soul ready to love his fellows. Only a young peasant girl had come to listen to him, her lips parted and her eyes wide. He sang to her with all his poetic soul. He celebrated before her the royal amours of Guinevere and Lancelot, and the magical amours of Merlin and Viviane. But, having recited his most beautiful songs before the peasant girl, he perceived that she had not understood them. She cherished him for himself, for the color of his hair, the gaze of his eyes and the laughter of his lips, and not for his sacred art. While sitting at his feet, she contemplated the man and did not listen to the singer.

He conceived a mild and poignant sadness because of that, and abandoned the amorous girl.

Dusk had fallen. The minstrel picked up his harp and tried to sing to himself, in the joy and anguish of his solitary soul; for a poet is only veritably a poet when he sings alone, uniquely for the joy of singing.

He experienced momentarily the charming bitterness of disdain. He praised himself for being scorned by the crowd, being greater than all its members. But the strings broke, one by one, under his willful hands, and the minstrel, sitting on the river bank, contemplated the mysterious visage of silence under the veil of the twilight.

Night came: a bewitching night. Night wandered over the mountains and the plains, like a barefoot witch collecting poisonous herbs for her philters. Night glided over the water like a witch in a silver chariot pulled by black swans. Night strayed beneath the foliage of the forest like a witch dressed in blue murmuring incantations in a low voice.

The minstrel, sitting on the river bank, contemplated the dark waves that ferried broken stars. The moon was not shining, in a sky only paled by starlight.

Suddenly, the profundity of the water and the night was torn by a faint distant light. A radiant boat was furrowing the black ripples and spreading around it a mystical glow. The minstrel considered the prodigy in amazement.

The light drew nearer, and he saw that the radiant boat was a coffin, drifting on the water, projecting the double white light of its candles and its lilies.

In the coffin, lying on the lilies, a young woman was asleep in the light of seven candles. She was miraculously blonde. Her hair seemed to be woven of pale candle flames, and her face seemed to be modeled in pale candle-wax. She was asleep, lying on the lilies.

Moved by an inexpressible amour, the minstrel rose to his feet and followed the floating coffin, ornamented like a nuptial boat with candles and flowers. He followed it for as long as the blue darkness lasted. Further downstream, the coffin passed before plains and villages, gardens and towers, but, borne away by unknown currents, it never slowed down or stopped.

Finally, at the somber moment that precedes the dawn, the minstrel saw that the river, narrower and more tumultuous, was rippled by a stronger breeze. A perfume of iodine and salt, vigorous and pure, refreshed the air. A vast rumor rendered the earth and the sky similar to the murmurous walls of a seashell.

The minstrel understood that the river was entering the sea.

The river was entering the sea slowly and placidly, as a human existence is lost in the infinity of death. Its waves seemed wearied by the long journey, glad finally to sleep in the bed of the tides. Its flow broadened out, and the broken stars ferried by its ripples shone with a more serene gleam.

The minstrel saw the candles of the coffin burning more limpidly still. The lilies exhaled a rarer perfume. The face of the dead woman shone more brightly in its virginal pallor. And the coffin, slowly and serenely, entered into the sea.

The waves carried the floating bier and the unknown corpse away. The waves carried the candles and the lilies into the distance. And the minstrel, his arms outstretched, remained standing on the shore.

The light of dawn finally shivered in the icy sky. A cold sadness invaded beings and things. The universe seemed to be regretting the consoling refuge of sleep in a cowardly fashion and waking up reluctantly, still bruised by the fatigues of the previous day.

Standing on the shore, the minstrel followed the vanished vision with his eyes, in vain. A murmur, simultaneously quavering and puerile, caused him to shudder. He saw a strange child with the face of an old woman, whose lips were contracted in an ancient smile.

She was murmuring bizarre prose to herself, set to a monotonous tune. That chant resembled the rusty music of a lamentable centenarian spinning-wheel. And this is what the child with the face of an old woman was muttering:

> *I have begged the wave*
> *To carry me away to the desired land.*
> *I have confided my destiny*
> *To the caprices of the wave.*
> *Carry me away to the desired land,*
> *O wave!*

The wave does not reach
The land that you seek;
The wave has told the gulls
And the gulls have repeated it to me,
The wave does not reach the land you seek,
Éliane!

I have begged the wave
To carry me away to the desired land.
I have confided my destiny
To the caprices of the wave.
Carry me away to the desired land,
O wave!

The wave has not brushed
The land that you seek:
The wave has told the foliage
And the foliage has repeated it to me
The wave has not brushed the land you seek
Éliane!

I have said to the wave:
"Do not wither my lilies,
O wave!"
And I have said to the wind:
"Do not blow out my seven candles,
O wind!"

The wave will not wither your lilies,
Éliane!
The wind will not blow out your seven candles,
Éliane!

And, standing up, the strange child quavered, in her ancient and puerile voice: "Éliane's coffin has disappeared . . ."

The minstrel was attracted by the enigma of those bizarre words, which, in their incoherence, dissimulated a mysterious meaning. Approaching the ancient and puerile being, he interrogated her about the mysterious words that he had just heard.

"Who was the Éliane of whom you speak and sing?" he asked.

"I don't know," said the strange child with the smile of an old woman. "I only know that she has been traveling for more than five hundred years toward the desired land where she will finally find the repose of the sepulcher."

And the strange child ran away in order to collect mauve and blue thistles on the dunes.

Thoughtfully, the minstrel picked up a dormant conch shell from the strand; for conch shells have learned all the secrets of the seas and repeat them in a confused and sonorous murmur. Conch shells contain all the echoes of the tides and all the dancing reflections of the waves.

The minstrel listened to the frail nacreous conch, and it was thus that he learned the story of Éliane.

Éliane was a royal princess who died before being queen. She conceived a great dolor in dying without being able to give substance to her vast and generous projects; for she wanted her reign to be an era of amour and peace, She wanted, with her fragile hands, to knead the clay of a confused realm in order to form a majestically beautiful work. She wanted the land that she governed to know no injustice, and that the women there might be happy.

But death took away Princess Éliane before she was queen, and before she died, the Princess said to her father the King: "Do not bury me in a shroud and do not seal my body in a sepulcher; for I shall only sleep in peace in a realm without injustice, where the women are happy. Set my coffin adrift on the greatest river of my homeland. The river will carry my coffin away to the sea, with my lilies and my seven candles, and the benevolent sea will carry me away toward the desired land . . ."

But for five hundred years, Éliane's coffin, with its lilies and its seven candles, has been drifting on uncertain seas, without ever reaching the desired land where injustice is unknown and the women are happy . . .

That is why Princess Éliane, who died without being queen, has not yet savored, and doubtless never will savor, the repose of the sepulcher.

Monsieur Berthier, Professor

MADEMOISELLE DE NOIRMONT had just attained her seventeenth year. That morning, she was radiant with a new pride. Poring over a schoolgirl's notebook, she was the image of studious grace. The errant light set her ardent brown hair ablaze. Her eyes, the imprecise color of waves and olive groves, were greener than usual. And her young smile was already subtly complicated. She incarnated the strophe of the American poet:

> *Standing with reluctant feet*
> *Where the brook and river meet,*
> *Womanhood and childhood fleet.*[1]

Nellie possessed the aerial charm of the first fragile rosy hours. Everything in her was capricious indecision, from the uncertain contours of her body to her vague and fresh gaze. Her eyes were open with astonishment to the vast Possible. Seventeen years is the April of the human spring, the first light of dawn.

And yet, one could already divine in that child the future woman. Her hair, which russet flames were slumber-

---

1 "Maidenhood" (1842) by Henry Wadsworth Longfellow.

ing, evoked a young autumn. Her eyes, saddened by the dream alone, presaged the dolors to come.

Monsieur Berthier, the old professor, was thinking about those things. He was also thinking how poorly the austere décor of the study room framed that feminine charm. Wall maps entangled their designs, like the bizarre shapes of clouds. A rigid cupboard bore with severity the burden of large dictionaries and encyclopedias. The young woman was sitting at a table overladen with volumes heaped in disorder.

The living image of studious grace, Nellie was plunged so profoundly in her old schoolbook that she did not see the melancholy tenderness of the gaze raised upon her. For melancholy and tenderness can be banal and ridiculous in themselves, and the old professor as condemned in advance to ridicule and banality. An entire monotonous and fastidious existence had left its imprint on that man of fifty.

Rather fat and very bald. With a disdainful stroke of her pencil Nellie had portrayed him thus to her companions. An old professor, rather fat and very bald. What a pitiful hero for a novel, or even a short story! And yet, that insignificant individual bore the sense of sadness within him, like the most delicate poet or the most picturesque lover. Nellie was for him the living chimera, toward whom all his best impulses rose recklessly.

Alas, he sometimes warned his vivacious and dolorous heart, *she's like all the young women who will one day marry. Nellie will marry . . . and I shall never see her again. I shall no longer have the anguish of this joy, not the ecstasy of this torment. I shall lose these hours, in which all the other hours are concentrated and go astray. And I shall no longer know this felicity of desolation into which I plunge so passionately. I shall never see her again. I shall then be nothing but a self-conscious void, nothing but a tenebrous despair. I shall have the fixed gaze of those who cannot forget. And I will sense that, in spite of the immensity of my despair, I am ridiculous and banal. I shall suffer as much from that as from my suffering. Why does Dolor not have the consolation of being beautiful?*

And he repeated, implacably: *I am ridiculous and banal.*

Fraülein Brillenstaub assisted in his lessons. She was touching in her modest ugliness and her poor dignity. She was very simple and very good. One day, having encountered Monsieur Berthier, she spoke to him incidentally about a project of betrothal sketched for their young pupil. The old professor went pale and tottered. Fraülein Brillenstaub was as sympathetic as she was astonished, but when Monsieur Berthier explained that lividity as a cardiac affliction, the excellent woman's astonishment disappeared and her compassion increased.

Since then, a heavy trouble had weighed upon the old master. Fraülein Brillenstaub summarized the situation in concise and clear terms: "Boor Monsieur Pedier is ill. At one dime, he always had a friently word to attress to me, but now he is sad. Ach, mein Gott! He only has one thought: to go as soon as bossiple!"

Nellie's hours passed, grayly, among atlases and large dictionaries.

One day, the young woman received a note from her professor, who was too gravely indisposed to continue his lessons. Fraülein Brillenstaub lavished over the old professor the exquisite pity of which her heart was full. And Nellie, very good in spite of her great youth, showed for Monsieur Berthier a compassion equal to that of Fraülein Brillenstaub. In response to her daughter's request,

Madame de Noirmont sent a domestic to obtain news of the invalid.

As majestic as an English footman, the valet entered Madame Berthier's drawing room.

Monsieur Berthier was old, fat and bald. Monsieur Berthier was ridiculous and banal, and to complete his disgrace, Monsieur Berthier was married.

Madame Berthier's "drawing room" was hung with rep. The once-bright green of the walls had faded to the gray of dusty olive groves. On the mantelpiece, a solemn pendulum clock was enthroned between two vases comical in their ugliness. The armchairs, of pretentious plush, maintained rigidly their outdated arrogance. The chairs affected a deplorable symmetry. In the exact center of the room was a lordly table that had never consented to abject utility. Only a portrait of a young woman contrasted, by its pensive grace, with the bourgeois mediocrity of its surroundings; it had Nellie's fugitive gaze, vaguely smiling lips and uncertain irises.

A fat woman irrupted into the drawing room hung with rep. The domestic considered her, exaggerating a sly respect. He saw before him Madame Berthier, née Zoé Froment, the irreproachable daughter of a very scrupulous bailiff. She took the letter from the domestic's hands. Her ample red flannel peignoir was inflated by irritated pleats. Her slightly puffy face expressed a haughty severity.

With a quasi-regal gesture, she sent the valet away.

Madame Berthier felt profoundly outraged in her conjugal dignity. Madame Berthier was having great difficulty containing her indignation. That morning, following the habit of bourgeois wives, she had been examining her husband's papers minutely, and among the letters from the provinces and the letters from the parents of pupils, she had found a piece of paper on which Monsieur Berthier had scribbled verses.

Madame Berthier reread, bitterly:

For Mademoiselle N. de N.

O virgin with furtive footsteps, virgin that I love
When will you come toward, light and smiling
The passer-by lingering in the shade of the cypress?

The dawns unfurl their solemn trails,
The flowers have shivered, sensing you pass by,
And your gaze has made the grasshoppers sing.

Your annunciators, the ingenuous Aprils
And your blue precursors, the mornings, have come:
The dew has starred their bare feet with golden nails.

They came to the attentive plain, to sing
The naïve song of the river bank.
It was the hour when red fires heightened the waves,

And the gardens, seeing that I was waiting too,
With an equal hope, with a similar care,
Said to me in a loud whisper: "Here she comes!"

Madame Berthier remained frozen in a pale stupor. Never had her husband celebrated her virtuous charms in verse. Standing next to the window, she meditated, ample and majestic, in her red flannel peignoir. And gradually, into that mediocre bourgeois soul, slid the obscure intuition and the obscure regret of melodious realms that she would never enter. Never would she know the illusory radiance that illuminated and set her husband ablaze, ridiculous and banal as he was.

Madame Berthier sensed confusedly that she was not one of those women for whom poets sing and suffer and die. Why? She did not understand that yet, and because of what she did not understand, a great anger flared up within her.

She went to the mantelpiece, seized the delicate virginal portrait with the indecisive gaze and the uncertain smile, and she tore it up angrily, with a vulgar gesture of bourgeois fury.

A few days later, Nellie's mother received a curt note from Madame Berthier announcing to her that her husband's health did not permit him to resume his lessons.

Nellie was saddened momentarily. But, being young and joyful, she did not worry about it for long. And what had to be accomplished was accomplished. Nellie was engaged to some young man. He was unremarkable, either by virtue of an abnormal intelligence or a troublesome individuality. He was an excellent young man who resembled all the others.

The marriage, in consequence of a family mourning, was celebrated in the strictest intimacy.

On returning from the traditional honeymoon voyage, Nellie found in her correspondence a large envelope bordered in black. It was a letter of notification that informed her of the death of her old professor, Monsieur Berthier.

"The tenth of October 1889—the day of my marriage," Nellie murmured, vaguely anguished.

She never penetrated the mystery of that death.

Those who are able to divine suffering will understand that Monsieur Berthier, professor, died as a poet, a beautiful amorous death; they will not ask any more.

Is not a beautiful death the hope and the inestimable dream of the poet, the compensation of a mediocre life and the consolation of a banal life?

Moonlight Over the Heath

Scene One

MOONLIGHT over the heath. Two peasant women enter slowly. One is carrying a basket of pancakes and the other a pitcher of milk. A thief is lying in ambush behind the pines.

First Peasant Woman: "Our dogs were howling mortally last night. Truly, I don't know what it can mean."
Second Peasant Woman: "How strangely the moon is shining over the dead fir trees! How strangely it's shining over the burned sands!"
First Peasant Woman: "The market opens at first light. I can't linger contemplating the moon or the dead fir trees, for I need to sell my pancakes at the market at first light."
Second Peasant Woman: "Let's hurry."

(They hasten their steps. An imploring voice calls to them.)

Lodda, *calling*: "I beg you . . . stop."

(The two peasant women stop.)

Lodda, *catching up with them.* "I went astray in the dark. Where can I find a shelter until first light?"

(*The two peasant women look at one another indecisively.*)

First Peasant Woman: "I don't know."
Second Peasant Woman: "I don't know."
Lodda, *to the first peasant woman*: "I'm dying of hunger. Give me one of your cakes."

(*The peasant woman gives her one of her cakes. Lodda eats it avidly.*)

Lodda: "I give you my thanks. You have a merciful and tender soul." (*She turns to the second peasant woman.*) "I'm thirsty. I'm very thirsty. Give me a little of that milk. I'll drink it from the hollow of my hands."

(*The second peasant woman pours her a drink in the hollow of her hands. Lodda drinks it avidly.*)

Lodda: "I give my thanks to you too, whose soul is merciful and tender. I would like to recompense both of you, but although I'm rich, more marvelously rich than any sovereign, I cannot give away that smallest part of my treasure."

(*The two peasant women laugh.*)

First Peasant Woman: "Are you rich, in truth? Why, then, are you so miserably dressed in rags on which flax flowers are fading?"

Lodda, *offended*: "I'm dressed in royal purple and precious stones."

Second Peasant Woman: "Where is your radiant and splendid palace, O Sovereign?"

Lodda: "Everywhere. Here before us."

First Peasant Woman: "She's a madwoman."

Second Peasant Woman: "She's a poor madwoman."

Lodda: "Oh, if only I could share my dreams with you! You'd be as rich and splendid and omnipotent as I am."

First Peasant Woman: "You were hungry just now, though."

Lodda, *confused*: "That's true . . . I was hungry just now."

Second Peasant Woman: "And just now, you were thirsty."

Lodda *sadly*: "That's true . . . just now, I was thirsty."

First Peasant Woman, *laughing*: "I don't care about sharing your treasures."

Second Peasant Woman, *laughing*: "Keep your treasures."

(*They go on, singing.*)

Scene II

Lodda, *alone*: "I can't do anything for those two, who were good and kind to me. It's very little, in sum, a wealth that one hasn't the ability to share. Without those two compassionate women, I'd be dead of hunger and thirst in the midst of all my magnificence. (*She shivers.*) How sad the moonlight is over the heath. I'm falling down with lassitude. I'm going back to my royal couch, to wait for dawn. (*She lies down on the sand.*) How soft this silver velvet is under the purple awning of the nocturnal pines. My maidservants have strewn pale golden flowers on my bed. They've burned perfumes in emerald cassolettes. Shut up, my murmuring heart. Leave the banqueting halls. Shut up. I can hear the first chords of the music that will lull my dreams . . ."

(*She falls asleep.*)

Scene III

The Thief, *emerging from his ambush, coming to Lodda and shaking her brutally*: "I heard you just now. Give me your jewels and your gold."

Lodda: "I can't give them to you."

The Thief: "Do you or do you not have jewels?"

Lodda: "My gold is as abundant as the sun's rays. My jewels are as luminous as the stars. But I can't give them to you."

The Thief: "You'll give them to me anyway!"

(*He approaches her, dagger raised.*)

Lodda, *recoiling, her hands over her breasts as if to hold and defend a treasure there*: "No! No! No!"

The Thief: "Give me your jewels. Living or dead, you'll deliver your gold and your jewels to me."
Lodda: "No! No! No!"

(*The thief plunges his dagger into her breast.*)

Lodda, *tottering and dying*: "My jewels! My . . . !"

(*She dies. The thief leans over her in order to rob her, but stops on hearing the voices of the two peasant women. He flees precipitately. Lodda remains lying in the shadows. The two peasant women advance with precaution.*)

Scene IV

First Peasant Woman: "That was like the scream of someone being robbed."
Second Peasant Woman: "It was more like the scream of someone being murdered."
First Peasant Woman: "A murder has certainly been committed on the heath."
Second Peasant Woman: "That's why our dogs were howling mortally last night."

(*At that moment, a ray of moonlight filters through the branches of the fir-trees and strikes the white face of Lodda.*)

Second Peasant Woman: "My God! My God! someone has murdered that stranger who asked me for milk."

First Peasant Woman: "Yes, it's her, it's the stranger in rags who said she was rich and omnipotent."

Second Peasant Woman: "She was a madwoman."

First Peasant Woman: "A poor madwoman."

Second Peasant Woman: "She must have killed herself."

First Peasant Woman: "Surely she's killed herself."

Daphne

DAPHNE, the daughter of the Earth and the Water, was more beautiful than all the other nymphs. The reflections of foliage tinted her blonde hair green and her eyes an indecisive blue. She was as supple and fresh as a wave on the river. Ge, mysterious and somber, and Ladon, the God of the River, had engendered her. She was beautiful under the Sun.

The Sun was infatuated with her. Phoebus Apollo loved her madly. At first he coveted her reflection in the water, and then he coveted her. He desired her for being undulating and uncertain. He desired her for attracting him and fleeing at the same time, as ungraspable as the water.

Phoebus Apollo loved the daughter of the Water in vain; for she did not love him. She feared him, as the waves fear the sun that draws their clear freshness from them and drinks it avidly.

Even the Gods, the impassive Blissful, are sometimes ravaged by the obscure ardors and tenebrous sufferings of humans. Phoebus Apollo no longer reigned with serenity over the placid skies. The empyrean All seemed to him to be too narrow to contain his divine torment.

One summer day, vibrant with bees and cicadas, Daphne was lying under the olive trees of Arcadia. She was lying down with her hair spread out. A spring was babbling quietly in a nearby orchard. The wildflowers were exhaling an odor of honey. The trees were asleep in the midday torpor. Grasshoppers seemed to be curious, delicately carved jewels. Some were flying like the birds. Their deployed wings quivered, green against the blue background.

Daphne was lying down, as blonde as the sun itself. She was the supreme outpouring, the perfect blossoming of that summer hour. She was the unique flower of the earth and the water of which she was the daughter.

Who will ever be able to describe the beauty of the vanished nymphs? They were more odorous than crowns of violets and more luminous than the first stars. And no nymph was comparable to Daphne, the unique flower of the water and the earth.

Phoebus Apollo saw her, lying under the olive trees of Arcadia; and Phoebus Apollo desired her in his ardent and cruel soul of a young God. Having descended from the serene sky in order to ravish her, he pursued her.

But Daphne, as ungraspable as the water that flows away eternally, fled before him. She fled, and her prompt sandals passed like silver lightning through the grass. She fled . . . and the God pursued her, ardent and terrible. The living grass paled and withered under his burning footfalls. Fresh streams dried up. His hair delivered its living flames to the still air. The Universe contemplated with amazement the course of the Sun through the terrestrial fields.

Fugitive Daphne, more beautiful than desire, sensed the torrid breath of the God getting closer. She sensed that Phoebus Apollo, hated and redoubted amour, was about to seize her in his arms of an ardent and cruel young God.

A distress greater than any human distress screamed within her. It was a mortal terror, mingled with an inexpressible shame. All the modesty of her feminine being, all the hectic pride of her virginal being, protested against the violence of the rape.

Remembering her childhood, she implored Ge, the good maternal earth; and Ge heard the prayer of her most splendid daughter. She opened her wide protective bosom, and the fugitive disappeared into the abysms where all things germinate.

And Phoebus, who was pursuing her, saw instead of the desired Form, an exceedingly green laurel.

The God, more sorrowful and more disappointed than a mortal, plucked the sacred laurel, weeping; and because he had lost the hope of his dream, because he was alone in the face of his dolor, he cursed the laurel. He cursed the laurel and all those which, in the future, would collect its deceptive leaves, in order to circle their temples with an illusory crown.

And that is why the laurel weighs heavily upon the foreheads that bear it. That is why Poets only ever collect their vanished dreams in memory. Having lost the hope of their dreams, they collect the accursed foliage. They collect it regretfully, and they circle their pale heads with the deceptive crown . . .

In truth, I tell you, Poets pluck the divine laurel weeping, weeping, weeping . . .

The Mystery of the Hands

A MESSENGER brought me a strange oblong packet wrapped in black cloth. It was like a minuscule coffin: a coffin for a dwarf or a kobold. Somewhat hesitantly, I opened the black oblong package, and I saw that it was indeed a minuscule crystal coffin. In the depths of the coffin, wrapped in yellow strips of fabric, lay two mummified hands. The strips were the color of antique papyrus and retained a vague odor of aromatics. The hands themselves were extended in an impatient repose beneath the sealed crystal. One divined the vigorous bones through the thin, blackened flesh. The brown fingernails retained a perfect form.

I interrogated myself momentarily as to who might have sent me that strange gift. Then, vaguely, I remembered Lady Scar, the bizarre old Englishwoman that I had met the previous winter. I remembered that she had offered to bring me back the hands of mummies from her next voyage to Egypt. I had accepted that baroque offer with a smile, as a joke on the part of the incomprehensible old woman.

I evoked the eccentric personality of Lady Scar. She resembled terribly the mummies of which she was so fond. The sun had darkened her meager visage to a bright brown.

She was more than old, she was ancient. Her garments, of an indescribably neutral color, exhaled an odor of faded aromatics. Her hands, above all, were disquieting by virtue of their impatient repose, their nervous mobility. One divined the vigorous bones through the thin, blackened flesh. In truth, that Englishwoman had ended up resembling the mummies of which she was so fond.

For a long time I contemplated those hands, which might have put on the pschent more than a thousand years ago and awakened the dormant soul of the kinnor.[1] They were doubtless imperious hands, to judge by the sensation of impatient repose that emanated from them. They were also gripping and cruel hands, considering the tenacity of the long fingers curled by the centuries, and the sharp ferocity of the brown fingernails.

Curiosity overcame my instinctive aversion. I respected the obscure decision that had sent those relics to me. I would not refuse them hospitality. Under the sealed crystal, they were extended in their eternal wait.

From the day that I received them, I was haunted by an indefinable malaise. The insipid scent of desiccated aromatics that the yellow strips of fabric gave off attached itself to me. And with that reek of dusty spices an insidious reek of the hypogeum was mingled. The vague emanations of an ancient putrescence were combined therein with a stale smell of the crypt. I came to fear entering my house.

Night, especially, rendered them redoubtable. The shadows intensified the impression of sly waiting. More than ever, I had the intuition that they were hands of prey

---

1 The kinnor was an ancient musical instrument, a kind of harp, mentioned in the Old Testament, but not usually associated with ancient Egypt. The pschent was a characteristic Egyptian "double crown."

and cruelty. An oblique moonbeam provoked an illusory scintillation of the ferociously sharp brown nails.

In dreams, I saw the hooked fingers advancing toward me, clenched in impatient repose; for they were hands of prey and cruelty.

The unquiet obsession pursued me with such obstinacy that I resolved to liberate myself from it, by returning to the soothing earth the hands so impatient in death. I dug a small grave at the back of my garden under the rose bushes, where I buried the little sealed crystal coffin. Having covered it again with red and greasy earth, I rejoiced in no longer having to breathe involuntarily the vague and insipid reek of desiccated spices and the subterranean tomb. I went to sleep delivered from the apprehension of seeing the ferociously sharp brown nails scintillating in the moonlight.

The following day, however, on going back into my house, I saw the hands in their accustomed place. The midday sun made sparks and gleams play upon the tenacious and cruel fingernails. An odor of fresh earth still corrupted the rising effluvia of desiccated aromatics. And I remembered having heard it said, by wanderers who brought back multiple superstitions from their long voyages, that relics sometimes attach themselves despotically to a person. Irritated by having been profaned and troubled in their long repose, it was said, they attached themselves to the person who had collected them in a transitory refuge.

The earth had rejected the redoubtable hands.

The gardener furnished me with a naïve explanation of the mystery. Frightened by the discovery of that strange subterranean deposit, he had returned them to the light, while refusing to bury them again. In his simple soul, perhaps he feared some enigmatic crime.

I resolved to leave my tenacious burden at the doors of some museum. The wardens would doubtless take them to scholars, who would study them with an anxious interest, those hands, which had put on the pschent more than a thousand years ago and awakened the dormant frissons of the kinnor. But the overly vigilant wardens obliged me, every time, to take back my package, deliberately left under a bench. Some politely, and others with hostility, made me take my importunate hands away, with the hooked fingers and sharp fingernails.

I was beginning to despair of being able to rid myself of the little sealed crystal coffin when a fortunate inspiration caused me to choose for a place of repose the nocturnal Bois. I abandoned it—finally!—in a pathway blue with darkness, and fled, my heart much lighter . . .

The adventure of the unknown hands, the first phase of which resembled a story by Edgar Poe, concluded in the most prosaic and the most imbecilically clownish fashion. My lunch the following day was cheered up by reading a headline reproduced in several daily papers: THE CRIME OF THE BOIS DU BOULOGNE. Shreds of journalistic phrases fluttered before my eyes: *Horrible details . . . freshly severed hands . . . bloody traces . . . is it a murder?*

The hands that, ten centuries before, had put on the pschent and awakened the frissons of the kinnor, sojourned for some time at the police commissariat, before finding their final sepulcher in the communal grave.

The Sirens No Longer Sing

ERMENTRUDE'S youth was studious and taciturn. She only took pleasure in the faded realms of olden days and books. She lived therein a radiantly distant life, wandering over unknown meadows among unreal forms. When winter traced pale arabesques on the windows, she did not see the snow flowering the world, for she was laughing at a summer of dreams ablaze with roses, where lilies consumed their perfumes. When spring sparkled in accordance with the indecisive laughter of the sun, she carried within her the melancholies of an artificial autumn.

The joys and dolors accorded to her by the magic of books enfevered her entire existence, which was externally serene. She was submissive mentally to beautiful tumults of amour and despair. She savored mentally the bittersweetness of renunciation and the cruelty of triumph. She bathed in the indecisive dawn of uncertainties and expectations. She traversed multiple existences and put on a thousand dissimilar souls. Alive, she had lain down in the shadow of death. Like Alcestis, she had returned, weary and mute, from long darkness.

Above all, Ermentrude sought the illusion of verses, more musical than streams, more imperious than the tides, more prismatic than fountains. The poems that charmed her most subtly were those whose imprecise verbiage prolonged an echo of the beyond; for she loved vaguely sensed but uncomprehended anguishes, and even more indeterminate ecstasies.

Her nostalgic spirit drew her toward vanished Hellas. She was the pious Belated of temples and legends.

Hera appeared to her, white under the glorious curve of the rainbow. At the feet of the goddess, a peacock opened the splendor of its ocellated adornment. Subjugated lightning bolts, tormented the creases of the snowy robe in which the divine body was flamboyant, Hera, who unleashes storms by shaking her black hair, smiled at the child. And Pallas favored her with the gaze of her eyes, as gray and green as the immortal olive trees. For her, Hermes made a lyre from a turtle shell again, and Phoebus Apollo revealed himself to her in golden laughter. But the best realization of her unconscious dream within the sunshine of Myths was the tempting apparition of the Sirens.

"You will find in your route the Sirens; they enchant all men who come close to them. Those who have the imprudence to approach them and listen to their songs cannot avoid the charm of them, and their wives and children never go to greet them and rejoice in their return. The Sirens retain them in a vast meadow by means of the sweetness of their songs."

With a tender precision, Ermentrude evoked those daughters of the foam, those white sisters of the waves, gemmed with reflections and must, and girdled with roseate algae.

One day, Ermentrude's studious life was brightened by a little living sunlight. The young girl was taken to the blue and black Mediterranean, which was the cradle of the Sirens. She loved that sea, which carried so many imperishable memories in its feeble tides.

Pines with curious and tenuous needles raised their violet trunks on the mountainsides. Through their ingeniously-wrought branches, the religious sunset allowed the incandescence of stained-glass to pour. They bore strange jagged fruits and a simple perfume of resin. Ermentrude admired the rude slenderness and the heroic grace of those northern trees, which neighbored palm trees and aloes.

The villa where Ermentrude had taken refuge overlooked the sea. Sometimes, the angry waves launched the mist of their crests toward the young girl's windows. Dominating her calmest slumbers, she heard the rumor of the sea. The hissing and rolling of the shingle, drawn one moment and thrown back the next, seemed to her to resemble a great breath abruptly resumed. And, because she cherished the sea and legends, she remained leaning on the terrace for a long time, evoking the vanished Sirens.

"Stop your ship in order to hear our voice. No one has passed before this island in a black vessel without first having listened to our melodious voices."

Not far from the coast, a smooth brown rock extended. The waves broke upon it with a white frisson of surf. The rock was shiny and polished, like onyx or agate. In truth, it resembled a marine couch ready to receive the beautiful body of a siren, the glaucous scaly body.

Ermentrude took pleasure in contemplating the smooth brown rock, in the unconfessed hope of glimpsing there, one evening, the lassitude or languor of a siren lying on the wrack.

She mentioned it one day to an old man who was instructing her in the law of Myths.

"The sirens no longer sing," replied the old man, devoid of chimeras.

"Why don't they sing any longer?" asked Ermentride, with an ardent incredulity.

"Because the world has changed," said the disillusioned and veridical old man. "The world has become as gray as ash since those melodious times. And people have changed too; they're rebellious to all splendor. Today, the companions of the ingenious Ulysses would listen to the song of the Sirens without peril. The Sirens know that. That's why they no longer sing."

"Why do you say that the world has become as gray as ash?" asked Ermentrude, obstinately. "Isn't the sea that was the cradle of the Sirens still as fecund? Isn't it still beautiful, with its blue and black waves and its bright reflections of summer?"

She interrupted herself in order to follow with her eyes the aerial passage of a sail.

"The earth is, in fact, still the same, but the times and people have changed," sighed the old man, as he went away, curbed by the burden of old age.

Ermentrude meditated for a long time on what the veridical and disillusioned old man had said: *That's why people have changed . . . the world had become as gray as ash . . . the Sirens are no longer singing . . .*

She meditated for a long time in the darkness before going to sleep, in a sad slumber.

A blue moonbeam woke her up.

The rumor of the sea had become subtle and caressant. A perfume of iodine and algae came in through the open window. In the air, there was I know not what insidious promise. Space was vibrant with a glad expectation.

Ermentrude got up, attracted by that indefinable appeal, and went down to the beach, where the shingle was shining like broken crystal. She stopped before the waves, struck by an adoring stupor. The shiny and polished rock was gleaming like onyx and agate. A strange nocturnal radiance was reminiscent of a living pallor.

Was it the double illusion of the sea and the moon? Ermentrude thought that she could see a Siren, languidly extended, whiter than the frisson of the surf, who was laughing at the waves. Her hair was bathed by the water, like floating algae. Her glaucous scales were blue-tinted in the starlight. And her green and azure eyes reflected the double clarity of the sea and the moon.

Ermentrude remained motionless, in ecstasy. It seemed to her that her entire being was nothing more than a melodic tremor. The flux and reflux of harmonious blood was singing in her veins. She was happy, like a wave under light. Her entire being was no longer anything but an exaltation and a heroic symphony.

But a cloud veiled Selene's face obscurely . . . and the form whiter than a frisson of surf disappeared, as if it had plunged into the waves. The sea became opaque and heavy again. All the musical clarity was extinct.

Ermentrude launched a desperate appeal into space. Only the monotonous sobbing of the metallic waves responded to her. And from the depths of her memory, the words of the disillusioned old man returned:

"The Sirens no longer sing . . . for the world has changed . . . the world has become as gray as ash . . . the Sirens know that . . . that is why they no longer sing . . ."

For the first time, the child doubted her dream. For the first time, she sensed within herself an incredulous soul in revolt.

In a supreme surge toward the fugitive chimera, she plunged into the opaque and heavy sea. A metallic wave carried her away. She disappeared, the prey and victim of the Mediterranean, which was the cradle of the Sirens.

What the Seasons Say

I
The Lady of Spring

THROUGH the foliage, I saw the uncertain smile of the Lady of Spring. As frail as an adolescent, she had the strange eyes of a disillusioned old woman. She was wandering barefoot, dispersing flowers. She was trampling them under her bare feet, throwing them to the wind with her youthful hands. She trampled them angrily and shredded them in rage.

And, having approached the Lady of Spring, I said to her: "How beautiful you are in all your youth! How charming you are in your cruel joy!"

She laughed, showing her pointed teeth, and replied: "I'm old beneath my blonde hair and the rosiness of my cheeks. I'm older and sadder than the world, under the weight of my flowers. I know the plaintive languor of convalescents, I know the dolorous ardor of the feverish, for I am simultaneously convalescent and feverish. I suffer from not knowing myself, even more than from not knowing the mysterious universe. I suffer from being young and desiring the unknown. For I love everything and nothing.

"Sometimes, I'm in love with the air and the sunlight, and songs on the road, and the sky, and me. I'm in love with existence for its own sake. The joy of breathing is sharper then than the voluptuousness of a caress. I rejoice in being and feeling.

"Sometimes, I'm sad for all my future sorrows, and I feel very old beneath my blonde hair and the rosiness of my cheeks. I cherish myself and I hate myself. I pity myself for weeping unjustly, and something in me cries: *Oh, the abominable, the hideous old woman!*

"And yet, I've been young since the commencement of the world.

"I suffer from being beautiful and loving myself. I suffer from being proud and hating myself. I suffer from everything, because I'm young. I sense that all marvels are possible for me. I suffer from wanting to be happy. I suffer from believing in happiness. How I suffer from being young!"

With her avid fingers, she tore apart the light flowers, before sighing again: "How I suffer from being young and old at the same time!"

And she looked at me for a long time, with her disillusioned eyes.

"Nothing is sadder than hope, and nothing is crueler than expectation. Memory is made of disappointed hopes, and hope already contains the bitterness of future memories."

She threw herself down on the grass, in an overwhelming languor.

"And yet, I'm glad to be alive. I'm glad that there's a sun. I'm glad that there's verdure on the earth. I'm glad to possess the senses of smell and hearing, in order to perceive living beauty, amorously."

She raised a little leaf with a slightly bitter juice to her mouth.

"When I bite this little leaf with a slightly bitter juice, it seems to me that I have the veritable taste of the universe on my lips. It seems to me that I'm eating living forests and prairies. It's by means of taste that one communicates most directly with the very essence of things. A child who bites a wild berry is closer to the primordial world that a thinker listening to the rumor of the sea or a sensualist complicating perfumes."

Suddenly, she started weeping.

"Why are you weeping?" I asked her, eventually.

"I don't know," she replied. "I'm weeping because I'm beautiful and because the sky is mild. And I'm also weeping because I have death in my soul. Oh, if only I could translate my anguish and the disquiet of my being!"

She continued, through infantile sobs: "How I envy the fever of summer, the satiety of autumn and the ennui of winter! I covet the bliss of empty hours. I covet desperately the repose of monotonous and dull hours. Who will give me blissful ennui?"

Birds were singing in the cool shade. The Lady of Spring listened to them, lying upon moss.

"Oh, the sweetness of being! How good tears are, and how exquisite terrors are! Expectations, and even regrets, are precious, since they prove that one still exists. Anything, rather than the great chill of Death. I dread slumber as a redoubtable enemy. I dread abominably the hours when I no longer feel alive.

"And yet, I'm weary of being reborn, weary of being resuscitated. I'm weary of seeing myself flourish again. I'm weary of loving, every year, with a different amour."

She was sitting under a limpid rainbow.

"I dread forgetfulness as much as memory. I'm terrified by life and by death. I'm a poor, uncertain soul, a poor disabled soul . . ."

The birds had fallen silent among the branches, and the rainbow faded away in the distance.

II
The Lady of Summer

I followed the tracks of the Lady of Summer. I followed her footprints through the dried up rivers and the desiccated plains. And I finally saw her, lying, like a fever victim, on a bed of burned moss. She contemplated me with her haggard eyes and murmured:

"I'm thirsty. I'm ill with languor and amour. The sun has consumed me all the way to the marrow. I'm burning. Nothing will ever extinguish my thirst.

"I've drunk the water of the sea in my fever, and the water of the sea has dried out my throat cruelly.

"The solitudes are afraid of my embrace; the prairies fear my implacable kiss.

"I've leaned over springs in order to smile at my reflection in the clear water, and the springs have dried up. I wanted to lie down on the fresh grass, and the fresh grass has withered."

She continued murmuring, with her ardent lips:

"I'm thirsty . . ."

And the echoes, like an invisible aerial choir, took up the plaint and the prayer: *I'm thirsty . . .*

"I've wearied that which I've loved, and I've wearied myself by my vain ardors," she sighed. "I no longer aspire to anything but a tenebrous slumber beneath the extinct stars.

"Every night I search for a peaceful river and let myself float downstream, like a dead lover. I allow myself to be borne away by the peaceful river, my eyes fixed on the glaucous light of the moon. But the moon fears my pale face, obstinately turned toward her own, for she knows that her cold mildness will never calm the bitter burning of my forehead and my eyelids.

"At dawn I flee, exasperating my wild cries, and, weary of suffering, sick with languor and amour, I rip up the clematis, I shred the honeysuckle and I crush the wild lilies underfoot.

"Sometimes, I divert myself with the drowsiness of my thought. I sit down amid the hay and the hayricks, like the peasant women, and I contemplate the red and brown landscapes without seeing them. My eyes are open, unconscious and stupid, and a bewildered torpor numbs my limbs. My wide ruminant eyes reflect the verdure of grass and the rust of spelt, I linger like that until dusk. Indolent snakes come to sleep in the pleats of my robe. I amuse myself ornamenting their living coils with emeralds and pale sapphires. But I sometimes throw them away with a weary gesture, for nothing amuses me for long.

"The imbecile crowd praises me, prefers me and desires my presence; but those who have seen me face to face fear the avid flame of my eyes. I kill those I love. I drink the sap of flowers with so much fever that I cause them to perish under my mouth. I'm like the cruel Empresses and Queens who kill those who love them, especially those they have loved."

She turned her thirsty and dry lips toward Infinity.

"Freshness!" she sighed. "Freshness!"

Her ardent sight was prolonged in the silence.

"Lizards and grasshoppers are my living hiccups," she said, eventually, cheered up by having seen a little greenness moving at her feet. "I've learned my most beautiful poems from cicadas. They're joyful or sad, in accordance with souls. In the times when humans had a less unquiet soul in a less weary body, an aede sang the praises of the cicada.[1] He compared it to the Gods, because it has no worries and doesn't carry the dolorous burden of human flesh and blood. Today, poets listen to its monotonous cry as a dull plaint.

"I alone am always the same, always burning with the same tormented ardor. I wander in the jungles like a lioness, and my yellow eyes pierce the curtain of the lataniers. Those who contemplate me fixedly lose their reason. I glide through the fields of rice like a furtive python. I cause paradoxical orchids and daturas to bloom in the lands where I reign solitary, for I have a despotic soul, and I want to dominate without sharing. In the countries where I reign solitary, I accord my subjects sparkling and bizarre birds, forests in which an eternal glaucous twilight lingers, and flowers, and flowers, and flowers . . . all flowers . . . the

---

1 The author probably has the ode to cicadas by Meleager of Gadara in mind, although that is by no means the only ancient Greek poetic tribute to the insect in question; the supplementary comment does not seem to refer to Socrates' famous symbolic employment of cicadas in *Phaedrus*.

most violent and the most delicate, the most barbaric and the most complex . . ."

The Lady of Summer laughed, with an excessive clarity.

"Oh, the sunlight!" she said. "Oh, the sunlight! It flows in my veins like molten gold. It's the very substance of my flesh. It clothes me, like a royal cloak. It ornaments me with translucent jewels. It weighs upon my shoulders, like a burden of blazing metal. I'm weary of the sunlight, and yet I cherish it; for one cherishes desperately that which makes one suffer."

She stopped among the grasshoppers. She picked one up at random and admired it.

"In truth, I have the vindictive soul of the sun. I have the vindictive soul of the sun, and I give death to those who love me."

The Lady of Summer fell silent. She went in search of a little shade under the blue foliage. The chant of the springs fell silent as she approached; and the sundial, gray in the midst of red rose-bushes, ceased to mark the torrid hours. Only the cicadas were singing, untiring and monotonous.

III
The Lady of Autumn

Toward the end of a nostalgic day I went into the sumptuous orchard where the Lady of Autumn was lingering.

Beautiful fruits weighed down the branches. Apples were reddening in their robust varnish. Pears were being gilded next to violet figs. Apricots were ambering their ripe freshness. The odor of vines soothed the air.

The pomp of colors unfurled like an Oriental procession. Red affirmed its plentitude and its profundity. It was majestic or tender, in accordance with the mysterious design of hues. Yellow was ardently velvety, warming up all the way to the fervor of orange.

There were no flowers in the grave orchard where the Lady of Autumn was lingering. Only the chrysanthemums were entangled eccentrically, surrendering their melancholy perfume as if regretfully.

On a bed of mown hay, the Lady of Autumn lay languidly. Vine branches ran through her loose hair, russet and brown, the color of dead leaves, and her eyes were the color of wine. Her orange robe and her red mantle brightened the shade. She was holding an empty cup in her hand. Her lips were laughing, but her eyes remained sad.

When she saw me she rose to her feet and started dancing, trampling scattered clusters of grapes. The juice of the grapes bloodied her beautiful rhythmic feet. And while dancing, she wept.

Overwhelmed by inebriation and lassitude, she finally let herself fall on to the bed of mown hay. With a hesitant hand she sought the golden cup in which she had moistened her avid lips. Being thirsty, she seized it and raised it to her lips. I followed her uncertain gestures with my eyes . . .

Being thirsty, she seized the golden cup and raised it to her mouth . . .

But the cup was empty; and the Lady of Autumn, disappointed, threw it away.

A malaise gripped me in the opulent orchard where the colors were singing. I approached the woman overwhelmed by inebriation and lassitude.

"Why aren't you rejoicing in your grape-harvest?" I asked. "Why are you weeping silently, among the heavy clusters of grapes and the weighty fruits?"

She looked at me with her sad eyes, while her mouth laughed. "I'm weeping," she said to me, slowly, "because I'm going to die."

For the first time, I perceived an indefinable odor that was exhaled by the orchard: the moist corruption of dead leaves and overripe fruit, the mortuary suavity of shredded roses, and the funereal perfume of chrysanthemums . . .

"It's in the plenitude of life," the Lady of Autumn continued, "that one senses with the greatest intensity the presence of death. It's in the blossoming of felicity that one savors with the greatest sweetness the charming bitterness of morbid memories."

Through the echoes of space, she sobbed: "I'm going to die! I'm going to die!"

She picked apart a cluster of grapes in her feverish fingers.

"Tomorrow, the whiteness of death will whiten everything. Great pure breaths will sweep away the dead leaves that are already rotting on the dried up ground. The snow will envelop with its ample folds the livid nudity of the earth. The dead wood will crack in the wind. Tomorrow, there will be the sepulchral Cold. Tomorrow, there will be the slumber of icy things. And today I am drinking to my imminent death."

While speaking, she shredded large red and yellow chrysanthemums.

"Today I've said a dolorous adieu to the heavy clusters of grapes and the weighty fruits. I've said a long adieu to the colors and the perfumes of my orchard. For tomorrow, I'm going to die."

Being thirsty, she seized the golden cup and raised it to her mouth . . .

But the cup was empty . . .

IV
The Lady of Winter

I was meditating in front of the captive fire, in which I rediscovered the redness of old sunsets; and the Lady of Winter tapped on the window panes.

She tapped on the window panes with fingers jeweled with pale sapphires; and her face appeared to me through the blue-tinted glass. Her face appeared to me, so beautiful in its sadness that I resolved to contemplate it at greater length. I followed the Lady of Winter to her palace of starry ice.

The Lady of Winter was sitting on a cathedra of ice encrusted with diamantine frost. A backcloth of stalactites emphasized her profile, rigidly sculptural. She was clad in a royal mantle of snow and crowned with a headband of glittering icicles. With her subtle and vigorous hands she was weaving, in the frame of the Frost, all the landscapes and all the enchantments of winter. She was evoking thus the boreal plains, traversed by snowy flocks of eiders and wild swans. She was evoking the blue slumber of glaciers and the meditation of mountains with limpid summits. With her vigorous and supple hands, she was weaving, in the frame of Frost, all the landscapes and all the enchantments of winter. I saw the fragile lace of branches stripped of leaves and florid with snow. I saw the black frisson of pines under the north wind. And I also saw the moon silvering the ice.

The solitary woman turned her proud and beautiful face toward me. Her hair cast the reflection of a polar sun. Her eyes harbored the glaucous azure of glittering stalactites. The North Wind was asleep in a pleat of her robe.

She said to me: "I'm the Lady of Winter. I'm the mistress of beautiful spaces. I accord, to those who love me, my aristocratic and melancholy soul. My servants are as indomitable and untamed as the storms, which also obey me."

She fell silent, and the North Wind, which was asleep in a pleat of her robe, woke up and flapped its wings. She soothed it with a sovereign gesture, and the North Wind went to sleep again.

Then the Lady of Winter said: "Ignore those who scorn you. Distance yourself from those who love you. Take refuge in solitudes, and the solitudes will murmur familiar words to you, like grave friends. They will advise you with good will. They with criticize you gently. And sometimes, they will praise you sagely.

"Distance yourself from human beings. Thus, you will contemplate the visage of your soul as if in transparent water that no other images have troubled. Learn the force of disdain. Know that men and things can do nothing against silent disdain.

"Only scorn is invulnerable. Be calm in your pride. Pride is the strongest and the most noble chastity. Pride is the savor of souls, for it drives away vulgar temptations and base covetousness. It teaches serenity throughout life and before death.

110

"Remember that you will die alone. Remember too that every individual ought to live as they would like to die. Prepare yourself for your solitary death by living alone.

"Do not look back. No thinking being is without regrets at the approach of evening or without remorse at the approach of night, but regret and remorse are vain things.

"Do not aspire to do good. It is a goal too high for a human soul to attain. Aspire to do as little harm as possible. The best of men and the saintliest of women are the man and woman who have done the least harm.

"Let your felicity be composed of noble sadness. Rejoice in the North Wind, ice, mists and lacy frost. The wind will be your guide, the snow your consolation."

She fell silent, and the North Wind woke up for the second time. It flapped its wings like a great wild swan. Like a great wild swan, the North Wind flapped its wings and flew away into the distance. I saw it soaring above the marvelous white landscape. I followed its imperious flight with my eyes, and I fashioned myself a soul in the image of its soul, cold and tumultuous and free.

I replied to the Lady of Winter: "Like you, I am calm in my pride. Like you, I have the strength of pride and disdain. And like you, I am a friend of solitudes."

The Lady of Winter, sitting on a cathedra encrusted with diamantine frost, smiled at me. And, while smiling, she was weaving with a subtle patience . . . weaving, in the frame of frost, all the enchantments of winter.

In the Shade of the Laurels

A SHEPHERD received, from the nymphs and pastors who had collected him at birth, the predestined name of Daphnis. The unknown nymph who had given birth to him had abandoned him at the foot of very green laurels, and that is why the nymphs and pastor who collected him had attributed the name Daphnis to him.

When he grew up, he wandered over the vivaciously forested mountains. He saw the blue flowers of dawn opening, and the red flowers of dusk intoxicated him with their feverish perfume. He wandered over the mountains amid the forests; and, having cut reeds on the edge of ponds, he blew into their sonorous hollows. The whisper of his pipes mingled with the murmur of nocturnal waters.

In winter, crouching near woods where the odor of foliage still lingered, he celebrated the vanished summer. Spring penetrated him with a fervent melancholy; and in autumn, he rejoiced among the trellises. Juicy clusters were crushed between his avid lips; he laughed ardently, his hair mild with vine-branches. He was as free as the Fauns. He was solitary among the fraternal plants. He was happy to be the equal of beasts in repose, for he did not love anyone and, more importantly, he was not loved by anyone.

He was not loved; that was because he was as free as the Fauns and happy to be the equal of beasts in repose.

One evening, however, a Naiad heard the harmonious pastor on the bank of the river. The whisper of his pipes slid with a strangely persuasive softness over the quivering water. She loved him for his beautiful vesperal music and for his melancholy youth.

She was insidious and jealous, like the water that had once conceived and given birth to her. She appeared, as if made blonde by the sunlit water, and Daphnis allowed himself to be enveloped by her imperious amour.

The Naiad put her fluid arms around the adolescent. In return, she had him make a solemn oath never to love any other beauty than hers, and never to contemplate tenderly any other face than hers. And Daphnis made the solemn oath that the Naiad as jealous as the water demanded of him.

For a long time he remained plunged in the amour of the one who incarnated all the multiple charms of the water. Her eyes appeared to him to be green at dawn, blue at midday and gray in the evening twilight. Her hair was burning gold under the sun and pale silver under the moon. Her flesh was an eternal refreshment offered to the thirsty. For a long time he loved her with an amour as oft-renewed as the appearances that she put on to please him.

One day, however, Daphnis contemplated another face than that of his lover. He was smitten with a wandering flute-player who was passing through the vines. He loved her eyes, intoxicated beneath their heavy lids. He loved the taste of her kisses, in which the juice of grapes was mingled with the honey of hyacinths.

The Naiad learned of his treason. She appeared, vengeful, before the forgetful lover, and reminding him of the violated oath, she afflicted his infidel eyes—the eyes that had retained an image other than her own—with blindness.

Daphnis sang and wept in the depths of his darkness. He sang to console himself by means of his own lies. Fallacious memories sobbed eloquently through the syrinx. And in the interior darkness, stars sometimes streamed, momentarily resuscitated. Often, however, the melodious words expired on his lips; and he wept, mutely, in the depths.

He lived thus for some time, under the jealous eyes of the nymph who loved him. For some time, he lived thus on memory and lies. An hour came, however, when the memories no longer charmed him, and the lies ceased to please him with their illusory glitter. The lies having ceased to please him, Daphnis the poet died in the shade of the shiny laurels.

And the Naiad wept for him, not realizing that she had killed him.

Often, it is the lot of individuals to cause the death of those they cherish most recklessly. Thus, we destroy our joys and we shatter our hopes; and we cause amour to perish under our kisses . . .

The Captive Princess

A severe chamber in a tower of gray stone. On the walls, very ancient tapestries, almost effaced; a mirror; a weaving-frame with broken threads; a cithara forgotten in a corner. Silence. Dusk gradually falls.

The Princess: "Evening, at last . . . Evening, already . . . How long and brief the minutes are! At this glaucous hour, everything becomes fluid. The roads are like rivers; they meander and they flow in the undulating light. In truth, everything becomes fluid at this hour, everything steals away, everything flees. It's the hour of water. The sky itself resembles a limpid pool. The fields evoke troubled eddies and the mountains make one think of motionless waves.

(She lingers in front of the mirror momentarily.)

"I'm weary of my own face. I'm weary of my beauty. My most ardent wish is to become someone else. Always myself before myself! I'm so bored with being me. I've put on barbaric robes, made up my lips and my cheeks, powdered my hair with golden ash and blue dust, in order to metamorphose myself, but always I've encountered in the mirror the same gaze in the depths of the same eyes, and the same smile on the same lips.

"To distract myself, I contemplate those tapestries, so old . . . as old as my ennui. I want to evoke the effaced figures of their antique characters, imagine them as they once were, joyful or funereal, amorous or menacing . . . but I'm weary of my imaginations. I'm weary of embroidering my dreams in that frame. Out of sadness and anger, I've broken the multicolored threads that tinted it.

"I must be old already. Veritable old age is the futile youth of those who are bored. I'm the Captive Princess who has been locked up, alone in confrontation with herself. And I've been waiting, for such slow years, for the Prince Charming who will liberate me."

(*A voice is heard crying out joyfully.*)

A Voice: "Free! Free! Free! I'm overwhelmed by fatigue, my feet are bruised by stones and lacerated by thorns, but I'm free! I've eaten the dust of roads and drunk the stagnant water of marshes, but I'm free!"

The Princess, *leaning over and striving to gaze through the bars*: "Oh, the pale beggar-woman who is lingering at the foot of the tower, her eyes raised toward me. She's wretchedly dressed and poor . . . poor . . . and yet she seems both happy and proud. There are very humble joys, which seem to want to hide, to shelter in the shadows. There are fearful and tender joys . . . But that woman is rejoicing overtly in her felicity, as if she had no fear of losing it, as if nothing and no one could take it from her. How proud she is of her happiness! And yet, she's so poor . . . so poor . . .

(*She summons the guards.*)

"My guards! My guards, who watch night and day, allow that highway beggar-woman to come to me. She'll distract me by telling me about her adventures. (*She picks up the broken threads from the frame.*) She has followed freely all the roads that evening blurs, which resemble rivers in the indecisive light. Perhaps she knows the legends of all the lands she has passed through. Perhaps she's sat in the corner of a ruddy hearth where a cauldron is simmering, among old men, very wise for having lived, and all the attentive children . . . but I know nothing beyond my own dreams.

(*The wanderer enters, clad in rags, escorted by the guards.*)

"Leave us.

(*The guards withdraw.*)

To the wanderer: "Who are you?"
The Wanderer: "I'm the Wanderer and the Vagabond."
The Princess: "You're the Wanderer, you say? Have you no other name?"
The Wanderer: "I have no other name."
The Princess: "Why do you rejoice so insolently, O passer-by? You're poor."
The Wanderer: "I'm free."
The Princess: "A lamentable joy."
The Wanderer: "The most profound joy is the sad joy."

The Princess: "How proud you are, stranger! How strangely proud you are. You're as proud as the daughter of a king."

The Wanderer: "I was the daughter of a king once."

The Princess: "Was your father vanquished in combat or expelled by his people?"

The Wanderer: "My father was neither vanquished not dethroned. My father reigns in splendor over a powerful people. I quit my father's place in order to be free."

The Princess: "Alas! I envy you and pity you."

The Wanderer. "Don't pity me. I was once a Captive Princess like you. Like you, I was locked up in a tower of gray stone. Like you, I was a sacred prisoner of guards who watched night and day."

The Princess: "And how did you escape, stranger?"

The Wanderer: "The ivy that covered the walls was very thick. The ivy was my verdant ladder."

The Princess: "Oh! How did you find that force and courage within yourself? Myself, I've been waiting for years for the Prince Charming to come who will liberate me."

The Wanderer: "No Prince Charming ever liberated a Captive Princess. The legend of the Prince Charming was invented to deceive the ennui of Captive Princesses whom no one will ever liberate."

The Princess, *despairingly*: "Whom no one will ever liberate, you say?"

The Wanderer: "Captive Princesses can and ought to liberate themselves. Their salvation is in their own hands. They alone cam set themselves free."

The Princess, *sobbing*: "How will I ever escape from here?"

The Wanderer, *going to the window and looking outside*: "The ivy that is crawling over these walls is even thicker than the ivy that once served me as a ladder."

The Princess: "Oh, I would never dare to attempt that! Oh, I would never dare to attempt that."

The Wanderer: "You'd be free."

The Princess: "But I'd wander, wretched, in wretched rags, along uncertain roads. The sun would burn me in summer and the north wind would chill me in winter. I'd be hungry and thirsty, like vagabonds. I'd be hungry under the bleak north wind. I'd be thirsty under the terrible sun. I'd go astray in unknown lands. Those whom I'd ask for alms wouldn't understand what I was saying. I'd be chased out of villages with insults. Children would stone me on their father's doorstep. In spite of my fatigue, I wouldn't dare to sleep, in my terror of murderers and wild beasts. I'd always be hungry, and always thirsty, and always afraid. I'd no longer be beautiful or charming. The passers-by would speak to me scornfully. I'd be someone who goes, fallen and rejected, from hearth to hearth and house to house."

The Wanderer: "You'd be free."

The Princess: "In truth, in truth, I don't dare. And I never will dare to attempt that effort."

The Wanderer, *sadly*: "Adieu."

The Princess, *resigned*: "You're leaving? You're abandoning me?"

The Wanderer: "I'm leaving you, because I can't do anything for you. For a long time, I've been trying in vain to free Captive Princesses. I try to free them, in vain. Some, like you, fear the hazards and perils of the unknown. Others fear the tears that their flight will cause to flow. They refuse to follow me, some by reason of timidity, and the others by reason of tenderness."

The Princess: "Are you happy, stranger?"

The Wanderer: "I'm so sure of my joy that I disdain to dissimulate it. I wear it in my face, like a noble sign. I throw it to the passers-by like a challenge."

The Princess: "Don't you regret the soft security of old?"

The Wanderer: "I've never regretted anything in my life, except the cowardice of others."

The Princess: "Will I ever see you again?"

The Wanderer: "Never."

The Princess: "Adieu."

The Wanderer, *dolorously but firmly*: "Adieu."

The Sun's Lie

TWO PRIESTESSES OF THE SUN, a mother and daughter, lived in a fecund plain, honoring the beneficent deity. The mother had a severe and vindictive soul, but the daughter was compassionate, like the Sun that she venerated.

The mother and the daughter labored in women's employments, and everything that they earned by their labor they gave to the temple of the Sun. They were content with a single maize cake each per day.

Having neither desires nor hopes, the two Priestesses of the Sun lived peacefully. The star ambered the brown flesh of the young woman with its reflections. It gilded her black hair and lingered over the radiant pleats of her mouth. At dawn the two Priestesses saluted with marveling hymns the triumphant revelation of the rising sun; and every evening, they lamented seeing their god dying over the sea.

One day, the mother went to the city in order to sell the products of their common labor. The young woman, being hungry, brought forward the customary hour of the repast and ate her unique maize cake. When she had finished, however, a pilgrim passed along the bright road. The sun had burned his eyes and bronzed his adventurous face. The pilgrim, famished and weary, begged the young woman, in the name of the Sun, to give him a little nourishment.

The young woman trembled in her every limb because, having eaten her share, she dared not give him her vindictive mother's. Firmly pious, however, she could not refuse alms implored in the name of the Sun. Taking the maize cake, she broke it, and gave half of it to the pilgrim.

Having eaten it, the pilgrim blessed her in the name of the Sun, and, having blessed the young Priestess, continued on his way.

When the vindictive mother came back from the city, she went into a terrible fury on learning about her daughter's pious action. The young Priestess promised in vain to yield her own share to her the following day. The old woman accused her daughter of having deceived her and of having eaten her own share in her egotistical gluttony, while abandoning her mother's; and her anger was so violent that she threw her daughter out, hurling harsh words at her.

Thrown out by her mother and abandoned to her destiny, the young Priestess wept bitterly on the road. Toward evening, exhausted by the long journey, she took refuge in the branches of a large pipal tree. The sun disappeared over the horizon, and, feeling that she had been abandoned by the Sun, the young woman sobbed desperately in the branches.

The night passed, slowly and dolorously. The star reappeared, merciful and magnanimous, and hope radiated again in the heart of the young Priestess with the renascent light. Exhausted by her sleepless night—she had not been able to sleep for fear of wild beasts—she went to sleep. When she woke up, the sun was blazing in the sky.

A young Rajah was returning from hunting. The ardor of the day constrained him to seek the blue shade of the pipal tree. He became drowsy in the shadow of the cool branches.

The young Priestess, not daring to quit the protective tree, remained silent, hiding in the branches. But in thinking about the bitterness of her past and the uncertainty of her future, she wept slowly, and for a long time . . . and her tears fell on to the face of the young Rajah, like a warm and odorous rain.

And the young Rajah, waking up, thought he could feel on his forehead and his face the drops of a warm and odorous rain. Seeing the blazing sun, however, he was amazed, and, seeking to clarify the enigma, he discovered the young Priestess of the Sun among the branches.

The star enveloped her in a protective glory. Sunlight was dormant in the creases of her robe. Sunlight emanated from all of the brown and gilded flesh. She appeared to the young Rajah, living light and perfumed and tender ardor. And the young Rajah shivered with amour before the splendid stranger.

The young Rajah, having taken the splendid stranger to his palace, married her with great honors, for he venerated the stranger of mysterious lineage. The new Rani conserved the secret of her name and her race, and when the Rajah's other wives interrogated her she maintained a smiling silence.

The happy peace of the young Rani was, however, troubled by a return of the old days. The bitter clamors and coarse speech of a beggar-woman resounded one morning at the gates of the palace, and penetrated as far as the young Rani; and, with a shiver of shame and disgust, she recognized her mother's voice.

She ordered that the beggar-woman be introduced into her presence. And when the old beggar-woman was admitted to her presence, she ordered the servants and maidservants to leave them alone.

The vindictive mother rained invectives and maledictions down upon her daughter. She accused her of ingratitude. She reminded her that, although she had expelled her from their communal hearth, that maternal abruptness had been the cause of her royal fortune. Mingling plaints with reproaches, therefore, she accused her daughter of ingratitude. In vain the young Rani represented to her the perils that she had escaped miraculously: the perils of hunger, thirst, wild beasts and the brutality of men. The vindictive mother did not cease her plaints and reproaches.

At that moment, the young Rani heard the footsteps of the Rajah, her husband. And, ashamed of her relationship with that coarsely-spoken beggar-woman, she begged the merciful Sun to spare her tender pride; for, being in love with the Rajah, she was jealous of her husband's esteem.

And the merciful Sun listened, and granted the prayer of the young Priestess. When the Rajah arrived in her presence, the coarsely-spoken beggar-woman had disappeared, and in the place where she had stood, spiteful and noisy, shone a golden throne, which appeared to be carved from radiance. In response to the Rajah's question, the young wife replied to him that the throne was a present from her mother and that it came from her mother's dwelling.

The Rajah, impressed by the prodigality of that gift, announced to the Rani his intention to visit the palace of that mother, whom he supposed to be a powerful sovereign; and the Rani, her heart heavy with anguish, consented to her husband's desire.

The Rani and the Rajah and their entire court traveled for a long time through sonorous verdant valley, across plains and through jungles. They reached the country where the little hut stood from which the young Priestess of the Sun had once been expelled by her vindictive mother.

When the travelers approached the place where the little hut stood, the young spouse prayed to the Sun to spare her tender pride for a second time, for she feared being covered by confusion before her royal husband. Above all, she feared being less beloved if, instead of a sumptuous palace, the Rajah discovered the miserable hut that had sheltered his young wife.

And the merciful Sun granted the prayer of the young Priestess, for, when she approached the place where the wretched hut stood, with the entirety of the traveling court, a vast radiation burst forth among the fields of sorghum. It was a golden palace, the walls and porticos of which were dusted like living flame. The terraces shone with a yellow and blue glow; the gardens were ablaze with ardent flowers; the fountains streamed with limpid fire.

The young Rani rendered thanks to the merciful Sun in her heart. "This is the palace were I was born and in which I grew up, attentive and docile," she said. And the Rajah, marveling at the beauty of the dwelling, went into the palace of living flame . . .

Blinded by the hot splendor, the Rajah and his court did not perceive the unreality of the edifice of radiance, the architecture of light. They did not perceive the emptiness of the large golden halls in which the throne was resplendent. Dazzled, they quit the miraculous palace proclaiming the glory and praising the magnificence of the Rani.

As he drew away, however, the royal husband looked round in order to contemplate the luminous dwelling of his young wife one last time.

To his great amazement and his great anger, the chimerical palace had disappeared. The golden walls no longer loomed up in the distance, which had become dull again.

The Rajah was unable any longer to be grateful to the Rani for the radiant illusion that she had accorded him. He had her strangled publicly by his executioners.

Thus the young Priestess of the Sun died of her impotent tenderness. For men, in their cruel thirst for an ugly truth, are not grateful to those who abuse them by means of a radiant illusion of amour.

The Enemies of Light

For them the morning is the shadow of death.
They experience all its terrors therein.

I THOUGHT of these verses of Job:

Others are enemies of the light,
They do not know its ways,
They do not travel by its paths . . .
For them the morning is the shadow of death,
They experience all its terrors therein.[1]

As the feverish fear the mortal approach of night, its memories, its terrors and its deliria, the Enemies of Light fear the approach of dawn. Its radiance, sharp and similar to arrows, pierces their weary pupils. They put a veil over their face, as warriors arm themselves with a breastplate. Some, out of sadness, and others, out of terror, remain indoors by day. Some are defending a fragile and culpable

---

1 This is a back-translation of the lines as they are given in the text. In the A.V., *Job* 24: 13 & 17 reads: "They are of those that rebel against the light; they know not the ways thereof, nor abide in the paths thereof . . . For the morning is to them even as the shadow of death; if one know them they are in the terrors of the shadow of death."

joy against the daylight, others fear the brutal revelation of their despair. Some seek the shadow in order to make love there and others in order to weep secretly there. "They do not know the light." And all of them fear the dawn. The future day, the unknown day, creeps up on them as a perfidious adversary, bringing with it all the treasons of destiny. It prepares, for those who hate it, all evils: the disappointment that aggravates wounds and the humiliation that envenoms them. It engenders expectations, sharp hopes, lassitude, angers and dolors. The Enemies of Light know that, and that is why they fear the dawn.

Darkness puts a cool blindfold over the eyes. It pours its balms and aromatics over the heavy eyelids. It is the friend of silence. It is the protector of felicity and the consoler of dolor. With a gesture, it makes the wind fall silent in the trees. With a gesture, it appeases the uncertainty of the waves.

The Enemies of Light take refuge in it, because they know that it is compassionate to the banished. The Enemies of Light feel that they have gone astray in a hostile world; they have a slight weight on the face of the waters; on land they only have an accursed part.

They never take the road of the vines. They will not mingle with the brown processions that go that way to tread the grapes. They will not see the beautiful bare feet of the virgins, the gilded feet amid the dark purple of the grapes. They will not see the sun redden, like henna, the funereal tresses with dormant reflections. They will not see the burning laughter of dark eyes in which the grapes are reflected. They will not hear the songs of those who pick the ripe fruits and cut the forage left in the fields. They never take the road of the vines.

And those who know the Light name them the Impious. To staunch their thirst, those who are named the Impious dig a well far from inhabited places. People clap their hands when they fall, and jeer them on their departure.

Sometimes they say to their oppressors: "But where is wisdom to be found? Where is the dwelling of intelligence?"

And their oppressors, who know the Light, stone them with words that they do not understand. That is why they go back into the darkness.

Their eyes are open during the night and only close at daybreak. They spy on nocturnal secrets. They hope to accumulate more wisdom thus, but the Unknown carries their thought away, and the terrors surprise them like floodwater. They are like the dead in the land of the living. They are weary of Olden Times. They listen to the mysterious footsteps of the Messengers of Death. Living, they have descended into the grave. And they have learned silence. Weary of vain rebellion, they have said to the Eternal:

"Look, I am too little a thing: what can I reply to you? I am putting my hand over my mouth. I have spoken once, I will not reply again. Twice, I will not add anything."

The Night lies down on the lotuses, amid the reeds of the marshes. The willows of the torrent surround it.

And the Enemies of Light come to the Night, in order to be consoled. They bathe their beaten brows and their feverish eyelids in the tenebrous water. They count the stars that the torrent carries. They rejoice in the shadows and the silence. And until dawn, they live an unreal life. For they finally possess recovered peace and the forgetful dream.

The Three Doors Open

THE SUN was bathing the venerable manor with yellow light; it seemed to be steeped in the golden waters of a fountain of youth. The sunlight vivified the walls and resuscitated the extinct splendor of the galleries. It caused living smiles to wander over the fixed lips of the portraits.

Oh, those bleak English country houses! They are grave, almost terrible dwellings, where time has lingered to the extent of making them appear immutable. The halls are vast, the hearth is immense. One could set fire to an entire tree trunk there, in accordance with the old custom, for the festivals of the North.

A gallery enclosed by light curtains is still quivering with ancient echoes of viols and clavichords. It is there that musicians charmed the digestions of the sated guests. There are hiding places in the feudal walls. The family portraits have the almost menacing aspect of solitaries that intruders are disturbing. The Past, more real than the Present, is enthroned in the massive armchairs, wanders through the corridors, and leafs through the gray books and the jaundiced parchments. The Past alone reigns there over a court of shadows and phantoms.

A young Englishwoman with ultramarine eyes, May Gore, blossomed like a charming antithesis in that tenebrous manor. She had come to visit one of those venerable houses. She had come to wander through the corridors blue-tinted by dusk.

She exhaled the charm of a bunch of wildflowers; and the old halls were illuminated by her limpid grace, as ancient forests are illuminated by a ray of spring sunshine.

However, May felt out of place and alone that evening, in a vast bedroom as severe as a sepulcher. Hanging on the wall, an old painting, darkened by time, evoked the solitary meditation of Saint Anthony, kneeling before a desiccated skull. The three doors seemed as if they ought to open at the same time, for a supernatural passage. No familiarity destroyed the austere harmony of the room to reassure its inhabitant. Everything there was rigid and ancient. The Past and Death celebrated their eternal union there, their hands joined and their gazes interlocked.

Somewhat disconcerted, May Gore felt ill at ease in being a living being, and young, amid all that Antiquity. She crossed the faded threshold of her bedroom with a furtive apprehension. She went to sleep, not without a certain mistrust.

The hours went by like a dark steam beneath leafy branches. The hours went by, and May Gore slept, very young amid that venerable Antiquity.

Suddenly, the sleeper raised her head, chilled by the abrupt impression that the three doors had opened at the same time.

She leaned over and looked, her eyes hallucinated.

The three doors were, indeed, wide open, but no presence was affirmed in the placid bedroom.

Enfevered by an involuntary terror, May sat up straight. There were muffled footsteps in the corridors. She listened to them gliding and passing by, in a whisper of trailing robes. Then the nocturnal silence, so different from the silences of the day . . .

Nocturnal silence is woven from frissons and mysteries. It is redoubtable, haunted by the Invisible, motionless and taciturn. It is perilous expectation.

May listened to the nocturnal silence. The fear of the unknowable entered into her, and the anxiety of the beyond chilled her to the bone.

She thought about the phantoms that popular belief render vivid, and, for the first time in her life, the insouciant and cheerful person that she was felt fearful and grave. She no longer found so ridiculous, nor so naïve, the opinion that holds that the spirits of the dead sometimes stray among us.

Who would ever dare to deny the possibility of something about which no one knows anything?

She imagined the obscure existence of those phantoms. She imagined herself as one of them: a dead woman wandering among the living, gliding through the familiar rooms inhabited by strangers, brushing them with her breath and the wake of her veils, brushing them without their having the perception of her presence. They gazed at her without seeing her, and their unconscious pupils transpierced her diaphanous phantom appearance. She touched them with icy fingers without them feeling the slightest frisson. She spoke to them without them hearing her unreal voice. They were not listening and they did not reply. And distress gripped her, at being unknown among the living, at being distant, and being dead, in the frame and the décor of old. The beloved places were the same, and yet mysteriously transformed. She was similar to what she had once been and yet different, living in death and dead in life. The horror took hold of her of being a specter on the earth. Avidly, she sought once again the darkness in which the Dead seek refuge, the consoling darkness that buries and enshrouds.

It was thus that May, the insouciant and cheerful person, imagined apparitions.

Only the souls that loved terrestrial things profoundly, she thought, *are constrained to the torture of returning to the light like this. Then they finally see the brief duration and consistency of everything that they once cherished with the greatest intensity.*

She also thought: *I have loved people and things, and all terrestrial nature, too much not to return. I love loved landscapes inverted in water, the odor of grass, the color of stones and tree trunks, smooth lawns and marine sunsets and the whiteness of winter too much. I have loved all those ephemeral and yet eternal things too much. Because I have loved those things that one can see, respire, hear, touch, taste and sense too much, I shall be enchained to them in spite of the vain impulses of my superior being. It is because I have been a very petty soul among souls.*

I shall go into the night uncertain and fearful, bewailing the joys of the light. Oh, the lost beauty of the earth! I shall be the vainest of shadows, because I was previously the most alive among the living.

She stopped, and stammered: "I shall never resign myself to no longer being alive. And yet I shall die."

She evoked the animal sweetness of being uniquely for the felicity of being. And she rejoiced in possessing eyes, hands, lips and ears. She rejoiced in being herself, and existing in the present moment. The horror of the Void and Nothingness were united with the voluptuousness of sensing her own materiality in a positive world.

But again she had the poignant sensation that the three doors were open at the same time.

The impression was so sharp that May was panting, agonized by horror and terror.

The past reigns alone, over a court of shadows and phantoms, in old English manors.

Litanies of a Grain of Wheat
(A Translation of a popular sequence of Hindustan)[1]

I

A PEASANT WOMAN was threshing wheat under the broad sun, expanded like a datura.

She was threshing the wheat when a passing bird paused in its flight and took possession of a grain more warmly gilded and more flavorsome than the others.

With a rude gesture, the woman threw a clod of earth at the bird. She threw it with such a rude gesture that the clod of earth broke the bird's wings.

The woman went to the bird, which lay there with its wings broken, and she said to it angrily: "If you don't return the grain of wheat that you stole from me, I'll wring your neck."

And the bird replied to the woman: "I'll return to you, woman, the grain of wheat that I stole."

But when the bird tried to pick up the grain of wheat that had fallen from its beak at the moment when the

---

1 The first part of this item is laid out in the text from which I am translating as if it were free verse, devoid of rhyme and scansion, but divided up into very brief lines; the second part is not, however, and I have collapsed the text of the entire translation into a matching prose form.

woman, with a rude gesture, had thrown the clod of earth, it saw that the wheat had entered so profoundly into a fissure in the tree, so deep that it could not reach it with its beak. And the bird said to the tree: "Return my grain of wheat, O mango tree."

But the tree refused to return the grain of wheat to the bird.

The bird, very angry, said to a woodcutter: "Fell this perfidious mango tree, which refuses to return my grain of wheat to me, for if I do not return that grain of wheat to the coolie's wife, she'll wring my neck."

But the woodcutter refused to fell the mango tree.

The bird, very angry, flew to the Rajah's palace and, very angry, said to the Rajah: "O Rajah, have the woodcutter whipped, for he refuses to fell the mango tree that refuses to return my grain of wheat, and if I don't return that grain of wheat to the coolie's wife, she'll wring my neck."

But the Rajah refused to have the woodcutter whipped.

The bird, very angry, perched on the Rani's shoulder, and, very angry, said to the Rani: "O Rani, torment the Rajah your husband with bitter words, for he does not want to have the woodcutter whipped, and the woodcutter didn't want to fell the tree that refused to return my grain of wheat, and if I don't return that grain of wheat to the coolie's wife, she'll wring my neck."

But the Rani refused to torment the Rajah her husband with bitter words.

The bird, very angry, said to the serpent: "O serpent, bite the arm of the Rani, who doesn't want to torment the Rajah her husband. The Rajah didn't want to have the woodcutter whipped, and the woodcutter didn't want to fell the tree that refused to return my grain of wheat, and if I don't return that grain of wheat to the coolie's wife, she'll wring my neck."

But the serpent refused to bite the Rani's arm.

The bird, very angry, said to the branch: "O branch, strike the serpent who has refused to bite the Rani's arm. The Rani has refused to torment the Rajah her husband with bitter words. The Rajah has refused to have the wood-cutter whipped, and the woodcutter has refused to fell the tree that refused to return my grain of wheat, and if I don't return that grain of wheat to the coolie's wife, she'll wring my neck."

But the branch refused to strike the serpent.

The bird, very angry, said to the flame: "O flame, consume the branch that refuses to strike the serpent. The serpent has refused to bite the Rani's arm. The Rani has refused to torment the Rajah her husband with bitter words. The Rajah has refused to have the woodcutter whipped, and the woodcutter has refused to fell the tree that refused to return my grain of wheat, and if I don't return that grain of wheat to the coolie's wife, she'll wring my neck."

But the flame refused to consume the branch.

The bird, very angry, said to the green and gilded sea: "O sea, extinguish the flame that refuses to consume the branch. The branch has refused to strike the serpent. The serpent has refused to bite the Rani's arm. The Rani has refused to torment the Rajah her husband with bitter words. The Rajah has refused to have the woodcutter whipped, and the woodcutter has refused to fell the tree that refused to return my grain of wheat, and if I don't return that grain of wheat to the coolie's wife, she'll wring my neck."

But the sea refused to extinguish the flame.

The bird, very angry, said to the elephant: "O elephant, drink all the sea, for the sea has refused to extinguish the flame. The flame has refused to consume the branch. The branch has refused to strike the serpent. The serpent has refused to bite the Rani's arm. The Rani has refused to torment the Rajah her husband with bitter words. The Rajah has refused to have the woodcutter whipped, and the woodcutter has refused to fell the tree that refused to return my grain of wheat, and if I don't return that grain of wheat to the coolie's wife, she'll wring my neck."

But the elephant refused to drink the green and gilded sea.

The bird, very angry, said to the lion: "O lion, bind the elephant's feet tightly, for the elephant has refused to drink the sea. The sea has refused to extinguish the flame. The flame has refused to consume the branch. The branch has refused to strike the serpent. The serpent has refused to bite the Rani's arm. The Rani has refused to torment the Rajah her husband with bitter words. The Rajah has refused to have the woodcutter whipped, and the wood-cutter has refused to fell the tree that refused to return my grain of wheat, and if I don't return that grain of wheat to the coolie's wife, she'll wring my neck."

But the lion refused to bind the elephant's feet.

The bird, very angry, said to the mouse: "O mouse, gnaw the lion who has refused to bind the feet of the elephant. The elephant has refused to drink the sea. The sea has refused to extinguish the flame. The flame has refused to consume the branch. The branch has refused to strike the serpent. The serpent has refused to bite the Rani's arm. The Rani has refused to torment the Rajah her husband with bitter words. The Rajah has refused to have the woodcutter whipped, and the woodcutter has refused to fell the tree that refused to return my grain of wheat, and if I don't return that grain of wheat to the coolie's wife, she'll wring my neck."

But the mouse refused to gnaw the lion.

And the bird, very angry, said to the patient cat: "Cat, O cat, devour the mouse. The tree doesn't want to return the grain; the woodcutter doesn't want to fell the tree; the Rajah doesn't want to have the woodcutter whipped; the Rani doesn't want to torment the Rajah; the serpent doesn't want to bite the Rani; the branch doesn't want to strike the serpent; the fire doesn't want to consume the branch; the sea doesn't want to extinguish the fire; the elephant doesn't want to drink the sea; the lion doesn't want to bind the elephant; the mouse doesn't want to gnaw the lion, and yet, I'll get that grain; I won't abandon my resolution."

II

Now, no cat ever refused to devour a mouse. The wily bird knew that as well as us.

The cat replied: "I'll devour the mouse right away."

The bird asked the mouse: "Mouse, O mouse, do you want to be devoured?"

"I'd rather gnaw the lion."

It asked the lion: "Lion, O lion, do you want to be gnawed?"

"I'd rather bind the elephant."

It asked the elephant: "Elephant, O elephant, do you want to be bound?"

"I'd rather drink the sea."

It asked the sea: "Sea, O sea, do you want to be drunk?"

"I'd rather extinguish the fire."

It asked the fire: "Fire, O fire, do you want to be extinguished?"

"I'd rather consume the branch."

It asked the branch: "Branch, O branch, do you want to be consumed?"

"I'd rather strike the serpent."

It asked the serpent: "Serpent, O serpent, do you want to be struck?"

"I'd rather bite the Rani."

It asked the Rani: "Rani, O Rani, do you want to be bitten by the serpent?"

"I'd rather torment the Rajah."

It asked the Rajah: "Rajah, O Rajah, do you want to be tormented by the Rani?"

"I'd rather have the woodcutter whipped."

It asked the woodcutter: "Woodcutter, O woodcutter, do you want to be whipped?"

"I'd rather fell the tree."

It asked the tree: "Tree, O tree, do you want to be felled?"

"I'd rather return the grain."

And the bird, having recovered the grain, took off and flew away.

The Silence of the Rocks

THE rugged Scottish landscape is bristling with the monstrous and tragic forms of rocks. They seem to be the pallid survivors of a chaos of indescribable terrors. As gray as Eternity, they prolong their taciturn dream indifferently.

Rocks are terrible by dint of their silence. They make one dream of somber mythologies. They evoke livid Niobes who have adopted the form of stone in order to commemorate their immutable suffering. Rocks are dolors enclosed in memory. They are icier than tombs. Their bleak rigidity saddens the brightest roads. They are the Eternal Past.

A torrent rears up in a ravine, a torrent drunk on rain and snow. On the mountainside, a granite quarry opens like a wound, red with the blood of the Titans; and everywhere, there are the cold attitudes and the rigid silence of the rocks.

There is a green oak tree amid those grim solitudes. Its leaves, curiously wrought, and its acorns, sculpted like jewels, seem to be the laborious work of a patient artist. And beneath its broad crown, shadows change color, blue at midday and violet at dusk. That druidic oak has its legend. And because I took pleasure in listening to it during one meditative sunset, a simple soul among simple things, I shall repeat it for those who would like to hear it with simplicity.

✳

A young, very young, shepherd was wandering through the rocks, gray against the gray backcloth of the cloudy sky. He was wandering through the rocks whistling a popular ballad, the ballad of "Annie Laurie" or that of "The Banks of Allan Water." They were naïve and plaintive words, following an ingenuous tune. And he discovered in the hollow of the oak the rosy slumber of an abandoned baby.

Gripped by compassion, the adolescent took the fragile forsaken child in his arms. He carried her to his father's house, a hut clinging to the wall of the rock.

A fine rain was combining its frail melancholy with the gravity of the evening. The drizzle veiled the horizon and the mountain with an incomparable sadness. Its nostalgic charm was similar to a charm of Regret and Memory.

In the crepuscular drizzle, the adolescent thought about the uncertainty that awaited him at the paternal hearth. The old pastor, his father, was cloistered in a bitter solitude. He had fashioned a soul honed by rancor and hatred. His wife had once betrayed and left him, and his rude peasant's heart had closed over the past, for his primitive brain, exaggerating the range and magnitude of that treason, also exaggerated the rancor it engendered. He had isolated himself in a hostile exasperation against the entire feminine universe. No woman had ever crossed the forsaken threshold since the day when the wife had fled. Dusk fell, enveloped by the drizzle, and the hesitant young man hid the little girl beneath his vast cloak. He went in, indecisively . . .

By the ruddy light of embers, the old shepherd was dreaming. The flames vacillated in his extinct gaze and revealed a dead ardor therein. He did not turn his eyes, in which dancing reflections gleamed, toward his son.

"You're late back," he reproached the young man.

"The road isn't easy, Father, and I was walking slowly because I was carrying in my arms a poor little creature gone astray in the mountains."

"A lamb?" asked the old man, indifferently. "Let it warm up next to the fire and give it a little milk."

And, turning round, the old pastor saw the sleeping child in his son's arms.

Suddenly withdrawn into a stubborn anger, he ordered his son to take the child—the future woman, the future enemy—elsewhere.

"Father," the young man implored, "we wouldn't leave a lamb outside that had gone astray on a foggy night."

Hearing the two voices of anger and supplication, the child opened her eyes, the profound eyes of a woman in a puerile visage.

And the old shepherd, before those wide open eyes, remembered. He remembered, and the spell of his former suffering bewitched him dolorously. He tasted the poignant softness of regret. And without understanding his own words, he stammered: "Let it warm up next to the fire and give it some milk."

But in his obscure soul he feared for the future. He sensed, for the second time, Fatality entering his house. And for the second time, on crossing the threshold, it had taken on the deceptive and charming form of a woman.

The years passed. The unknown child had become the mysterious woman. Her hair, as blonde as gorse in the sunlight, harbored all the wild and penetrating odors of the mountain. And her eyes were as blue as bluebells trembling in the wind. That was why the young shepherd who had discovered her in the hollow of the oak tree called her Bluebell.

At first he had loved her with a rude and protective tenderness. He surrounded her with the solicitude with which a vigilant shepherd surrounds a lamb temporarily gone astray. Gradually, however, on seeing her become candidly beautiful, he loved her with a complex and wild tenderness, in which a little dread, hostility and suspicion were already mingled.

The young woman lived alongside those two simple men, who loved her, one with a paternal goodness and the other with an amorous suspicion. The old pastor considered the girl who had once been an intruder as an inexpressibly dear daughter. The cordiality of a common hearth and a warm mutual affection united the three individuals.

But a stranger came into the region. Passing by the farm one day he stopped, dazzled by the young woman's golden hair. That rustic freshness pleased him. He liked the young smile of those unrouged lips. He liked the limpidity of her puerile eyes and all the perfume of the rural dawn. And gradually, the young woman felt herself attracted by the indefinable charm of his speech. He pleased her, by virtue of being a stranger to her world, coming from far away and possessing unknown splendors of which, being a woman, she dreamed. She glimpsed, in his discourse, the scintillation of the unknown, chimerical gleams. And all the glitter of luxury, which is rendered real by the most ingenuous desires, was revealed to her soul.

Luxury—which is to say, the possession of submissive Beauty, the domination of Joy! To savor life like a rare fruit, to respire it like a flower, to listen to it like savant music! To multiply her existence by multiplying her sensations infinitely! Oh, the jewels of Gretchen![1]

She loved the stranger, therefore, who enabled her to glimpse all those things. And when he implored her to go with him toward those luminous regions of gold and sunlight, she said, very simply: "I'll go with you."

But the vigilant shepherd had heard those words of consent. He surged forth before her when the stranger, having taken the mountain road, had disappeared behind the far slope.

"You belong to me," he said, "as a stray lamb belongs to the shepherd who picks it up. You belong to me, because I loved you first, with a persevering love. You belong to me in life and in death."

He caused a terrible silence to enter into her. The young woman, slipping away hastily, tried to flee by the road that the stranger had just taken—but, menacing, imperious and resolute, the shepherd held her back.

____

1 The reference is to Goethe's _Faust_ Part I, in which Mephistopheles tempts the innocent Gretchen by means of jewels that he leaves in her house.

The old man was half-asleep, as before, in the corner of the hearth. The dancing flames were mirrored in his eyes. As before, he did not turn round when his son crossed the threshold. As before, he spoke first.

"You've come back alone, my son. Why isn't Bluebell with you?"

"I left her asleep under the old oak, Father."

The wind was weeping in the nocturnal pines. The tenebrous wind was moaning in the anxious pines. Cold stars were shining too brightly in the cold sky.

Old Dirk turned toward his son eyes in which an as yet uncomprehended anguish was interrogating.

"How have you left her asleep at this hour, in the icy air?"

Stupidly, the young man replied: "I found her once asleep under the old oak. Father, she has gone to sleep under the old oak where I once picked her up. She's asleep under the old oak . . ."

The wind was weeping in the nocturnal pines, and the tragic rocks loomed up, pallid in the darkness, fixed in their immutable dolor.

The Poisoned Garden

Scene I

A GOTHIC chamber in an old manor. The bright garden can be seen through the open window.

Madelaine: "How gray the sun is outside! How dull the spring is! I live all day in anticipation of nightfall, the consoler of fatigues, like salvation. And when night has come, I await the sunrise, like a deliverance. For the dawn dissipates nocturnal fevers and terrors. But the night doesn't bring me the consolation of my fatigues, the cherished slumber; and the dawn doesn't dissipate the burning of my torments. During the day, I pull the heavy curtains. The light collides in vain with their ample and rigid pleats. Thus, I create artificial darkness, where I take refuge, dazedly exhausted. When evening comes I light all the candles, in fear on the dark. Thus, artificial light protects me against my own terrors. But nothing soothes my tumultuous soul. (*She weeps.*) I have even lost the bittersweetness of regret. I am like those who dare not sob in the depths of twilight, frightened by their own dolors.

(Old-fashioned music becomes audible outside.)

"Oh, that quavering guitar, as rasping and as worn as the voice it accompanies!"

The Old Woman:

The sun sings over the plain,
The sun sings in the woods,
And is mirrored as of old,
In our chatelaine's rings

Little hesitant laughter
Melts at the edge of the spring,
But your chatelaine's ennui
Is reflected in the ponds.

You invite, O chatelaine
To the joyous feasts of old.
The sun singing over the woods
The sun singing over the plain.

Madelaine, *leaning outside*: "What a strange old woman! She's dancing and singing in the sunlight. The horrible and charming old woman! Her red eyes are blinking in the bright light. Her hair is hanging lamentably down her cheeks. Her face is furrowed by wrinkles. She's hideous, and yet beautiful in her inexhaustible joy. How has she kept that self-confident felicity intact, through so many long years? And I, who am as rich as that woman is poor, as young as she is old, am consuming myself in perpetual suffering. Why am I sad, without hope, when that beggar-woman displays such an insolent joy?

"I'm going to make that old woman come here, and learn from her the enigma of her persistent and untimely joy. (*She runs to the window.*) Old woman! Old woman!

The Old Woman, *from outside*: "I dare not approach you. I'm afraid of you, beautiful Lady."

Madelaine: "Have no fear. Only see in me a woman who is suffering."

The Old Woman: "I'm afraid of your dogs."

Madelaine: "Me little maidservant will escort you. (*She claps her hands.*) Dixa!

(*Dixa comes in.*)

"Run, Dixa, and bring me that old woman who is singing and dancing in such a strange fashion under my windows.

(*The maidservant goes out.*)

"I'm reassured in seeing that old woman so bizarrely joyful; and yet I feel oppressed all the way to the soul. I have hope in that old woman, but I fear her coming, I am obscurely fearful of what she is about to say.

(*The door opens. The old woman appears, clad
in brightly colored rags. She salutes Madelaine,
making comical reverences.*)

"Come in, come in, have no fear. I heard you singing. How cheerful you seem, with an old quavering gaiety that imposes itself on young anguish! Come closer.

(*The old woman shivers.*)

Are you shivering with cold?"
The Old Woman: "No . . . no . . . I don't know."

(*She contemplates the tapestries and sculpted furniture admiringly. Madelaine claps her hands. Dixa comes in.*)

Madelaine: "Set the table and prepare a meal."
The Old Woman: "You're very kind, Chatelaine, but I'm not hungry. I ate a few chestnuts at dawn. One meal a day is sufficient for me."

(*Dixa returns. She sets a sumptuous table. The old woman moves away, smiling, with a gesture of refusal.*)

Dixa, fearfully: "Madame, she's a witch. She doesn't eat, and yet she's never hungry."
Madelaine: "Are you a witch, old woman? Can you read the future, and within souls?"
The Old Woman: "I possess all the secrets of the future."
Madelaine: "How can you decipher the fate of individuals?"
The Old Woman: "I look at their shadows."
Madelaine, *uncomprehendingly*: "How does that tell you the future?"
The Old Woman: "Every individual is accompanied by their future, under the appearance of a shadow. Sometimes destiny follows the individual, sometimes it precedes them.

It bears a bizarre resemblance to the individual it escorts, while exaggerating their contours. Our destiny is ourself deformed, subject to the mysterious caprices of light. Our destiny accompanies us, like our shadow. That's why I always see the destiny of individuals under the appearance of their shadows."

Madelaine: "Reveal my destiny to me, old woman."

The Old Woman: "I dare not. In truth, I dare not. Last year, a young woman came to ask me to reveal the unknown form of her future to her, and I saw a shadow elongating at her feet similar to the one projected by a bier. I saw a coffin in front of her, and I predicted her imminent death."

Madelaine: "Was your prophecy realized?"

The Old Woman: "The young woman died, my beautiful chatelaine. Her relatives and friends accused me of having put a spell on her. Since then, children stone me, with insults harder than stones. I'm hated and feared throughout the hostile country. I no longer decipher futures, my beautiful chatelaine. I no longer pierce tenebrous futures."

Madelaine, *drawing nearer to her, supplicant and seductive*: "Tell me why I'm eternally sad. Tell me what obscure perils are lying in wait for me. Have no fear. No one will learn from my mouth what you have revealed to me. As for me, I have no fear of the words you might pronounce. (*To herself*:) I no longer have anything to fear. (*Aloud*:) Speak, old woman."

The Old Woman, *staring at the young woman's shadow*: "You will never be happy."

Madelaine: "Why? Why?"

The Old Woman, *looking around*: "However, you will live in beauty. You will respire beauty. That is all you see.

It surrounds you. And, slowly, it has impregnated your flesh with its light and its perfumes. You know nothing of life except its beauty, but you aren't happy. You will never unlearn melancholy. And yet . . . and yet . . . oh, all the possible joys that radiate around you! You hold them in your hands without possessing them. Oh, the sun on the roses! And every night, that miracle renewed: moonlight on lilies! One might believe, on seeing you inexplicable bleak, that an invisible corruption is fermenting under the fortunate earth and spoiling the breath of dawn among your flowers. Beware of the death that is poisoning your garden."

Madelaine, uncomprehendingly: "Death? What do you mean? Is a cadaver buried in my garden, then? What is this putrescence whose emanations are corrupting even the roses under the sun and the lilies in the moonlight?"

The Old Woman: "You'll know one day."

Madelaine: "Renounce these obscure phrases. My reason's going astray. You're keeping quiet? (*Imperiously:*) Speak!

The Old Woman: "I ought not to have said anything. I did well to swear to myself never to decipher redoubtable futures again. My God!"

Madelaine, *her head in her hands*: "A dead man in my garden? Has one of my ancestors committed a crime? For the Bible says that he who has sinned will be punished in his descendancy unto the seventh and the eighth generations."

The Old Woman, *weeping*: "I'm afraid."

Madelaine, *more mildly*: "Go, go."

> (*The old woman leaves, weeping. Scarcely has she gone, however, then all her gaiety rises to her lips again. She is heard singing.*)

The Old Woman, outside:

The sun sings over the plain,
The sun sings in the woods,
And is mirrored as of old,
In our chatelaine's rings

Little hesitant laughter
Melts at the edge of the spring,
But your chatelaine's ennui
Is reflected in the ponds.

Madelaine, *alone*: "I don't understand . . ."

(*She sits down, in a dejected pose.*)

Scene II

Madelaine's garden, in which large ditches have been dug, like profound graves. Madelaine is wandering feverishly through the garden. She stops in front of the gardener Hendrik, who is digging a hole.

Madelaine: "Haven't you found anything yet, Hendrik?"
Hendrik: "No, Mistress."
Madelaine; "Search, search."
Hendrik: "For three months now I've been digging and turning over the soil, and I haven't found anything. (*He leans on his spade.*) Nothing, nothing, nothing."
Madelaine: "And yet the old woman affirmed it to me: death is poisoning this garden. That invisible putrescence is

corrupting the flowers. One dies of respiring near the dead. My garden has to be purified. Dig the ground, Hendrik. Dig the ground more deeply."

Hedrink: "Yes, yes . . . (*Aside:*) I don't believe there's a corpse in this garden. But if I find one I won't fear it. It's unnecessary to fear the dead. The poor dead! They're such a little thing: a little dust in the bottom of a worm-eaten coffin."

(*He shifts the earth.*)

Madelaine: "Have you sounded the pond, Hendrik? The nenuphars floating on those stagnant waters resemble mortal flowers. They're such pallid flowers, so strangely pallid, flowers of the dead. One might think that they harbor a poisonous juice. Have you sounded the pond, Hendrik?"

Hendrik: "Yes, yes. There's nothing in the pond. Nothing, nothing, nothing. (*Aside:*) It's certainly not necessary to fear the dead. I married a vindictive and jealous woman once. Then she died. When she was dying, she made me swear not to remarry. More than death itself, she abhorred the thought that another woman might sit down by the hearth after her. (*Philosophically:*) That didn't prevent me marrying another woman a year after her death. Well, my first wife has never appeared to me, even in a dream. If the dead possessed the power to rise up among the living, she would have come back to avenge herself on her rival."

Madelaine: "Resume your labor, Hendrik. Keep searching."

Hendrik: "I can keep on turning over the earth, but I won't find anything. (*A pause.*) Nothing, nothing, nothing."

(Madelaine weeps, her head bowed. Hendrik digs silently. Two young women pass along the path bordering the garden, looking over the hedge, contemplating Madelaine with pity.)

First Young Woman: "How sad our chatelaine is!"

Second Young Woman: "And yet she's so beautiful, so rich, and again and especially, so beautiful!"

First Young Woman: "What unknown dolor can be torturing her mysteriously?"

Second Young Woman: "An unhappy amour, no doubt. You know full well that only one thing is real and alive: amour. All the rest is as vain as a gust of wind over the water."

First Young Woman: "Is it true that amour alone is of any importance in this world? Is it unnecessary to love, desire and search for anything but amour?"

Second Young Woman, *with conviction*: "Undoubtedly."

Madelaine: "They're ingenuously and graciously stupid. They're charming simpletons. And what a felicity is theirs, to have no thoughts! (*Angrily, to the two young women*:) Don't look at me any longer with your excessively bright eyes. Don't smile at me any longer. Leave me alone. I hate you. I hate you mortally for being happy. My poor intelligence is such a little thing before your triumphant, radiant imbecility!"

First Young Woman: "Our chatelaine has lost her reason."

Second Young Woman: "Undoubtedly, our chatelaine has lost her reason."

(They flee.)

Scene III

The same décor as Scene I, a few years later. In the distance, the last notes of the old woman's song are audible. Already wrinkled and withered, Madelaine is pensive.

Madelaine, *leaning out*: "Come here, come here."

The Old Woman: "Who are you, and why are you summoning me with such imperious sadness?"

Madelaine: "I'm the unknown woman to whom you once revealed the enigmatic future. I'm the one to whom you said: 'You will never be happy.'"

The Old Woman: "I no longer remember. All that was a long time ago, a long time ago. I no longer remember."

Madelaine: "Come here, come here."

(Silence. The door opens. The old woman comes in. She has not changed at all. She has the same face. She considers Madelaine.)

"Look at me carefully. Don't you recognize me?"

The Old Woman, *after having looked at Madelaine carefully*: "I don't recognize you."

Madelaine: "Don't you recognize this place?"

The Old Woman: "I seem to find the confused image of this place in my memory. But everything here appears different from my memory."

Madelaine, *softly*: "Yes, everything has changed around me, as it has within me. However, everything around me is despairingly similar to what it was before, and I remain, myself, despairingly similar."

The Old Woman: "I no longer remember."

Madelaine: "You lied to me brazenly, old woman! You lied to me cruelly and stupidly. All searches have been in vain. There is no dead man in my garden."

The Old Woman: "Dead man? Oh! I remember now!"

Madelaine: "Speak, tell me the truth today. I'll pour gold and jewels into your extended hands."

The Old Woman: "Keep your gold, my beautiful chatelaine. Keep your jewels. You'd be paying too dear for a verity as distressing to hear as it is to see."

Madelaine: "The truth! The truth!"

The Old Woman, *after having contemplated Madelaine's shadow for a long time*: "I've already told you."

Madelaine: "You're lying! You're lying!"

The Old Woman: "I enabled you to glimpse the truth under the veils of Symbol. In the garden of your soul, bitter discontentment with yourself and others has been putrefying for a long time, like a corpse eaten by worms. As long as that hatred for everything that exists is fermenting within you, you cannot escape your perpetual melancholy. You are your own prisoner, for you are the sole cause of your own torment. All of us carry happiness or suffering within us. Nothing exists by itself. It's through our gaze that people and things put on illusory appearances. We are our own benefactors and our own torturers. We are our own dupes and victims. We alone can free ourselves. Extract yourself from the languor that is too dear to you. Don't seek death any longer. For one only discovers what one is searching for at the moment when one stops searching. It's so simple to be happy! (*She leaves, laughing.*) I'm happy, me, the old pauperess."

Madelaine, *left alone*: "O my soul!"

NETSUKE

Preface

WITH an untiring slowness, Japanese artists elaborate netsuke.

Netsuke are patiently-sculpted figurines of ivory and wood. They are attached by a cord to an inro, which their weight retains and prevents from slipping out of the belt; for an inro is a small work of studious love: it is a lacquer box encrusted with nacre or gold, with several compartments, which once contained remedies against fevers.

Netsuke are carved in ivory or wood, with a patina like bronze. Sometimes they evoke a symbol, sometimes they resuscitate a legend. They are eloquent, like a poem.

The carvers of netsuke collected the mysterious traditions of the Chinese or Koreans. They follow religious ancestors, the Butsuki, sculptors of idols and liturgical ornaments.

Netsuke have their enlightenments and their glories. Toyomasa was able to bring out the tenebrous forms of dragons. Ikkwan has the keen curiosity of rats. Ryumin, Masaichi and Gyokuzan Asahi, having leaned for a long time over tombs, reproduce the grotesque and admirable solemnity of grimacing skulls and skeletons. Giokumin is fond of majestic turtles. He is also able to convulse the bizarre hideousness of demons.

Like the sculptors of netsuke, I have evoked symbols and resuscitated legends. Like them, I have lingered over enigmas, and like them, I have tried to fix in narrow lines a fleeting universe of dreams.

The Humiliated Violet

IN a distant time a child was born in Nara who was named Murasaki. She was given that name because of her suave soul and his humility.[1]

Murasaki, the odorous violet, flourished during her puerile years, but when she entered adolescence her mother died, and Murasaki's father, Toyonari Fujiwara, a very wise counselor of the Mikado, took a second wife. In accordance with the custom of old men, he chose a young woman.

Toyonari Fujiwara's second wife was named Terute. She was a woman with a narrow heart and a jealous soul. She hated Murusaki, the fragile violet, who was not her child.

Murasaki exhaled the divine perfumes of simplicity. Guanyin herself would have envied her beautiful eyelids.[2] She loved slow and tenacious music and obsessive verses. Her voice recalled the song of the cuckoo amid the wisteria. She composed religious stanzas.

Terute gave birth to a son.

Everything that maternity contains of unconscious egotism swelled that rough heart. Terute was a mother

---

1 Author's note: "Nara was the ancient capital of Japan; Murasaki means violet."
2 Author's note: "Guanyin [which she renders Kwannon] is the goddess of mercy, the equal of Buddha."

in a primitive and savage fashion. She cherished her son grimly and despotically. She hated the daughter of the first wife with the same passion that she brought to loving her own son.

Murasaki, the humiliated violet, suffered in silence the injustices of the excessively fervent mother and the implacable stepmother. Knowing that the superficial events of exterior life are a small thing, and that the intensity of the interior life can count for everything, she accepted the proofs of destiny disdainfully. The rudeness and the ugliness of reality heightened the beauty of her young dreams. She lived in the palaces, gardens and temples of fantasy.

When Murasaki had attained her twelfth year, she was taken by her stepmother to the solemn festival of the cherry-trees.

The Empress and the entire court celebrated with pomp the resurrection of spring embalmed under the snow. The cherry-blossom, white amid the white flakes, was revealed by its subtle odor.

The Empress was not unaware that the pleasure and dolor of mortals find their supreme expression in the divine babble of music. She therefore made the most gracious maidens and the most savant women of the court play and sing for her.

Solitude had taught Murasaki profound thoughts. Silence had taught Murasaki unheard melodies, all the sweeter for being chimerical. Patiently, she had been able to triumph over recalcitrant meters and notes. The young musician and poet had learned from the very lips of suffering her most harmonious secrets.

On the orders of the Empress, Terute and Murasaki were to perform a very naïve song together, which an ancient female poet had once composed.

Murasaki made the bright samisen sob limpidly under her fingers, but Terute, who had neglected all other cares in the fervor of her maternal tenderness, accompanied her stepdaughter without skill. The flute obeyed her breath and her fingers poorly. Confused by her blameworthy inexperience, Terute dropped the rebellious instrument and excused herself piteously before the Empress and the assembled court.

Murasaki sang alone. She celebrated the languor of spring, the sadness of cuckoos and cicadas, and the dolorous light of fireflies consuming themselves in vain desire before the indifferent night. All of her constrained youth revolted and protested in those strophes against futile anguish.

The Empress listened, moved to the point of forgetting her own regrets.

And the Empress, grateful to the person who had made her forget her troubles in order to enable her to suffer foreign and illusory troubles, offered the musician and poet rare presents.

The hatred of Terute increased because imperial favor had shone upon Murasaki, the disdained and sadly odorous violet. She concealed her hatred in the utmost depths of her silence, as other women conceal an unadmitted amour in their mysterious hearts. But Terute's hatred became envenomed from day to day and from hour to hour. She finally resolved to cause her stepdaughter, the melancholy violet Murasaki, to die.

Hatred is more obstinate than love, Terute watched for a propitious occasion.

As spring bloomed, the festival of the moths brought the young women and adolescents together. In Terute's dwelling, all of them stimulated one another with the mystical delight of winged souls.

Terute, who cherished her secret hatred as others cherish their fearful tenderness, distilled a poison and mixed it with the sake that animates festivals. She had the mortal sake and rice cakes brought into the garden where Murasaki was celebrating the beauty of the Daughters of the Moon for the infantile joy of her brother.

At intervals of a thousand years, the Daughters of the Moon come to swell among humans. They are sad and grim so long as the daylight lasts, but when darkness falls they appear, ringed by an aureole. They do not respond to the covetousness of men who implore them . . .

Murasaki fell silent when Terute advanced, smiling falsely. The stepmother praised the young poet and offered her—as a recompense for her beautiful songs, so she said—the cup of poison. But, her eyes blinded and her mind clouded by the horror of her crime, she confused the two cups, the poisoned cup that she destined for her stepdaughter and the cup of sake, simultaneously ardent and sweet, prepared for her own child. With her tremulous hands, the excessively passionate mother gave the mortal cup to her son.

Stupefied by terror, she saw the face of her child decompose. She saw the agony and the death of the only being on earth that she had loved.

A new bitterness swelled her heart. She hated her stepdaughter for being the innocent cause of that death. The passion of the mother intensified the hatred of the stepmother.

In her envenomed soul she meditated on the surest means of causing the death of her stepdaughter, Murasaki the dolorous violet.

The time of the rains approached. They fell implacably. The river Tatsuta, which ran iridescently through the imperial gardens, swelled monstrously. It rolled its tumultuous waves amid the giant bamboos, drowning the melancholy wisteria, the camellias and chrysanthemums.

The Empress, who cherished her gardens fervently for their magnificence and their freshness, fell ill with sadness on seeing them submerged by the river. She wept night and day over the destruction of her wisterias, her chrysanthemums and her camellias, for those flowers unveiled their mysterious personality to her. She knew the soul and the muted life of each of her chrysanthemums, which differed from one another as one face differs from another.

Alone behind the screens, the Empress wept night and day over the death of her gardens.

The Mikado, in love with his young wife, was alarmed by the fever of languor and sadness that was consuming her to the marrow. Seeing her perishing, he sent an order to all the temples to offer prayers to Guanyin and Buddha, for the appeasement of the angry waters.

In spite of the supplications of monks and priests, however, the waters were not calmed.

Overwhelmed by despair, the Mikado remembered that a virginal poet more beautiful than the fir-trees florid with snow, Ono-no-Komachi, by means of the spell of her poems, had once ended a mortal desiccation that was splitting the earth. Rain fell from the sky and blessed the torrid ground at the moment when the last words of Ono-no-Komachi died away, confounded with the expiring murmur of the koto. Having learned from her father that Murasaki, the ignored violet, was the most melodious poet in Japan, the Mikado ordered her to go to the imperial gardens at dawn. Surrounded by the entire court, she was to recite her most beautiful strophes before the rearing waves.

Murasaki, the fearful violet, obeyed the imperial order, palely tremulous. She dared not hope, solely by the magic of her verses, to repress the violence and rebellion of the waters.

On a bridge that was defying the bounding waves, Murasaki unrolled the fragile poem with which her brush had ornamented the rice paper. She recited the first words in her ingenuously and expertly cadenced voice. And in order to listen to her, a great silence fell.

The river quieted its stormy din. It flowed less furiously between the devastated banks. Gradually, the torrent eased in accordance with the languid rhythm of the poem. It calmed down, like a weary dragon going to sleep.

Slowly, slowly, the waters retreated to their bed . . . and the torrent became once again the pleasant river that bathed serenely the gardens of chrysanthemums and wisterias.

The imperial bushes flowered again splendidly. On seeing them as beautiful as before, the Empress rediscovered her health and joy. That is why the grateful Mikado accorded Murasaki the title of Princess. The Empress, in her turn, heaped her with honors and presents.

But Terute's silent hatred was exacerbated. And when Toyonari Fujiwara left with an embassy to the Emperor of China, the stepmother resolved once again to kill her stepdaughter.

She summoned an old and faithful servant of Toyonari Fujiwara and, a thousand times crueler in the calumny that in the plotted murder, she accused Murasaki, the immaculate violet, falsely, of having lowered herself to the rank of courtesans. Murasaki, she said, was pregnant by the work of some stranger. In order to dissimulate that shame and scandal from everyone's eyes, it was necessary that the reproved individual perish. Tenute, counterfeiting a virtuous wrath, ordered the old and faithful servant, Katoda, to put the young woman to death.

Katoda remained perplexed in his loyal soul. He dared not infringe the order of his mistress, the redoubtable wife of his master, but, having known Murasaki since infancy, he knew that she was innocent of the crime with which her stepmother charged her. That is why he used a stratagem. He pretended to obey Terute's command, and, having had Murusaki's palanquin prepared, he took her into the depths of the wilderness.

Murasaki, the yielding violet, submitted to the orders of her stepmother, incomprehensible to her. She went with Katoda, the old and faithful servant, through the mountains.

Katoda, being a just man, built a bamboo hut for the innocent and immaculate maiden. He brought his aged wife in secret, and they both watched over Murasaki, the chaste violet.

Murasaki's father, Toyonari Fujiwara, return to the house. Terute welcomed him with a simulated dolor. Prodigal with lying tears and fake sobs, she convinced him that Murasaki, pregnant by the work of some stranger, had gone to hide her shame and despair far away.

Toyonari did not have a heart great enough or strong enough to believe, against all appearances, in the one he loved. He accepted the calumnies of his wife, the unjust stepmother; and because paternal tenderness protested within him, albeit very feebly, he wept.

Wanting to free himself for a few days from the anguish that was weighing him down, he went hunting in the mountains. A hare bounded through the thickets. Toyonari was in advance of his servants. He found himself alone in front of a bamboo cabin, the work of unskillful hands; but the primitive hut was surrounded by an odorous wild garden. A nostalgic perfume of violets rose toward Toyonari. He stopped, his heart gripped by memories.

Suddenly, a voice rose up, as melodious as the koto of Benten.[1] It was the voice of a maiden, similar to a stream of molten snow, and that voice was intoning sonorous strophes nobly.

Toyonari approached, struck by a stupor of admiration. He hesitated before crossing the flowery hedge that protected the garden.

A young woman, more supple than willows in spring, was reciting those verses to the charmed solitudes. And Toyonari, his soul illuminated by a boundless joy, recognized his daughter Murasaki, the immaculate violet.

Everything is explained in naïve popular legends. Calumny, necessary to the action, leaves no imprint or burn. It slides over souls. It does not penetrate. Everything is explained, I tell you. Innocence is recognized immediately after the ordeal. Doubt, vanquished, dissolves. Evil engenders good, and dolor joy, in naïve popular legends.

---

1 The author inserts a footnote defining Benten as the goddess of the sea, but she is actually the goddess of all things that flow: water, music and eloquence—which fits the story better.

The Moon Reflects . . .

AN old bamboo-cutter once lived on the daily product of his labor, and because he led his simple existence among simple things he was happy.

He cut and carved his bamboos, as slender and flexible as a woman's body, with serenity. He loved them for their fresh suppleness, but he felled them without remorse. No sadness ever came from the human destiny that obliges a murderous cruelty with regard to the living world, of plants as of animals.

From dawn onwards, the bamboo-cutter was obstinate in his labor. He was laboring one morning, his eyes rejoiced by the hour and the beautiful location, when a prodigy was accomplished. Through the bamboos, yellowed by the early morning sunlight, an unreal moonlight filtered.

The old man considered the mysteriously silvered trees. He perceived that the dreamlike light was coming from a bamboo taller and suppler than the rest.

In the hollow of the tree the brightness was intensified, more splendid. Bending down, the old bamboo cutter perceived a strange little being.

The body, as small as that of an infant, was rounded by the voluptuous contours of a woman. Supernaturally beautiful, that living splendor was diffusing a pale radiance around her.

The bamboo-cutter was only slightly astonished, and did not fear the prodigy, for the soul of simple folk is in unconscious communion with marvels and chimeras. Miracles are only accomplished before credulous eyes.

Having picked up the enigmatic being, the bamboo-cutter brought her up in his cabin.

From that day onwards, an incomprehensible fortune gilded the old man's existence. He discovered gems and valuable ingots in the hollows of felled trees. Enriched by those treasures, the old bamboo-cutter became the most opulent man in the region.

Gradually, the stranger hatched in the hollow of a bamboo grew in strength and grace. Her flesh seemed to be molded from moonbeams, and her eyes were distant and limpid, like the reflection of the moon on water. A perpetual lunar light emanated from her. Sad people who contemplated her went away consoled; feverish people who sought her presence went away cured.

All day, numbed by a bizarre torpor, the radiant un-known awaited the awakening of darkness. Then she ap-peared to be reanimated. Her eyes, extinguished by the brutal sunlight, suddenly lit up. The light that radiated incessantly around her became brighter and burned like the nocturnal flames of Djoga.[1]

Every night she contemplated the rise of the moon with a singular fervor. When the diminished star languished in the sky, the maiden seemed to waste away with it, and

----

1 The author inserts a note defining Djoga as the goddess of the moon, although that name appears to be idiosyncratic. The story is, however, a transfiguration of an old Japanese story in which the mysterious foundling is named Kayuga. The name she receives in this version, Teruko, is defined by the author as "Moonbeam."

when, in its fullness, it triumphed in the depths of the dark azure, she seemed to revive.

The old bamboo-cutter was naively astonished by that. Sometimes, he criticized her for spending long hours bathed by the light of the moon, her gaze fixed upon it, lost in the infinity of prayer and ecstasy.

Finally, the day approached when the old bamboo-cutter, in accordance with custom, had to prepare a feast in order for the mysterious child to receive her name publicly. He therefore invited a giver of names, the most celebrated in the land, a poet of great brilliance. Such was her ingenuity that she divined, on seeing children for the first time, their future personality. The names that she gave them were adapted to their souls, as a subtle kimono envelops the body harmoniously.

Because the woman was a poet she attributed rhythmic and tender names to young girls: Kohachi, puerile flower; Asakichi, fortunate gem; Katsukichi, happy dawn; Tchiyoe, flower of felicity; Tchiyotsuru, glorious victory; O-Kayo, years of happiness; Wakagusa, tender spring grass.

The giver of names considered the unknown for a long time. She became sad, sensing that all her art could not dictate to her a name sufficiently melodious or evocative for that miraculous virgin. Because of the magical light emanating from the stranger, however, she named her Teruko.

Teruko became so beautiful that the old bamboo-cutter, who devoted a paternal tenderness to her, had to surround his dwelling with a formidable palisade in order to protect that beauty against the profane gaze of crowds. In spite of the solitude in which the stranger was cloistered, however, the renown of her splendor spread. Such was the charm and power of her distant image that amorous individuals came from the most remote lands in order to catch a glimpse of her unknown face. They lay in wait day and night in anxious expectation, but the virgin never crossed the bamboo-cutter's threshold. Her fervent seekers never saw her desired face though the windows of diaphanous paper. For three years they waited in vain.

The disdainful silence broke the noblest courage and drove the most tenacious adoration to despair. The crowd of suitors gradually abandoned the wait. Only five young samurai remained beneath Moonbeam's windows, without sleeping or taking nourishment. Every spring enfevered their brows; the summers consumed them; and the funereal winters chilled them to the bone. Thirst desiccated them; hunger twisted their entrails; but they did not buckle for an instant. They did not abandon their amorous vigil.

For a further three years they were obstinate in their hope; and the old bamboo-cutter, having mercy on all simple souls, took pity on their long patience. He interceded in their favor with the radiant being that he called his daughter, but whom he treated with the veneration due to distant goddesses.

Teruko listened with a sad tenderness. It was a suffering and a remorse for her to respond by a refusal to the pleas of the old man who had collected and raised her, and yet she could not consent to those sacrilegious betrothals.

Her suffering and her remorse suggested an innocent ruse to her. She replied to the old bamboo-cutter:

"You who treat me as your daughter, I grant you the tender submission that a beloved child willingly grants to her father. I accede to your desire. But the man who aspires to marry me must win me by means of terrible proofs, for I am of another essence than terrestrial women, and I only want for a husband a man superior to other men.

"This is the proof of the first samurai. He must bring me from India the stone cup in which Buddha once steeped his divine lips. The proof reserved for the second is to climb Mount Horai and bring me a branch from the marvelous tree that grows at the summit; the roots of the marvelous tree are silver, the trunk is bright gold and the branches are jade. The third samurai must bring me from China the skin of a fire-rat, which lives in the midst of flames like the salamander, without being consumed. The fourth samurai must vanquish the dragon that possesses the stone of five colors and bring me that incomparable treasure. The fifth samurai must capture the fleeting swallow and extract from the belly of the bird, in order to offer it to me, the seashell that it contains."

On hearing those words, the bamboo-cutter lamented.

"I am old," he said, "and my present existence is nearing its end. Soon, my four souls will quit my worn-out body. Who will watch over you and protect you after my death? Listen to my prayer, you whom I once collected: do not impose on these valorous samurai proofs too rigorous for mortal strength, and deign to choose one of them as your husband."

The old bamboo-cutter lamented in those terms, for he was only a simple man astray in a complex universe. He did not understand that divine fragility retains within it a force superior to the will of giants.

Smiling with a lunar smile, Teruko remained inflexible in her determination. Sadly, the old bamboo-cutter took the message to the five amorous men.

The five amorous men were afflicted by the enumeration of the enterprises they had to attempt, but they did not revolt against the implacable sentence, for they were blindly submissive to the power of the name of Teruko and the melodious spell of her grace, celebrated by musicians.

✳

The first samurai, having accepted the conditions imposed by the mysterious virgin, prepared to depart for distant India; but, thinking about the perils and privations of such a journey, he lost heart and resolved to obtain the living recompense by a ruse. Shrewdly, he went to a temple in Kyoto. The bonze, whom the samurai covered with gold and gems, gave him the sacred cup with which the altar was adorned.

Having wrapped the stone cup in an embroidered cloth, the suitor took it to his dwelling, and after waiting patiently for a year, he charged an old woman to take the cup to Teruko.

The mysterious virgin received the cup from the hands of the envoy. Nightfall was approaching, as well as an amorous dread. Tremulous as the Night itself, Teruko unwrapped the embroidered cloth. She took the stone cup in her extended hands and offered it to the Night . . . but no radiance emerged from the dull cup. And Teruko understood that the dishonest samurai had abused her with a cowardly lover's lie. In her haughty soul, she was scornful of the man, for she knew that an amorous lie is the only irreparably infamous lie. Silently, she returned the fake cup to the messenger.

The samurai, seeing that his ruse had been discovered, returned to his own country, weeping. He remained inconsolable for that destruction of a dream.

The second samurai set forth in his turn for the impossible enterprise, but he feared the criticism and mockery of his family. He gave as a pretext for his long voyage the accomplishment of a vow. Disavowing his own temerity in his soul, he went in search of Mount Horai.

Mount Horai whitens in the fortunate island where weary spirits repose. In that island, storks fly that live for a thousand years. Fir-trees raise their proud and sad glory there. Imperishable tortoises nourish themselves on flowers and dew there. Mushrooms are verdant there, and as beautiful as ancient stones and ruined palaces. And whoever drinks the water of its springs never dies.

The air around the fortunate island is never troubled. Silence is prolonged there, limpid and smiling. The waves are never angry there. All desires are extinguished among the mortals who land on its shores. But no mortal has ever discovered the fortunate island. And those who do not believe in the reality of chimeras say, incredulously: "The fortunate island is not of this world . . ."

A monk had once said to a young man: "The sacred mountain is so high that its crest disappears in the azure. On its summit grows the tree with silver roots, a trunk of bright gold and branches of sculpted jade."

The samurai, having for a moment the divine faith of amour, attempted the enterprise. But when he asked bonzes, diviners, and even passers-by for the location of the fortunate island they all replied, mockingly: "The fortunate island is not of this world . . ."

The samurai lost the faith of amour and he too resolved to obtain the mysterious virgin by means of a ruse.

He summoned six Chinese jewelers. Slowly and patiently, they sculpted a jade branch heavy with foliage. The smallest veins were scrupulously and delicately traced there. The work of the Chinese jewelers was so perfect that one divined the lightness of leaves ready to quiver in the morning breeze. Efflorescences of precious stones were resplendent amid the fresh verdure.

The labor of the jewelers lasted for long months. When the jade branch was finished, the samurai tore his kimono and made up his face in order to give himself the appearance of a voyager weighed down by fatigue. Having sheathed the jade branch in a red lacquer case, he had it taken to Teruko.

The aged messenger who brought the case containing the sculpted branch to Teruko praised the intrepidity of the victorious samurai and depicted the lassitudes and perils of the adventure insidiously. Teruko listened to her silently, opened the lacquer case and took out the sculpted branch.

She respired it, not without a great sadness, for the flowers of precious stone did not exhale any perfume. She knew that the living gems, the precious flowers of Mount Horai, exhale an inexpressible fragrance.

Nevertheless, she listened to the mendacious story reeled off by the samurai's messenger

The old woman recounted the long voyage over a tormented sea.

"Storms harassed the vessel," she said. "Hostile winds spun it round like a sheet of rice paper. For forty nights and forty days the ship was carried away by the currents. And after sufferings heroically endured, the voyagers were hurled against the rocks of an unknown island.

"Beautiful pines darkened there, outlining their night against the immutable azure. Wing-beats quivered there perpetually. Noisy flocks of storks were seen passing overhead. Tortoises were resplendent in the sunlight, causing their carapaces coruscating with precious stones to sparkle.

"The voyagers came ashore, but a whirlwind of oni, angry malevolent spirits with sharp teeth and menacing claws, descended upon them. The samurai having soothed them with sage words, the oni showed themselves favorable to the castaways and aided them fraternally to repair their vessel, broken by the winds. One day, the samurai asked the oni what the name of the island was, and the oni replied 'You have landed on the fortunate island.'

"He begged the fraternal oni to guide him to Mount Horai. They showed him the path that led to the summit. It was there that the valorous samurai collected the jade branch with the gemmed flowers."

Teruko listened to the aged messenger, her eyelids lowered over an incredulous scorn.

At that moment, shrill clamors went up, becoming louder. They were threats and cries proffered in an incomprehensible language. Teruko wondered what the cause of the tumult was. The six Chinese jewelers, whom the samurai had been unable to recompense, were demanding the price of their patient labor bitterly.

Smiling, Teruko distributed the salary they were demanding and imploring by turns. The six Chinese jewelers took the road to their own country again, happy and recompensed. They set out, but their satisfaction was brief, for the samurai, having learned from the aged messenger about their inopportune intervention, was waiting for them not far from the city with armed men, and the six unfortunate Chinese jewelers perished under the blows of the vindictive samurai.

✳

The third samurai set forth in his turn on the impossible enterprise. He had to bring the virgin of his desires the skin of the miraculous rat that lives in the midst of a furnace, which breathes the flames and nourishes itself on the smoke. Now, the third samurai had a Chinese ally. With an eloquent brush he traced an urgent prayer to that ally, imploring him to obtain for him, for the price of a treasure, the skin of the miraculous rat.

A year later, an envoy came to announce to the samurai that his Chinese ally had taken possession of the skin of the rat, after superhuman efforts. His heart rejoiced, the suitor raced on horseback along the road that led to the port where his ally was expected.

For seven days and seven nights the suitor galloped over the road without sleeping or taking nourishment. He met his Chinese ally and, with tears of gratitude, gave him a treasure in exchange for the skin coveted by the mysterious virgin. The Chinese ally returned to his native land.

Having rolled the rat-skin up in the bottom of a nacre casket, the samurai sent it to Teruko.

Smiling, the luminous stranger plunged the rat-skin into the flame of a lantern, for the skin of the prodigious rat is not consumed by contact with fire. But the skin brought by the samurai crackled and burned wretchedly in the sharp flame, and was immediately reduced to ash.

In despair, the samurai then understood that the soul of friends is as perfidious as the lies of lovers. Sickened by others and by himself, he went to live in solitude on the summit of a mountain.

✳

In his turn, the fourth samurai attempted the impossible adventure. He had to conquer the stone of five colors that the blue dragon bears in its forehead. In his turn too, however, he wanted to obtain by duplicity what he could not conquer by patient valor.

He had the servants and men-at-arms who inspired the most confidence in him depart for China. In a blindly optimistic expectation, he wished for their return, for he was certain that he would see his emissaries return as possessors of the inestimable stone.

The servants and men-at-arms departed for China but, infidel to their master's orders, they did not want to attempt the impossible enterprise. They settled peacefully in Chinese cities and spent the samurai's gold on feasting and amorous magnificence.

In the meantime, the excessively credulous samurai arranged his house in order to receive Teruko, the living moonbeam. He felt sure that he would soon see that virginal bride cross the threshold of his dwelling.

A slow year went by in silence, however. No message of hope, no promise of imminent triumph—no news at all—soothed the suitor's impatience.

Feverishly, he made the resolution to depart himself in search of the indolent servants who were late in bringing him the miraculous stone. He chartered a vessel, and in a dawn warmed by hopes and promises, he embarked for China.

The samurai's heart was free and light, like the seabirds that were following the wake of the ship.

On the third evening, however, the sails swelled under an evil wind that grew angrier by the hour, and there was the majesty of a storm at sea.

During tenebrous days and spectral nights, the voyagers drifted at the whim of the waves and the hurricane. They endured hunger and thirst, for the waves had swept away or soiled all the provisions on board.

The samurai, his throat desiccated by thirst, followed his dream with haggard eyes as it flew away. For the suffering and the terror of death had extinguished the chimerical amour within him. The luminous image of the virgin no longer loomed up before his eyes. He shivered dolorously during the day; he burned with fever during the night. He ceased to be the master of his thoughts. Abominable hallucinations haunted his mind. He learned to hate the proud and distant lunar apparition, the cause of all his woes. He blasphemed his amour as others blaspheme their gods . . .

Finally, the evil wind broke the vessel, a lamentable wreck, on the coast of China.

The inhabitants of the port where the ship had been wrecked pitifully, gave the castaways a cordial welcome.

The news of the adventure of the very noble and very powerful samurai reached the ears of the Sons of Heaven, and the Sons of Heaven sent the samurai a present of rare works of lacquer and jade.

The infidel servants ran to their master, for the rumor of the shipwreck had spread throughout the country. Tremulously, they stammered a mendacious story to the samurai and showed him their empty hands. Their efforts, they said, had been vanquished. They had not brought their master the stone of five colors.

Fearfully, they awaited punishment; but, not without an astonished joy, they heard the samurai praise them in terms of gratitude. His rebellion against amour had been exasperated. He cursed Teruko, the mysterious virgin, in the name of all the suffering he had undergone for her. He cursed her for being inaccessibly pure, in the image of distant moonbeams. Hatred had corrupted in his soul the chimerical tenderness that had momentarily enlightened and inflamed him.

The fourth samurai did not dare go back to his native land, for fear of the winds and the waves. He lived for long years in the Imperial Palace of China, esteemed by the Sons of Heaven and honored by the courtiers. He adorned himself with a magnificent illustriousness. Chinese poets celebrated his heroic amour, and the most beautiful among the noblewomen loved him, some in secret and others overtly. He was a legendary hero. In the naïve stories, he appeared to be ornamented with all audacities and all virtues.

The fifth samurai, discouraged by his rivals' lack of success, did not attempt the impossible adventure. He avenged himself for his fruitless wait by decrying the beauty of the living moonbeam. He had possessed Teruko, he said, without delight and without difficulty. Thus he consoled himself with a scornful lie. His vanity being assuaged, he did not suffer from his disappointed covetousness.

Teruko, the luminous virgin, remained alone in the peace of her dreams. The renown of her mysterious splendor increased, like a sonorous tide, and reached the Mikado himself. He sent messengers to Teruko's dwelling charged with reporting back to him as to whether the lunar virgin was truly as beautiful as her name, and whether she merited the melodious glory that the singers had awarded her.

The virgin, however, retreated into a grim solitude, and refused to receive the Mikado's envoys.

The Mikado was astonished by that proud refusal. Until that day, no one had rejected him, for he lived surrounded by the women of the court, who, indifferent to passion, only desired honors and treasures from him. The magnanimity of that disdain surprised him, and imposed on him an admiration for the proud unknown woman.

He resolved to contemplate her with his own eyes. He therefore organized a hunt in the forest that surrounded the dwelling of the former bamboo-cutter. Alone, having deliberately surpassed the host of courtiers, he crossed Teruko's threshold.

The old bamboo-cutter welcomed his august guest deferentially. Hidden behind a screen, the sovereign was put in the presence of the young woman.

The Mikado was struck by amazement. A velvet light emanated from the virgin, silencing the strident clarity of midday. She was like a moonbeam that had slid through the sunbeams: a living moonlight, a nocturnal mildness, a cool consolation, Teruko was chimerically radiant.

Having contemplated her with his dazzled eyes, the Mikado tried to approach her and to brush her long blue sleeve. He begged her to take her place among the imperial concubines—but the virgin recoiled. The Mikado saw that radiant flesh become pale and attenuated before his eyes. She disappeared, aerial vapor, like the halo of the moon . . .

Bewildered, the Mikado implored the unknown woman not to resume her lunar form and to remain, a mortal among mortals. He promised her never to profane the mystery of that sacred body with the slightest touch.

Immediately, the mysterious virgin reappeared, in all the splendor of her beauty, simultaneously terrestrial and supernatural.

The Mikado prostrated himself before the stranger, whom he divined to be the issue of a divine race.

He quit the dwelling of the former bamboo-cutter, taking away an incurable amour, and he felt better in coveting in vain an inaccessible splendor.

That fervor for a living and distant light rendered the soul of the Mikado similar to the dolorous souls of poets. They too are vainly infatuated with impalpable gleams. They too exhaust themselves and consume themselves in hopeless adorations. The Mikado knew the bitter joy of singing his dolors. Every day he composed a hymn, which he sent to the intangible virgin.

She responded to him with strophes as fluid as a moonbeam gliding over calm water. Nocturnal perfumes emanated from those verses and frissons of pale foliage.

The mysterious virgin had composed those poems in unknown modes. The Mikado learned from her rhythms that one would have thought borrowed from another sphere. In those stanzas she praised virginity and celebrated her unshakable decision never to consent to a terrestrial union.

In that epoch, the former bamboo-cutter observed a bizarre quietude in his adoptive daughter. She seemed to be

waiting for moonrise with more impatience. Her entire being was no longer anything but a hope, silently contained.
And the former bamboo-cutter, thanks to the intuition of
simple folk, understood that an incomprehensible law was
weighing upon the stranger, whom he did not know, even
though he loved her with all his human tenderness.

Often Teruko considered him with a sad softness, as if
words that she dared not pronounce were burning her lips.

Finally, she spoke. Already, night was approaching, insinuating and imperious, like a lover who flatters and gives
orders at the same time.

Teruko revealed her supernatural origin to the former
bamboo-cutter who had collected her.

She had previously been one of the seventy-one
Daughters of the Moon, who die at dawn and are resuscitated with the darkness, but she had disobeyed an order
from Djoga, the Goddess of the Moon, her mother and
her redoubtable sovereign.

Djoga had subjected her rebellious daughter to a terrible
punishment. She had condemned her to dwell on earth
for twenty years, as a mortal among mortals. She gave that
living light the form of an abandoned child.

But now the time of the terrestrial sojourn had elapsed,
and Teruko had to rejoin her luminous sisters, the seventy
Daughters of the Moon.

On hearing those words, the former bamboo-cutter
sobbed. In his distress, he went to beg the Mikado to send
the imperial guard, in order to retain the Daughter of the
Moon on earth.

The Mikado armed his troops. He sent them to guard
the dwelling of the former bamboo-cutter.

For forty nights, the warriors waited around the dwelling. A thousand archers were watching on the roof and a

thousand more in the gardens. The Mikado had chosen them all for the precision of their eye, experienced at aiming at the most distant targets. Their quivers were abundantly provided with arrows.

The former bamboo-cutter made Teruko sit behind screens. He hoped to hide her thus from the penetrating gaze of the Moon. But the virgin smiled, a smile of pride and disdain. What could all the efforts of human power and tenderness do against the will of the Moon?

One day, Teruko said to the former bamboo-cutter: "The Moon, my mother, and my sisters, the seventy Daughters of the Moon, will take me away tonight."

The former bamboo-cutter, exhausted by lamentations and alarms, prostrated himself vainly at the feet of the individual he loved as he would have loved his own daughter. Vainly, he implored her to remain mortal among mortals.

All day long, the former bamboo-cutter was sunk in apprehension and dolor.

Finally, night fell.

The Moon, in her fullness, set the nocturnal sky ablaze with cold flames. The Moon dominated and reigned in her omnipotence. The universe, subjugated by her, seemed happy in that soothing servitude. The Moon was shining, in her fullness . . .

The hours passed and the old bamboo-cutter conceived the tremulous hope that Teruko would be left to him. He gradually relaxed, and no longer feared the vigilance of the Moon . . .

. . . But at the hour when the star was at its zenith, a luminous cloud veiled the opaque silver. Then, detaching itself, the cloud moved toward the earth. The old bamboo-cutter, terrified, understood that the cloud was about to descend upon his dwelling.

. . . The cloud finally floated above the roof that sheltered Teruko, the Daughter of the Moon.

The old bamboo-cutter and the two thousand archers saw, with an ecstatic stupor, the seventy Daughters of the Moon, who had come to take their exiled sister back to Djoga.

All of them were diaphanous in their light pallor. All of them were as beautiful as the very soul of the Night.

The one who appeared to be in command of the others advanced to the edge of the cloud and said to the former bamboo-cutter in an assured tone: "Old man, return our sister, whom you once collected. You have raised her piously, knowing that she was of a superior essence. In order to recompense you, my sisters and I once filled with gold and gems the trunks of the bamboos that you felled in your quotidian labor. The Moon will be favorable to you, old man, because you collected one of her daughters, chastised for having disobeyed an order of our sovereign mother."

The former bamboo-cutter wanted to trick the Daughter of the Moon by means of a subterfuge. He spoke to her in these terms:

"For twenty years, O redoubtably beautiful Envoy of the Moon, I have sheltered under my roof the person you imagine falsely to be your exiled sister. During the twenty years in which I have raised and cherished her, she has never resisted the most futile of my prayers, and she has never disobeyed the least of my orders. How could it be, O Messenger of the Moon, that she was the rebel who dared to brave the commandments of her sovereign mother? Seek elsewhere for your exiled sister."

But the Daughter of the Moon did not listen to the deceitful words of the former bamboo-cutter. With an imperious softness, she called: "Come, our exiled sister!"

At those words the screens parted and revealed the luminous beauty of Teruko. She was radiant, like her brilliant sisters, the Daughters of the Moon. And the old man who had enveloped her in a paternal tenderness for twenty years despaired. In the midst of the silence of the archers, he wept as one weeps for a dead person.

Limpidly smiling, Teruko advanced among her divine sisters, the seventy Daughters of the Moon. They dressed their recovered sister in an aerial kimono woven from silver thread. Then the one who appeared to be in command of the others handed Teruko a jade flask containing the elixir that renders immortality.

Teruko begged her sister to let her share the elixir that renders immortality with the former bamboo-cutter, but the elder Daughter of the Moon refused, with a tender firmness.

Having traced a poem in haste, Teruko held it out to the man who had cherished her for a long time as a father cherishes his daughter. She begged him to give those farewell stanzas to the Mikado, who had become a poet for love of her.

Then the living moonbeam joined the radiant host of her divine sisters.

The old bamboo-cutter followed them for a long time with his eyes, blurred by tears.

Teruko had sent the sovereign, with the permission of her sister, the jade flask containing the elixir that renders immortality, but the Mikado, in the sadness of his incurable amour, confided the inestimable present to monks. They broke the flask and burned the letter on the summit of Mount Fuji, the sacred mountain. That is why, even today, one can see smoke there rising up to the clouds.

Which is the Stronger?

KINTARO, the Golden Child, was born and grew up in dolor. Base maneuvers of jealous courtiers had caused his father, the valorous Kintoki, to lose the favor of the Mikado, and, unable to live far away from the blindly adored master, the samurai had died of the imperial disdain.

Tracked by her husband's enemies, Yama-Uba,[1] his young widow, took refuge in the mountains. And beneath the great violet pines, she gave birth to a posthumous son, whom she subsequently named Kintaro.

When the child reached the age of eight, he felled trees as ably as the most vigorous woodcutters. He constructed a dwelling with them for his mother, who had lived until then with no other shelter than the moving pagoda of branches.

Sometimes, in his puerile games, the child hero tore up rocks and broke them between his strong hands.

Having no friends or comrades in the depths of the wilderness, Kintaro chose the fraternal animals for com-

---

1 Author: "Enchantress of the Mountains." This popular legend exists in various versions, most of which do attribute the hero's early care to the mountain witch in question, but only one or two credit her with being his mother

panions. He learned their mysterious language without difficulty, and the animals cherished him for his strength and his mildness. Those he preferred among all of them were a she-bear, a stag, a hare and a monkey.

The she-bear brought her cubs, in order that they could amuse Kintaro by means of their maladroit and naïve gentility. Often, the monkey wrestled with the hare, in order to distract the child by means of his wily agility. Then, the she-bear evened out a platform of earth for the wrestlers. The monkey with the red back and the hare awaited the signal to fight. Kintaro dropped a leaf and appointed himself a judge along with the stag. Immediately, the two adversaries fell upon one another, uttering the cry: "Yoisho! Yoisho!"

One evening, Kintaro was coming back from the heights of the mountains with his four friends when they stopped before a torrent. The disorderly waters were throwing foam toward the willows thicker than white smoke. They were carrying uprooted camellias, trophies from destroyed gardens.

Perplexed, the four friends stamped their feet on the edge of the waters. In order to get back to their lairs and dens it would be necessary for them to make a long detour through the mountains. Night was already approaching.

But Kintaro placed himself beside a pine that was standing there in its proud slenderness, and with his powerful hands, he uprooted the tree and threw it across the seething waves. Thanks to the improvised bridge, the animals filed across one by one, and he preceded the animals to the other bank.

An old woodcutter had contemplated those things with his dull eyes, in which a gleam was ignited, for he rejoiced

in seeing a future hero before dying. Standing up, he followed the predestined child, who was walking escorted by
docile animals.

He followed the predestined child as far as a turning
where five paths intersected. The she-bear, the stag, the
monkey and the hare each took a different route, and
Kintaro went along the path that led to the dwelling of
Yama-Uba.

The stranger, having followed him, was present at the
welcome of the woman, rigid in her white kimono. Smiling
majestically, she interrogated her son.

"Where have you come from, Kintaro, my son?"

"I've come from the distant mountains, Okkasan."[1]

"What were the friends who accompanied you on the
route?"

"The she-bear, the stag, the monkey and the hare escorted me as far as the intersection of the five paths."

"Which is the strongest of the five of you, my son
Kintaro?"

"I'm the strongest of all of us, you know that,
Okkasan."

"And after you, my son Kintaro, which is the strongest?"

"The she-bear is the strongest after me, Okkasan."

"And of the other three, which is the strongest, my son
Kintaro?"

"The stag is the strongest after the she-bear, Okkasan."

"And which is the stronger of the monkey and the hare,
my son Kintaro?"

For the first time the child hesitated.

---

1 Author: "Mother."

"I don't know, Okkasan. Today, the monkey and the hare wrestled one another, and both appeared to me to be equal in strength."

The stranger was listening silently. At that moment he raised his voice and said: "When the hare and the monkey wrestle one another again, Kintaro, let me contemplate the struggle. I will tell you which of the two I deem to be the stronger?"

Yama-Uba and her son turned round. They considered in silence the face of the man who had spoken. Finally, Yama-Uba said to the unknown man: "Who are you, then, stranger?"

"My name doesn't matter," replied the unknown man, "but I know another question more interesting: that is discovering whether Kintaro or me is the stronger. Let's wrestle together, in order to settle the matter."

Laughing confidently and joyfully, Kintaro accepted the challenge. And during the nocturnal hours, the two adversaries prolonged the struggle, without either one of them emerging victorious.

Finally, at dawn, the unknown man proposed that they suspend the equal contest. Kintaro, marveling at the suppleness and strength of his aged adversary, consented with a good grace.

The unknown man spoke in these terms to Yama-Uba: "Your son will be, in the course of time, the most robust and the most glorious of men. He ought not to let his youth slumber in these mountains. Your son, Yama-Uba, ought to take his place among the samurai."

Yama-Uba replied, sadly, that they were alone and without support near the Mikado. She dared not hope, therefore, that her son would ever wear the sword and dagger of the samurai.

But the old man, who could read the future, predicted for the child the glorious future of a hero. In time, he would be merciful as well as valiant, would fight dragons and oni, and aid the afflicted. Until the most distant posterity, musicians and poets would celebrate the splendor of his name and immortalize his strength and his courage.

Then, recovering his veritable form, the unknown man assumed the aspect of a yellow dragon. The dragon flew away, leaving a golden wake in the air.

Yama-Uba, seeing that the destiny of her son had to be accomplished, bade him adieu, weeping. First light was already showing over the pink summits, and perfumes were reanimating in the sunlight, refreshed and renewed.

Kintaro's four friends, the she-bear, the stag, the hare and the monkey, alerted by a mysterious prescience, were waiting for him in front of the dwelling. While the sun rose over the peaks, Kintaro departed, escorted by his fraternal companions.

The dawn quivered with a proud expectation. It was already triumphant, in a confident hope. Its assured gaze illuminated the roads.

At the intersection of the five paths, Kintaro and his four friends separated. Divining that, for the young hero, they were already a vain past, the melancholy animals returned to their lairs and their dens.

Kintaro, alone and confident in the promise of the dawn, departed toward the future.

The Monkey's Five Livers

BENTEN, the Goddess of the Sea, neglected her fluid realm for a few months in order to teach the Gods the art of the samisen and the koto.

In those days, the Gods were still ignorant of the modes and rhythms of music. They knew the shrill and clear song of the little bells accompanying the dances of Uzume, the Goddess of Laughter, and when they wanted to draw Amaterasu, the Goddess of the Sun, out of her cavern, they imagined an infantile harmony. The Goddesses struck branches against one another, and the Gods made their bowstrings vibrate with bamboo stems. Fujin, the God of the Thunder, caused the celestial assembly to marvel with the resonance of his formidable gongs. But the Goddess had not weakened at the sweetness of notes on which charmed dolors swooned.

Benten, therefore, forsook the realm of the sea, carrying her koto of silver and crystal. Before quitting the submissive waves, she confided their sovereignty to Rin Jin, the blue dragon, her faithful servant.

Rin Jin received from Benten's hands the two pearls Nanjiu and Kanjiu. Those two pearls assured the one who possessed them of the command of the tides. The pearl of the flux, Nanjiu, when Benten wore it on her finger, caused the tides to rise up to assault the strand; and the pearl of the reflux, Kanjiu, when the Goddess wore it on her forehead, made the mollified and weary waves retreat toward the ocean bed.

Rin Jin sat on Benten's throne in the palace of the Goddess. The beauty of that palace was unimaginable. In the surrounding gardens the mollusks blossomed, more magnificent than the camellias of the land; and the algae undulated, softer than grass bending under spring breezes. Everything was mysterious and rare in the realm of Benten, governed by Rin Jin.

The blue dragon, acting as Benten had ordered him to do, governed the realm of the seas. But one day, the peace of the waves was troubled. Rin Jin was stricken by a mysterious illness.

The octopus, very wise and very wily, prescribed all the marine remedies, in vain. Rin Jin was weakening by the hour; and the fear of death took possession of him. His terror was exacerbated to the extent of rage. He summoned the octopus and commanded her, under the threat of the most terrible tortures, to cure him immediately.

The octopus, very wise and very wily, was frightened momentarily; but, recovering her self-possession, she searched for a subterfuge that would protect her from the anger of Rin Jin. And the octopus told Rin Jin that the only efficacious remedy against his malady was not found in the realm of the sea. It was necessary, she said, to capture a living monkey and extract its liver.

Rin Jin was perplexed. The enterprise was arduous. He remembered once having passed, during his dragon flight, above an island that was known as the Isle of Monkeys. That island was bathed by a southern sea. Paradoxical vegetation burst forth there, and the monkeys, sitting among the branches, jabbered while throwing mangoes like pebbles at reckless navigators.

He decided to send a messenger to the island in order to capture one of the monkeys, which quarreled untiringly there. But he thought that his subjects, the marvelous fish with humid colors and bizarre forms, had no power outside their native element. How could they bring him the sole efficacious remedy?

The octopus, consulted by Rin Jin, advised him to choose as his emissary the kurage.[1] Now, in those distant times, the kurage possessed a carapace and feet, similar to the carapace and feet of a turtle.

Rin Jin summoned the kurage to appear before him and gave the order to bring him a living monkey. The kurage listened reluctantly. He objected that, since monkeys could not swim, it would be impossible for him to bring his captive back to the marine palace.

"What use is the carapace of which Benten has made you a present?" replied Rin Jin. "You must carry the monkey on your back through the waves."

"Won't the monkey weigh heavily on my carapace?" enquired the kurage, hesitantly.

"What does a little physical pain matter if it is endured for the one whom Benten has appointed as king of the seas?" asked the blue dragon, imperiously.

---

1 The author inserts a note here defining *kouragé* [kurage] as "*poulpe*," a word that is difficult to distinguish in French from *pieuvre*, used in the story to refer to the deceptive physician, and is invariably defined in dictionaries as "octopus." The story subsequently employs *poulpe* to describe the animal in question, so it is not a simple misprint. As sushi-lovers know, the Japanese word actually refers to a kind of jellyfish, and that makes far more sense in the context of the story.

The kurage did not reply. Submissively, he quit the marine palace, swam through the gardens of algae and conches and reached the open sea.

After long glaucous days and long fluid nights, the kurage finally reached the Isle of Monkeys. A wave cast him up on the sand. Wandering through the pines on foot he saw a monkey hanging on to dark green branches.

After having exchanged the usual greetings, the monkey said to the kurage: "Who are you, stranger? For I've never seen your like. Who are you and where do you come from?"

"I'm the kurage, and I've come from the palace of Rin Jin, king of the sea," the other replied.

"Why have you come among us?" interrogated the monkey.

"In the submarine countries, I've heard the splendor of the land you inhabited praised," replied the naively wily kurage. "I'm one of the servants of Rin Jin. In order to come here I left the marine palace, the walls of which are prismatic nacre. I left the sonorous gardens where the corals stand up as vigorous as your pines. I left the realm of the sea, where everything is rare and mysterious."

"Is the realm of the sea more beautiful than this island where I've lived thus far?" asked the monkey.

"Certainly," affirmed the kurage. And he caused all the magnificence of the sea to shine before the attentive monkey.

The monkey was so charmed by the kurage's description that he came down from the tree and sat down next to the stranger. The latter, naively wily, rejoiced in the success of his stratagem. He spoke for a long time about the medusae, which projected their pale radiance, and the starfish, living stars illuminated above the undulating walls of the marine palace.

The attentive monkey listened, and the kurage talked about sea urchins and sea anemones, pink algae and madrepores. The monkey saw all the marvels of the sea blossoming before his eyes.

Eventually, the kurage proposed to him to take him to the palace of Rin Jin. The monkey objected, not without regret, that he did not know how to swim. Hastily, his interlocutor offered to carry him on his impenetrable carapace. The monkey consented joyfully.

Thus, the two of them traversed the waves, the monkey crouched on the kurage's back.

The monkey sniffed the salt spray avidly. The waves swelled around him. The sun ignited dancing reflections on the water. The distances became blue and indefinite.

A terror sometimes gripped the monkey's puerile soul.

"Slow down, I beg you," he implored, "in order that I don't get vertigo. I'm afraid of falling into the water."

Half way, the kurage became anxious. Knowing nothing about terrestrial things and not possessing the wisdom of the octopus, he feared that the monkey might not be in possession of the liver that was the only thing that could cure the dragon Rin Jin. Naively, he asked the monkey if he had bought his liver with him.

Surprised by the strangeness of that question, and suspecting a peril, the monkey, in his turn, interrogated the kurage about the bizarre interest that his liver inspired in him. Ingenuously, the kurage told the monkey about Rin Jin's illness and the remedy prescribed by the octopus; for the kurage was as naïve as he was wily.

The monkey listened, shivering. The horror of the fate that was in store for him became apparent to him. Collecting his scattered thoughts, however, he searched for a subterfuge. Dissimulating his terror, he replied to the kurage that nothing would have been easier or more agreeable to him than to make the sacrifice of his liver.

"Monkeys," he said, "possess five of them, which they remove as they please when their weight hinders them in climbing up trees."

Falsely sorry, however, the monkey added that he had forgotten to bring his five livers with him, and that all of them were still suspended from the branches of a pine tree.

The kurage was desolate. The guileful monkey suggested that they return to the island, where he had left his five livers hanging.

While deploring the delay it caused to his return to Rin Jin, the kurage resumed the fluid road that led to the Isle of Monkeys.

Reassured, the monkeys breathed the freshness of the marine breeze with a renewed joy.

The kurage and the monkey came ashore on the island of beautiful pines, and the monkey, under the pretext of fetching his five livers, joyfully took refuge amid the dark verdure. Then, grimacing through the jagged fruits and sharp needles of the pine, he mocked the kurage, who was waiting at the foot of the tree. With a snigger, the monkey thanked the kurage for the marvelous voyage that he owed to his helpful amity.

The disappointed kurage implored and threatened in vain. Sometimes he begged the deceptive monkey to remember his promise. Sometimes he reproached him with invectives for the falsity of his words. But the monkey, inaccessible among the branches, made fun of him with mocking jeers.

The kurage was obliged to return, frustrated and vanquished, to the realm of the sea. He trembled with fear in thinking about the anger of Rin Jin. How could he tell him that he had not brought the monkey's liver?

The sunlight on the waves burned him. The waves laughed coldly. The sea seemed to be rejoicing perfidiously in his defeat.

The glum kurage cleaved through the waves and traversed the gardens of coral and algae again. Rin Jin had come to meet his envoy personally. He was accompanied by his guards, the dolphins, and his ministers, the turtles. Courtiers were crowded around him: well-born lobsters with delicate pincers, humble swarming crabs, plaice, angler fish, red mullet and dorados. All of them hastened around the kurage as if to augment his anxiety involuntarily. They lavished expressions of delight on him, for they did not doubt for a single instant that he had brought back the efficacious remedy. They did not believe it possible that the kurage, defeated, would have dared to confront the wrath of the redoubtable Rin Jin.

The blue dragon welcomed his messenger with all the marks of royal favor. But when quaking with dread, the lamentable kurage was obliged to confess how he had been tricked by the malicious monkey, Rin Jin's benevolence turned into fury.

In his vindictive disappointment, Rin Jin summoned his torturers, the sharks. He ordered them to remove the patient's bones, cut off his feet and rip off his carapace.

The kurage was subjected to the abominable torture. Then, in accordance with the order of the implacable Rin Jin, the torturers whipped him so cruelly that there was nothing left of the miserable kurage but a mass of flaccid and formless flesh.

In order to prolong the memory of that punishment until the remotest tomorrows, Rin Jin clad the descendents of the Chastised with his exact resemblance. That is why the descendants of the kurage, who was once similar to a turtle, are now amorphous and gelatinous.

Tea-Flowers

DARUMA was a Hindu nun whose soul exhaled rare perfumes.[1] For nine years she remained motionless, in silent meditation. When she wanted to return to the human world, in order to teach them the wisdom of her long dream, she could not stand up, having lost the use of her limbs.

Later she traversed the sea on a reed and reached the shores of Japan. It was thus that the mysterious Guanyin, having transformed the hells into luminous paradises, had once traversed space on a lotus flower.

Again the nun sank into a dream. Spiders wove their marvelous webs around her. She appeared through the silvery networks as if through a mist.

One night, in spite of the fixed ardor of her thought, she drifted into slumber. When she woke up, the nun's contrition was so intense that she cut off her eyelids, as beautiful as the amber eyelids of Guanyin, and threw them on the ground. Such was the magical virtue of that almost

---

1 Daruma is the name given in Japan to Bodidharma, the Buddhist monk credited with importing Buddhism to China. This story refers to the character as a *moniale*, which is a female member of a religious community, and then uses the pronoun *elle* in referring to the individual in question, so the change of sex is clearly deliberate.

divine flesh that each of the eyelids became a bush with odorous foliage.

Since that day, tea has flourished on the earth, the tea dear to poets and slender mousmés.[1]

1 The term "mousmé" was popularized in France by Pierre Loti's novel *Madame Chrysanthème* (1887), where it is employed to refer to a Japanese girl; Vincent van Gogh's painting "La Mousmé" (1888) is now better known, but would not have been when the present story was written.

Death Exiled

WASOBEI, rocked by the rhythm of the boat, allowed a dream to enter into his soul that was as vast as the radiance of summer on the sea. Sometimes he evoked the Isle of Eternal Youth where Mount Horai rises. Fishermen and mariners had searched for it in vain among the distant verdant islands; even the most adventurous sailors had never been able to approach that divine land.

Wasobei's meditation was so radiantly vague that he did not notice the menacing clouds that were accumulating like tenebrous dragons. Eventually, the tempest enveloped him in the rumble of a squall. Carried at hazard through the waves and eddies, Wasobei raced over a disorderly sea for three nights and three days.

A wave finally cast him up on an unknown shore. Storks furrowed the air with their luminous flight; innumerable tortoises were basking in the sun; and marvelous seashells starred the shining sand.

The tempest having eased, Wasobei contemplated the land where his junk had run aground.

Against a backcloth of black pines there were pale cherry trees, like a florescence of moonlight outlined against a background of darkness. The green and gray leprosy of sacred mushrooms was reminiscent of the leprosy of very ancient stones. Like nocturnal rain, blue wisteria flowers were falling, quivering.

Everything in the isle with limpid horizons was simultaneously strange, simple and radiant. The sea lulled it with a feverishly caressant chant. In the distance, the azure summit of Mount Horai was lost in the ether, and its snows espoused the clouds.

By virtue of an almost superhuman intuition, Wasobei understood that, without looking for it, he had discovered the Isle of Eternal Youth. An immeasurable pride swelled his breast. He was henceforth inaccessible to terrestrial evils, superior to laws and similar to the gods.

For twenty centuries the chrysanthemums shed their perpetual autumn over him and the pines refreshed him with their solemn night. But gradually, a distress choked him.

He bore in his heart the melancholy of those distanced by destiny from flat common routes, those who do not know the bliss of stupidity. He regretted normal suffering and necessary ugliness. He hated the purity of his wrinkle-free face. He was no longer intoxicated by the sky and the sea, and even the multiple beauty lost its mystery, no longer oppressing him with a religious anguish.

Wasobei was weary of living.

One evening, he dreamed about death in the heroic and dolorous shade of the pines.

He evoked the meditative attitude of the dead, huddled in tombs. The perpetuity of their blind contemplation gained him in its turn. He saw them incessantly, in the fixed ecstasy of solitaries drunk on thought.

The desire or annihilation penetrated him, more tenacious than the haunting of hope or even the obsession of amour.

He finally resolved to quit the isle from which death was banished, like a beautiful and somber exile. An obliging stork transported him, and in a magnificent dusk he returned to the terrestrial places where everyone suffers and everyone dies.

In the hour of his death, a sad smoke, as if weary of its vain effort, dissipated in melancholy fashion among the fraternal clouds.

Amaterasu's Piebald Horse

THE STAGE is plunged in the most profound darkness. One divines rather than sees the Gods and Goddesses quivering in the blind night. They are shivering in dolorous attitudes. At the back of the stage is the cavern where Amaterasu has taken refuge. Seibo, the Goddess of Longevity, enters, feeling her way. She is carrying a basket of peaches.

Seibo, *talking to herself:* "I'm walking blindly in the blind night. I've groped my way through forests of bamboo and gardens of camellias. I've run the risk of drowning in streams. What will become of me? And what will become of the entire earth? For seven years the world has been plunged in darkness. What does that strange and cruel law signify? (*She listens.*)

"I can't hear anything. I'm looking for the sky where the Goddesses and Gods, my sister and my brothers, assemble. I want to penetrate this formidable mystery. I rejoiced in living in the orchard where my miraculous peaches reddened. It takes them three thousand years to ripen, and the individual who picked them would have become like us, eternal in an immutable world. The individual who would have detached my miraculous peaches would never have died. But now, no longer being bathed by the sun, my beautiful fruits won't ripen. The three thousand years haven't elapsed yet. My peaches require another century before ripening. Oh, my poor hopes!" (*She weeps.*)

Fujin, God of the Wind, *carrying two blue bags in which the winds are enclosed*: "To judge by your speech, you're Seibo, our sister who grants longevity. You've doubtless come to deplore with us the interminable night that weighs upon the world."

Seibo: "And who are you?"

Fujin: "I'm the God of Winds. But since this disaster I haven't opened the blue bags in which the hurricanes and breezes are enclosed."

Benten, the Goddess of Beauty, *with a serpent around her neck*: "I'm dying of ennui. What point is there in being the Goddess of Beauty and Amour, since no one can any longer see my face through the darkness?"

Tajikara, God of Dragons, *seated on a dragon*: "My dragons have lost their golden and glaucous scales. In their fright they've taken refuge under the fountains of the sea. They no longer fly among the clouds. They're deprived of their strength and their valor."

Daikoku, God of Commerce: "The rice-fields are like deserts. Talkative transactions between humans have ceased. I used to delight in stubborn quarrels between wily merchants. Now they sit, taciturn, in the shadow of death. The human race is ready to end."

Benten: "I shall no longer see the dances of geishas trading wisteria and chrysanthemums underfoot. I shall no longer be the smiling protector of little amorous courtesans."

Amenoko, God of Trees: "The priests will no longer plant sacred trees in the temple gardens."

Sarasvati, Goddess of Languages: "No one will speak the multiple and bizarre languages that I teach those who seek my sanctuaries."

Uzume, Goddess of Joy: "What will become of me, who loves laughter and fine celebrations and fears solitude like death, in a depopulated world?"

Tajikara: "What is certain is that the human race is going to perish."

Seibo: "But why is the human race on the brink of perishing? And why does daylight no longer rise over the world?"

Fujin, *striking his gongs with an angry gesture*: "Seven years ago, Amaterasu, the Goddess of the Sun, offended, took refuge in that cavern, from which she refuses to emerge. Chagrined, she is hiding her radiant face."

Seibo: "Why is Amaterasu so indignant against the world that she wants to make it disappear?"

Benten: "Do you remember Amaterasu's piebald horse?"

Seibo: "I remember that she once rode through the clouds on a piebald horse, to which she testified a great affection."

Benten: "In her azure palace, among the immortal virgins, she was weaving the pattern of dawns and sunsets while the ether darkened when Fujin appeared."

Fujin: "I brought her, with lamentations, the mutilated cadaver of the piebald horse."

Seibo: "Who would have dared to kill Amaterasu's sacred horse?"

Fuhin: "The cruel and maleficent Susano-o, her brother."

Seibo: "A curse upon the cruel Susano-o, who does evil for the love of evil and dolor!"

Sarasvati: "Amaterasu's pride revolted against the outrage. She went to weep in the depths of the cavern where, for seven years, she has remained far from her sisters and brothers, the Goddesses and Gods."

Seibo: "But why can't you persuade her, with soft words and pleas, to show herself, as before, in the reassured sky? Why can't you persuade her to render light and warmth to beings and things?"

Benten: "I've sung Amaterasu my most beautiful songs in vain. She didn't want to hear them."

Amenoko: "I've transported, weeping, the sakaki, the holy trees that shade the highest summits of the heavens. I've surrounded the entrance to the grotto with sakaki, and I've ornamented their branches with magatama, the jewels of crystal and jade that Izanaghi, the God of the Air, the father of us all, once gave to Amaterasu because she is his eldest daughter. I hoped that Amaterasu would quit her retreat in order to recover her jewels, which were once so dear to her."

Sarasvati: "I've implored her to come out. I've employed all human and celestial languages to appease her, in vain."

Seibo: "What shall we do, then? The human race will die out, and we, the Goddesses and Gods, will perish in the darkness."

Benten: "Ishi-no-Kore has forged lightning, in order to dissipate the darkness that enshrouds us for a few instants."

Ishi-no-Kore, God of Fire: "But it closes again, more opaque, after my brief flashes."

Uzume: "Ishi-no-Kore, you who are the most patient and the most cunning of us, what do you propose in this evil hour?"

Ishi-no-Kore: "I have, in fact, thought of a ruse."

Benten: "Speak, Ishi-no-Kore. Speak and save us."

Ishi-no-Kore, *taking from the folds of his kimono a large golden mirror and illuminating the stage with a flash of lightning*: "Look."

Sarasvati: "O marvel!"

Benten: "O marvel of marvels!"

> (*The Goddesses and Gods crowd around Iski-no-Kore, contemplating the mirror by the intermittent light of lightning flashes.*)

Seibo, *aside*: "Why these cries of surprise and delight?"

Ishi-no-Kore: "I have created the first mirror."

Uzume: "I will dance before you, my sisters, my brothers! I shall dance to attract the attention of Amaterasu."

Benten: "Strike these long pieces of wood together harmoniously, my sisters! You, my brothers, take your bows and make the strings vibrate with reeds and bamboo stems. Thus the first music will be born."

> (*Uzume gets up and dances to the sound of little bells suspended from her kimono. The music of the Gods accompanies her movements. The Gods laugh loudly, in chorus, giving marks of approval.*)

Fujin, *loudly*: "Our sister Uzume is more flexible than a willow sapling.

Tajikara: "The sound of her bells is more harmonious than the song of the cuckoo."

Benten: "Well done, Uzume!"

Seibo: "The three thousand years that ripen my peaches would pass by like an hour in contemplating you dancing, Uzume."

Raijin, God of Thunder, *striking his gongs*: "Glory to our sister Uzume!"

> (*A light is seen illuminating the back of the stage, emerging from the cavern.*)

The voice of Amaterasu, invisible: "Why are you dancing, my sister Uzume? Why are you rejoicing, my brothers?"

"Uzume: "We're dancing and rejoicing to honor the new Goddess, as beautiful as you, who has just taken her place in our assembly."

> (*Long rays of light emerge from the cavern, preceding the Goddess of the Sun.*)

Benten: "She's advancing slowly, in order to contemplate her unknown rival."

Saravasti: "She's advancing in order to contemplate the new Goddess, as beautiful as her."

Uzume, triumphantly: "She's advancing. Her long rays are preceding her. On perceiving her unknown image in the mirror, she'll see herself so beautiful that she'll remain among us."

> (*Amaterasu appears, enveloped in an exceedingly bright splendor. The entire stage lights up. Amaterasu reflects herself in the great mirror for a long time.*)

Benten: "The Goddess of the Sun has reappeared."

Seibo: "And now light and warmth have returned to the world."

Uzume, *to the Gods*: "Rejoice!"

(*She resumes her joyful dance. The curtain falls.*)

The Inexhaustible Gifts

LAKE BIWA is, in truth, one of the Seven Wonders of Japan. Pines mirror their melancholy shade therein. The little bells of the evening, traversing the waves, launch into the distance a music more limpid than elsewhere. And the vesperal veils that furrow the waves, as weary as them, incline with a more painful languor. The wild geese form noisy flocks reflected in the waters and troubling their calm with a flutter of wings. The autumn moon takes pleasure in contemplating herself in Lake Biwa, as in her most beautiful mirror. And who can ever depict the pomp of the sunsets that die over the transfigured lake?

Once, a very valorous samurai, Fujiwara Hidesato, who was wandering through Japan in quest of adventures, stopped on the edge of Lake Biwa. The bridge of Seta-no-Karashi was suspended like a prodigious thread of spider-silk above the waters. Wanting to pass over the lake, Fujiwara Hidesato was approaching the tenuous bridge when he saw, to his amazement, that a dragon was enlacing the piles with its vast glaucous coils. The bridge was shining in the sunlight, a living pile, an architecture of scales.

Although he was the most valorous samurai in Japan, Fujiwara Hidesato hesitated momentarily at the sight of the monster; but he had never retreated before an obstacle and never feared to confront a peril.

Fujiwara Hidesato considered the dragon. It appeared to be asleep, its golden claws clinging to one extremity of the bridge and its stony tail wrapped around the other. Serenely, Fujiwara Hidesato traversed the formidable bridge.

Having attained the other shore, Fujiwara Hidesato drew away without turning his head. Like all strong souls, he disdained the past. But a voice behind him called him by his name in a sob of prayer.

Merciful, in the fashion of heroes, Fujiwara Hidesato turned round, sensing that a weakness or a suffering was imploring his aid.

An old man weighed down by the years was sending him the appeal of his distress. Fujiwara considered the supplicant with surprise. His wrinkled skin resembled stony coils; his yellow fingernails were curved like golden claws; and his white hair was drifting in the breeze like pale smoke. The unknown man was wearing, regally, a crown of green scales, which scintillated like living emeralds, and his kimono was embroidered with reeds, dragonflies, irises and nenuphars.

Fujiwara Hidesato divined that the strange old man was not human. He was not astonished, accustomed as he was to the most surprising aspects of Adventure. Supernatural things did not appear to him to be incomprehensible or formidable. He knew that foxes are terrible gaki who delight in tormenting mortals. Sometimes they assume the appearance of a woman who smiles as she pours sake at feasts. Sometimes they borrow the venerable body of a bonze. Fujiwara Hidesato also knew that oni transform themselves into hideous old women who nourish them-selves on human flesh. Having learned to consider illusory forms with suspicion, he divined that the dragon and the old man were two dissimilar aspects of the same individual principle.

The mysterious old man was contemplating Fujiwara Hidesato with an anxious gaze. The samurai finally asked him why he had uttered the appeal. The old man replied that, knowing him to be magnanimous and merciful, he had cried out to him in his distress.

Hidesato immediately promised the old man his aid, and the latter, grateful for that spontaneous impulse, revealed his origin and his name to the samurai. Fujiwara Hidesato thus learned that the dragon who reigned over Lake Biwa had adopted the features of an old man in order to manifest himself to him. A gigantic spider with a thousand feet had devastated his fluid empire and devoured half his empire, including his children. And the monster was extending its ravages every day. Before long, the populous abysm of Lake Biwa would be nothing but a desert in which only death and silence wandered.

Respectful before any calamity, Hidesato listened to the royal dragon's story. The latter added that, in extremity, he had resolved to implore the aid of a valorous man, and for long days he had coiled himself, in his veritable dragon form, around the bridge of Seta-no-Karashi.

Anxiously, he had awaited the coming of a Hero; until now, however, no one had dared attempt the terrifying passage. The boldest warriors had fled at the sight of the attentive dragon.

Hidesato was as prompt to relieve unfortunates as to commiserate with them. He asked the dragon to conduct him to the lair where the spider with a thousand feet went to ground, but the royal dragon replied that he did not know in what obscure place the monster hid. Courteous

even in his misfortune, he invited Hidesato to descend
with him into the depths of his domain and share the evening meal with him.

Hidesato consented, having no more fear of deep waters than devouring monsters. With his eyes open and his
head held high, he descended alongside the royal dragon
into Lake Biwa.

The adventurous Hidesato had never had, even in his
most distant excursions, the revelation of such splendors.
The water blurred lines and contours with a transparency
of dream. Light undulated over things, glaucous and fugitive. Reeds as tall as fir trees elevated their vigorous slenderness, and nenuphars outlined their jade calices beside
irises. Golden red fishes darted their living flashes amid the
floating vegetation.

Hidesato considered that fluid domain with wonder.
He had listened in the past to the popular songs that celebrated the marine empire of Benten. Those stories had
evoked for his eyes the coral and the gardens of brown,
green and pink algae; but no song or legend had ever celebrated the empire of Lake Biwa.

Welcoming and majestic, the royal dragon invited the
samurai, his unexpected guest, to sit on his jade throne.
The meal was sumptuous, equaling the ceremonious feasts
of the Mikados. Crystallized lotus petals were served on
diamond platters. The ivory of the chopsticks was studded
with beryls. Carp, submissive servants, poured the sap of
reeds into a cup formed from an emerald. At the end of
the banquet, fish performed undulating dances before the
samurai; they described luminous spirals and circles in the
water, their movements sparkling with moist light. It was
the most harmonious of beautiful spectacles . . .

In the midst of that magnificence, however, a sudden rumble resounded, like thunder falling on a mountain and causing it to shake. The water darkened and was agitated violently. And the royal dragon said to the samurai: "My enemy is coming. Its approach causes the rocks and the abysms to tremble. Listen and see . . ."

Raising his head, the samurai saw the monster above the waves, still distant. Its thousand feet resembled a procession of ardent lanterns. Its eyes were like two accursed suns, two irritated and red suns.

Without trembling, Hidesato picked up his quiver and his bow. Being the most skillful archer in Japan, he was not afflicted to see that only three arrows remained in his quiver. He believed that he would attain the redoubtable target with the first effort. Confident and full of hope, he aimed between the two ruddy eyes. The arrow departed. To his amazement, however, Hidesato saw it rebound immediately and fall back, without having penetrated the rough hide of the monster.

Hidesato took aim for a second time. The arrow, launched at the exact center of the forehead, was blunted by the scales and rebounded, defeated.

Anxiously, Hidesato considered his last arrow. Life and death were trembling, suspended in that decisive moment.

Now the spider was descending gradually toward the lake. In a bleak anguish, the royal dragon awaited the outcome of the combat.

As he took aim, Hidesato remembered the popular belief that human saliva is mortal to spiders and centipedes.[1]

---

1 The more familiar versions of this legendary episode in the life of the tenth-century warrior Fujiwara no Hidesato have him battling a giant centipede on a mountain rather than a spider in a lake.

He therefore moistened the tip of the arrow between his lips.

Like the other two, the arrow departed. A din more terrible than the fall of the skies rent the nocturnal calm. The flamboyant eyes were veiled, like two extinct suns. With a formidable gasp, the wounded monster collapsed at the foot of the mountain.

Rocks split. The entire mountain vibrated. The darkness thickened. The obscure earth seemed oppressed by uncertainty.

Finally, like a deliverance, dawn broke in the liberated skies, and the cadaver of the monster was floating in the scarlet water of the lake, stained with blood.

The royal dragon rejoiced in a loud voice, surrounded by his people of fish. Gradually, the waters of Lake Biwa recovered their limpid transparency. They glittered in the sunlight, sparkling in happy peace, their waves iridescent with fugitive prisms. They turned a blue purer than the soul of snow.

The palace of the royal dragon was radiant, like a rainbow architecture, and the joyful fish made her scales resplendent.

The grateful dragon had his valorous savior served a feast even more splendid than the first. At the end of the meal, in spite of his host's pleas, Hidesato bade him farewell.

When the words of adieu had been pronounced, a procession of fish filed past, bearing presents that the royal dragon offered to his valorous savior. There was a sack of rice, a bale of silk, a cauldron and a bronze bell.

Hidesato refused, politely. On the insistence of the dragon, however, he accepted the magical gifts, without understanding their inestimable value—for those presents ensured their possessor an unlimited wealth. The sack of rice was inexhaustible; as soon as it was empty it filled up again, miraculously, with milky grains. The bale of silk renewed itself eternally, and the cauldron cooked the most delicate dishes without fire and without servants. Finally, the bronze bell sent the most unimaginable sweet sounds toward the heavens; it was an aerial music made to float over waters appeased by the evening. Hidesato resolved to dedicate those harmonies to Celestial Benevolence.

That is why he had the enchanted bell suspended in the temple of Guanyin. And that is why, today, the bell of the evening chimes such limpid notes above the waves of Lake Biwa.

The Inferior Brothers

THE poet Abe no Nakamaro, having long pored over nature, as well as a gulf of blue radiance, glimpsed a few gleams of the multiple enigma.[1] Like the meditative Buddha, he understood that animals have souls, indecipherable souls, and ought to be respected, like the idols in the sanctuaries.

He understood that an unknown power avenges obscurely the animals tortured by the base ferocity of humans. He also divined that the merciful Guanyin smiles, with her eyelids eternally lowered, at people who protect those sacred weaknesses.

The poet took pleasure in dreaming for slow hours in the gray shadow of the temple, for his dream was impregnated with mystery there. The aspirations of his soul were confounded with the ritual perfumes.

The fragile tinkle of little bells and the grave sonorities of gongs supplied rhythm to his fugitive thoughts.

One day, while he was evoking piously the splendor of the Gods, Amaterasu, the Goddess of the Sun, emerged, luminous, from the cavern of shadow, preceded by long sharp sunbeams. Djoga, Goddess of the Moon, was medi-

---

1 Abe no Nakamaro lived in the eighth century, and spent the greater part of his life in China, where he was known as Chao Heng.

tating under the tree of immortality. In the varnished foliage, fruits of a radiant blondeness were shining feebly. The blue kimono of the Goddess was embroidered with pearls brighter than the stars. By way of a belt she wore a red cord. That cord linked mysteriously the heels of those who, separated for the moment, unknown to one another, were to love one another in the future. A hare was crouching at the feet of the Goddess.

The God Fujin, clad in azure, was loading on to his strong shoulder the swollen bag that contained the winds. Uzume, the Goddess of Joy, was smiling the closed smile that nevertheless lit up her entire face, her eyelids closed over an interior contentment. Daikoku, the laborious God of Commerce, astride two sacks of rice, was brandishing a carpenter's hammer. Shioki, the God who masters demons, was imprisoning an oni under his vast hat as if under the bell of a pagoda. Benten, the Goddess of the Sea and Music, was singing while accompanying herself on the biwa with dreams of limpid water. She was riding a dragon with silver scales. Her eyes were radiant over the gray sea. The poet contemplated her lips, which had once elaborated in beauty all human speech, informing the first lovers of the art of kisses.

Suddenly, outside, the sound of a pursuit cut through the attentively solemn silence, and the singer saw a hunted fox take refuge in the enclosure.[1]

Moved by the compassion that links being to being and creature to creature fraternally, Abe no Nakamaro took possession of the animal—which, with a strange confidence,

---

1 Author: "Foxes are hunted in Japan not for the inept and ferocious pleasure of hunting them, but in order to procure the animal's liver, reputed to be a precious remedy."

allowed itself to be seized by those sympathetic hands. He hid it under a fold of his poet's ample white kimono.

The hunters entered the temple tumultuously. Disappointed, they were obliged to abandon their prey. And when solitude had fallen again over the pagoda, Abe no Nakamoro returned the rescued animal to the blue forests and the inviolable mountains.

A year later, a virgin as beautiful as moonlight on snow traversed the poet's path. She was as slender and luminous as a willow florid with fireflies. Her voice was as fascinating as the distant voice of the cuckoo, and her body undulated like faintly perfumed wisteria in the evening breeze.

Djoga linked with her red cord the heels of the poet and the unknown woman. The young woman became a wife, more ardently cherished than the most coveted mistress.

One day, however, she saw Karu, the Goddess of Fevers, who mocks the dying, grimacing beside her bed. Karu appeared to her with her ordinary attributes, astride a fish, her forehead crowned with a yellow toad.

And Karu took the young wife away to the realm of Yen-ma, the master of the dead.

On the third night after the death of his young wife, Abe no Nakamaro was visited by a dream. The dead woman revealed herself, surging from a pink lotus and smiling through an auroral radiance.

The poet understood her radiant silence, as one understands the speech of music. The mute lips of the apparition revealed to him that the fox once hunted in the temple had been reincarnated in the incomparable form of the virgin that Abe no Nakamaro had espoused amorously.

In delivering the hunted beast, he had saved his most ardent joy and his most beautiful grief.

Among Ten Thousand Musiciennes

AMONG the Emperor's concubines, like an iris among bamboos, the musicienne Kogo no Tsubone flourished.[1] No one was able to caress the swooning koto like her, nor reanimate it, as she could, with a strange and mortal ardor.

Sometimes, the imperial choirs sang to the combined sounds of the Chinese flute and the samisen, whose union is so narrowly perfect that it symbolizes the divine accord of souls. Kogo, hidden behind a screen, noted down the sinuosities of the rhythm with aligned beans, and was able to repeat the melody impeccably as soon as the final note sounded.

Kogo was the perpetual joy of the Emperor. She ornamented herself with seashells more beautiful than gems. For long hours she listened to the murmur of a conch, and the echo of the distant sea inspired her with fugitive and fluid music. Often, she composed strophes in which she praised mountains capped with snow and reminiscent of the dappled fur of a hind. She also sang about the undulation of wisteria, which recalls the undulation of waves

---

1 Kobo no Tsubone was a favorite of the Emperor Takakura. History records that she became a nun, but there is a Noh play with a heroine of the same name whose plot is very similar to this story.

and the melancholy flight of the yellow heron among the reeds.

But the Empress Hatsu hated Kogo with an unrelenting hatred, and such was the paltry violence of her persecutions that the concubine fled the imperial palace.

For three years the Mikado had people search for her in vain. His couriers traversed the realm in vain. The incomparable musicienne had disappeared.

Finally, the Emperor ordered a poet skillful in the art of songs, Nakakimi, to find the fugitive—for the poet had boasted that he could recognize, among the instruments of ten thousand musiciennes, the magical touch of Kogo.

For a long time, Nakakimi wandered through solitudes and cities. But one evening, as he was riding through the village of Saga, near Araski, playing naively sad tunes on his flute, he perceived the response of a koto, expertly brushed, which took up the refrain distantly, subtilizing it to the extent of the unreal. And with a frisson of great mute joy, he paled as he recognized the unequaled artistry of the rediscovered musicienne.

The Threshold of Silence

Minamoto No Yorimitsu was a magnanimous warrior.[1] The sentiment of his strength had never oppressed frightened or confident weakness, for Minamoto was not like other men; he was the gentle hero who only hates cruelty and injustice.

Minamoto fervently revered the three Gods of War.

He was the servant of Kwangu, the God who menaces the insubordinate elements with his spear and tugs his ragged beard angrily. Marishiten appeared to him, grimacing and standing on a wild boar. He was also favored by Fudo the avenger, whose right hand brandishes the saber that carves and whose left hand unrolls the cord that strangles. But the hero cherished above all Shoki, the God who seizes the fleeing oni in flight and imprisons them under his vast hat; for Shoki is the good strength who only punishes some in order to protect and save others.

Minamoto was followed in his campaigns by a servant with a very simple faithful soul, Tsuna. Both of them traveled Japan, delivering the oppressed, bringing down unjust provincial governors and combating the gaki.

---

1 The warrior Minamoto no Yorimitsu (948-1021) features in numerous legends, often accompanied by four retainers, including Watanabe no Tsuna, the hero of the story here translated as "Watanabe, Valiant and Joyful."

One evening, they were wandering in the plain of Rendai when a strange and terrible apparition was manifest. A skull borne by the evening breeze was floating in the air. The gleams of the setting sun haloed it with a red aureole.

Minamoto and Tsuna understood that a divine order was being mysteriously sent to them. The skull, whitening in front of them, seemed to be tracing their route. They followed the vision as far as the plateau of Kagura-ga-Oka.

In the middle of a field of pale grass was a desolate ruined house. An old woman in a white kimono was waiting on the threshold, whose face was similar to the pitted faces of old seeresses. Her hair was reminiscent of withered snow not bathed by the consoling moon. Her eyelids were so heavy that she lifted them up with an ivory rod, and so large that if pushed back they would have covered her entire head like an ample veil. With her hands she was retaining the burden of her dugs.

Minamoto harassed the bizarre solitary with questions. She extended her hand to the ivory rod. Her breasts fell down to her knees in the flaccid abandonment of a punctured balloon. Slowly, the unnamed woman opened her lips with another rod, and, in a quavering voice, she spoke.

More than two centuries weighed upon her weary head. She had existed for two hundred and seventy years, like the gray vegetation of the rocks. She had been the servant, subjugated by terror, of nine masters, of whose redoubtable names she remained silent. She warned the wanderers about the peril that awaited them in a country subjugated by demons.

Having said that, she crossed the threshold of silence again.

Minamoto and Tsuna went into the banqueting hall. Oppressed by the obscure air, which weighed heavily, they leaned over paper window-panes, on which a firefly was dying. A storm was about to espouse the night, accompanied by a nuptial procession of terrors. Fear intensified in the depths of the universal stupor.

In the expectation of the air there was a sound of multiple footfalls, like the tread of a disorderly crowd. A strident tumult of gongs and tambours burst forth. Revealed by an abrupt illumination of lightning flashes, innumerable demonic bakemono were howling. Some of them were folding up their long scaly green necks like the coils of a python. Others greeted the hero, extending their palms toward him and putting their feet in front as a sign of deference. Others swelled the flaccid bellies of cephalopods or opened their unique eye, situated in the location of the navel, suspiciously. Some were swarming in the form of tortoises with carapaces covered in thick fur, or monkeys with a gaping hole instead of a liver. As boneless and gelatinous as medusae, amorphous gaki allowed their inorganic flesh to crumble.

But, like fire-follets dissipating before the spectral clarity of the moon, the bakemono disappeared before a strange form. Naked to the waist, she proudly erected the shadow of round breasts. Her stature was mediocre, but her visage, implausibly diminished and thin, measured two feet from the forehead to the chin. Her arms, more tenuous than threads of silk, were troubling and disconcerting.

She laughed with all her teeth, which were admirably black, and disappeared in her turn.

Suddenly, in the swarming shadow, there was a lunar radiance, a diffuse dream-light. A strange woman, as beautiful as Djoga, the Goddess of the Moon herself, was sparkling, her forehead circled by pearls.

Yorimitsu stood speechless before that incarnation of all ungraspable feminine grace. His eyes were troubled. His thoughts vacillated, like the light of a lantern.

Suddenly, he felt mysteriously enveloped by fog. Innumerable spider-webs gripped him in their gray mist. It was a perfidious tangle that imprisoned him in a lukewarm twilight.

A languor insinuated itself within him, like the lassitude of the end of the day. The complex threads clasped him implacably in their mesh. The hero had the divination of latent peril. He straightened himself and sliced through the subtle weave with his sword. Blindly, he struck out in mystery. A hoarse moan rent the air. The ambiguous twilight dissipated. The vision had vanished, and Yorimitsu's saber was steeped in a blood milkier than drops of moonlight.

The two warriors understood that they were wandering randomly in a magical domain. They followed the trail of milky blood.

For a long time they wandered in strange subterranean passages. Finally, they penetrated into a grotto with jade walls, in which a monstrous spider was huddled dolorously.

A little gleam shone in the mass of the body. It was the broken tip of Yorimitsu's sword. The same bright blood of a wounded star emerged from the open wound in the belly. Yorimitsu invoked Shoki, whose merciful power triumphs over oni and dragons. Then, raising his sword religiously, he cut off the spider's head—a head twenty-five aunes wide[1]—and also plunged the sacred iron into the gulf of the belly.

From the entrails, laid bare, sprang nineteen hundred and nineteen skulls of warriors previously devoured by the monster, and a hundred spiders the size of a seven-year-old child.

Yorimitsu and Tsuna understood that they had vanquished a mountain spider, of a race even more redoubtable than the obscure race of dragons. And with the gravity of heroes stirred by the solemnity of victories, they went back up toward terrestrial existence.

Invisible flowers begged with all their eloquent perfumes, and the brilliant and gentle night advanced the heavy hands of camellias.

----

1 An aune is about four English feet.

For the Long Joy of Humans

YOHIKI, the favorite companion of the Empress Tokiwa, was as beautiful as a maple and as harmonious as nocturnal rain. The Empress listened for long hours to the fluid murmur of the koto beneath the young woman's hands.

Sometimes, too, clad in gray and blue wings, Yohiki danced before her imperial mistress the mysterious dance of the moths.

One evening, however, as she formed her rhythmic gestures and poses, she made slight contact with the cushion of the Empress.

The ministers and the officers demanded vigorously a punishment for that involuntary act of lèse-majesté; and the Empress, in spite of the tender weakness that inclined her toward the musicienne, was obliged to sentence her to exile. Before her departure, however, she taught her the Marvelous Words collected from the lips of Benten by a nun. The Marvelous Words, by their incomparable sweetness, drive away dolor forever and assure the person who pronounces them an entire existence of felicity.

Yokihi took refuge in a profound valley. By contemplating the flight of clouds above the mountains she learned the dance of the clouds.

The Virgin Star, Tehih-Nu, appeared to her one solemn night. On chrysanthemum leaves, the dancer traced the Sacred Words that obsess like music and intoxicate like perfume. It was thus that the first poem, written on flower petals and steeped with odorous dew, was inspired by a goddess for the long joy of humans.

The charm of the Words was so powerful that the dew, bathing at dawn the chrysanthemum leaves where Yohiki had traced them the previous evening, became a powerful elixir. The inhabitants of the country who drank those magic drops lived in the peace of equitable years.

And the sweetness of the Words was so insidious that in reciting them, Yohiki forgot the dolor of not seeing her imperial friend again.

When she died, Yohiki went to dwell on the distant bank of the Celestial River, but in order to honor amity, as white as snow over the countryside, the Gods permitted Tokiwa, admitted to the paradise of Buddha, and Yohiki to meet on the seventh day of the seventh month every year. A flock of magpies then hovered in space and formed a bridge of fluttering wings, over which the Empress went to join the dancer.

The Twilight of Spring

THE warrior Ota Dokwan[1] was wandering on horseback in the environs of Yeddo when a squall flagellated him cruelly. He took refuge for a few hours in an inn scented by tea and peaches.

When the wind and the rain did not ease, he decided to return to his hearth, and he asked the innkeeper's daughter to lend him a mino.

The young woman listened to him deferentially and came back a moment later, but instead of the expected garment she was caring a yamabuki flower on a fan.[2] Confused and blushing, she waited without saying anything.

Ota Dokwan, astonished, did not understand at first the hidden meaning of that mute response. The young woman then murmured a verse of an ancient poem:

> *Although having seven petals,*
> *To our great regret,*

---

1 Probably the warrior poet Ota Dokan (1432-1486), who became a Buddhist monk.

2 The author insets notes defining a mino as a kind of garment protective against rain and the yamabuki as *Kerria japonica*. The commonly cultivated artificially-modified versions of the plant in question are generally known in English as "golden guinea" and "bachelor's buttons."

The yamabuki
Has no seed.

For as well as signifying a garment, the word mino also means "seed."

Charmed to find such a profound and unexpected knowledge of old poets in the young woman, Ota Dokwan improvised a few lines for her:

> *The twilight of spring advances, and you repose*
> *   under the tree*
> *The flowers of which agitate their petals gently,*
> *Flowers like the gaze of your hostess, O stranger.*

A Wind of Madness in the Branches

IN the province of Omi, where the beautiful pines refresh feverish middays with a perpetual night, a redoubtable tree grows mysteriously. For a thousand years and more, the inhabitants of the country have passed the enoki with a muted dread, for enokis are inhabited by maleficent spirits.[1] Those trees are strange and sacred. The spirits that they shelter protect them sovereignly, and whoever touches their slightest branch is struck by unknown evils.

A daimio, Satzuma Bshichizaemon, acquired the domain in the middle of which the enoki stood. The tree displeased him by virtue of the desolation of its ancient grandeur. He resolved to have it felled, because, in the curiously ordered garden, the enoki masked the view of a pond with heavy crepe pleats; on the stagnant waters nenuphars reddened, similar to multiple autumnal moons. At the edge of the pond, a junk slumbered. Often, the young wife of the daimio indulged her puerile dreams at length, over the magical slumber of the torpid waters.

On the eve of the day when the fatal order was given by the daimio, his mother was troubled by a dream. Unknown powers reveal themselves more readily to beings

------

1 The author inserts a note identifying the enoki as *Celtis sinensis*; it is known in English as Chinese hackberry.

whom time has impregnated with its slow wisdom. It is not by chance that Guanyin, the meditative Goddess, has incarnated knowledge under the aspect of a tortoise.

A dragon appeared to Satzuma's mother. Its scales were shining somberly, like nocturnal rain. Gems like accursed stars illuminated the monster's forehead. And the envoy predicted the end of her race if the daimio did not abandon his design.

As soon as dawn quivered, Satzuma's mother came to press her son with prayers. In vain, she exhausted all her eloquence. In vain, she shed tears.

The local peasants came to knock on the daimio's door, bringing him, by way of offerings, wildflowers and the fruits of orchards. They implored him to spare the venerable tree. Satzuma sent them away without any response. His servants, confronted by his severe visage, were obliged to hold back their supplications.

Even the daimio's young wife attempted a timid and futile request. For Satzuma's mind was one of those that opposition exasperates to the point of defiance. With the obstinacy of limited souls, he went toward the Irrevocable. He gave the order to fell the tree.

The massive trunk fell like a wounded dragon. And with the rustle of the branches and the rude impact of the fall, an inexplicable sound was mingled: a hoarse groan of menacing suffering . . .

The next day, Satzuma's mother was wandering in the gardens. Her eyes, like demonic furnaces, stoked up their somber flames through her disordered hair. Dementia had confused the exactitude of her gaze and her thoughts. Her howls filled anyone who went near her with a religious terror.

There was a contagion. To the howls of the old woman responded, like an echo, the howls of the young wife. She too descended the spectral path, groping, among phantoms and larvae. From all the corners of walls where they were hidden, the mysterious beings took flight, grimacing . . .

One after another, all the servants of the chastised house succumbed to delirium.

The wind of madness that blew over those souls attained Satzuma last of all. Cruel dreams tortured him by his bedside. He saw the implacable tree again in his dreams. Its foliage shone under a gray and blue rain. A feeble breeze stirred it. The branches straightened and curled up like writhing snakes. The damp leaves shone with the sly glimmer of scales. And shrill hisses were prolonged, filling the man's miserable soul with horror.

The verdure of the tree oscillated like waves. The branches extended like the tentacles of cephalopods. The trunk swelled, like the monstrous pocket that swallows the limbs of shipwreck victims . . .

. . . And now long fingers advanced toward the fever victim, which tore and strangled. Terrible and clenched, they decomposed the violet greenness of putrescence . . . they were the fingers of vengeful death.

Satzuma hanged himself from a trapeze. The face of his cadaver retained the imprint of an unspeakable terror.

For a long time, the chastised house was prey to the phantoms of solitude. One day, however, the clamors of the people protested against the abandonment of the once-splendid dwelling. The shokujo[1] went to a beloved convent of Guanyin, where a bonzesse of the imperial family prated

---

1 Author: "A kind of magistrate."

in perpetual whiteness. The nun yielded to the envoy's supplications. She purified the dwelling by her presence and liberated it from evil spirits.

The servants of the shadow retreated before the chaste clarity of her eyes. The tormented oni that had once inhabited the tree returned to the subterranean darkness where temporary fevers and forgotten dolors sleep profoundly.

The White Hare and the Crocodiles

IN the time when the animals had the use of speech, a little white hare passed serene hours on the isle of Oki. In the days of summer the happy island laughed at the sea. Pink and green and singing, it laughed at the sun. And in the moonlight, it dreamed infinitely, silvery and blue.

In the distance, the coast of Inaba was visible, hemmed by white-capped waves. Forests of flowering cherry trees were snowing out there, at the whim of the breezes. It was like a vast undulation of perfumed foam. In the long middays, the appeals of the samisen implored, languidly tenacious.

The white hare contemplated the distant coast with staring eyes, for the thirst for the unknown was in him. He was weary of places that were always the same, even if they were the most beautiful in the world . . .

That desire increased imperiously within him and grew to the point of obsession; but the sea unfurled between him and the land that was so beautiful and so unknown.

On a day streaming with warm light, the hare waited for the arrival of Hazard. He waited, his eyes obstinately turned toward the mysterious land. And suddenly, he perceived an enormous crocodile lying on the sand, warming himself in the sun.[1]

---

1 In the version of this story contained in the eighth-century chronicle

A project crossed the hare's small brain. Adroit and cunning, he approached the crocodile and greeted him in flattering terms. Then, with a simulated interest, he said to the crocodile: "Our two fates are different, my brother, and separate us forever. You are the son of the water and I am the child of the land. I have a sharp curiosity regarding your race, so dissimilar from ours. Tell me, are you Crocodiles more numerous on the face of the waters than we Hares are on the face of the land?"

"Certainly," replied the Crocodile, proud of the race of which he was the chief. "We are more numerous than all of you, for the water is vaster than the limited land."

The hare interrogated the crocodile again. "Could you, my brother, line all the crocodiles up all the way to the coast of Inaba?"

"Certainly," the monster replied. "Assembled thus, we would form a living line all the way to the distant coast."

The hare then feigned incredulity. And, piqued in his racial pride, the crocodile offered to prove that his words were not an idle boast, but were the simple truth.

Plunging into the sparkling water then, he sank to the sea bed.

The hare waited patiently on the shore. Eventually, the crocodile came back, followed by a multitude of other crocodiles, like green rocks floating on the water.

At the request of their chief, duped by the hare, all the crocodiles arranged themselves in a line, and their backs formed a vast bridge that extended all the way to the coast of Inaba.

With a noisy admiration, the hare contemplated the living bridge cast over the sea. He asked the naïve crocodile

Kojiki, it is probably sharks rather than crocodiles that the hare exploits, although the term employed in the story is ambiguous.

for permission to count the exact number of aligned crocodiles by passing over their rugged backs, and the crocodile,
full of an ingenuous vanity, consented.

The hare thus traversed the sea on the backs of the crocodiles. He counted them aloud as he went. The number of
aligned crocodiles was seventy thousand. Triumphant, he
reached the other shore and leapt on to the sand.

On turning round, however, he had the imprudence to
mock the crocodiles. He boasted to them of having made
use of them to carry out his plans. Thanks to the vanity of
one of them, he had abused them all . . .

Angrily, the crocodiles attacked the perfidious and
boastful hare. They tore off their victim's fur and abandoned him, skinned alive, on the sand of the realm so
much desired, the beautiful realm so long glimpsed.

In his furious torment, the hare rolled on the sand, uttering the gasps of a dying animal. He reached the limit of
pain. Fever was devouring him with its hollow teeth. The
poor tortured hare was shivering and burning at the same
time, an open wound, a living suffering, flagellated by the
morning breeze.

The morning breeze, which aggravates wounds, had
carried away and dispersed the white fur of the lamentable
little hare.

Those who suffer by their own fault are more worthy
of pity than those who are struck by an unjust destiny, for
those who suffer by their own fault combine repentance
and remorse with their other tortures. The little hare felt
utterly miserable.

At that moment a procession passed by. In the middle of
a file of samurai, two splendid palanquins were radiant. Two
adolescents were pompously crouched on cushions therein.

Having heard the little hare groaning on the road, the adolescents made a sign to the bearers carrying the two palanquins. The servants stopped, in accordance with their masters' orders. And, in a pitying tone, the strangers interrogated the hare as to the cause of his cries and moans.

The little hare told the sad story of his boastfulness and his punishment.

The two adolescents considered him in silence. They possessed the cowardly and cruel heart of young men. And, counterfeiting pity, the elder of the adolescents prescribed the little hare a remedy that, he said, would ensure a prompt cure. He ought to bathe in the sea and then, sitting on the beautiful silver sand, dry himself in the wind.

Naïve and abused in his turn, the little hare thanked the two royal adolescents. The procession drew away and disappeared round a bend in the road.

Filled with hope and confidence, the hare bathed in the bitter waves . . . and the salt bit his wounds and corroded the blood that was sweating from the flesh laid bare.

The horror of that suffering twisted the poor hare. Imploring a little coolness for the living fire of his wounds, he delivered himself to the sea breeze . . . and the sea breeze sharpened the pain of the recently flayed flesh. The bloody flesh tightened again and wrinkled atrociously. Exhausted, the poor hare lay down on the sand, preparing for death.

Suddenly, a man went by. He was walking in solitude, with no escort of samurai and no palanquin carried aristocratically by servants. By the simple majesty of his forehead and his eyes, however, the hare recognized the passer-by as one of the sons of the Mikado.

Sympathetically, he interrogated the hare regarding his horrible dolors, as the two perfidious adolescents, his brothers, had already done. The two adolescents were the sons of the Mikado and his legitimate wife, and the imperial passer-by was the son of the Mikado and a concubine.

Having interrogated the hare, the passer-by awaited his response, but the wounded animal kept silent. The hypocritical cruelty of the legitimate sons of the Mikado had informed the animal's little brain with a just suspicion and dread of men.

The wandering and solitary son of the Mikado spoke again, and his tone was so soft and his mildness so firm that the little hare recovered courage and confidence. For a second time, he told the sad story of his adventures. And the august passer-by advised the hare to bathe in the water of a spring that was gushing from the foot of the bamboos.

The little hare obeyed the stranger's instruction. The fresh water washed away and dispersed the salt, and soothed the burns divinely. A balmy freshness consoled all the dolorous flesh of the hare.

He crawled with humility and gratitude to the feet of the merciful passer-by. The latter considered him, and a Buddha-like smile illuminated his face with serene splendor. Bending down, he picked the kaba flowers that perfumed the water of the spring and, strewing the flowers in the grass, he instructed the hare to roll over that embalmed couch.

The hare submitted to the master's order. Miraculously, the white fur of the flayed animal velveted his new skin. He leapt with delight, as he had been before provoking the vengeance of the crocodiles.

His heart overflowing with gratitude, the hare prostrated himself before the unknown man.

"Reveal your name to me, O benefactor," he implored, "for the name of a benefactor is sweet on the lips of the one he has helped."

"My name is Okuninushi no Mikado," the stranger replied. And, smiling at the attentive hare, the imperial magician told him that he was wandering, solitary, in the country, oppressed by sadness. His brothers, the two legitimate sons of the Mikado, were departing on an embassy to Yakami, a luminously beautiful princess of the province of Inaba, whom he, a concubine's son devoid of honor, loved in vain. The two imperial adolescents would prostrate themselves before the princess, who would choose one of them for her husband.

Having listened piously to the enchanter's story, the hare responded with prophetic words. He predicted to Okuninushi no Mikado that Princess Yakami, disdaining the two perfidious bothers, would choose for her husband the concubine's son devoid of honor.

Okuninushi no Mikado listened to the hare's prophecy with a grave joy, for he knew that animals harbor an obscure part of the universal wisdom.

Everything happened later in accordance with the hare's prediction, and the hare, under the beneficent influence of the Moon, the protector of hares and serpents, lived for a thousand years.

The Three Azure Scales

DURING the reign of the Emperor Karhiva,[1] the island of Enoshima was ravaged by a dragon that bore desolation and death in its five long claws.

In their distress, the people of the island offered Benten a desperate prayer. The Goddess heard their appeal favorably. The spell of her koto put the dragon to sleep, intoxicated by music. For Benten's koto unites the poignant ardor of joy with the distant suavity of Memory; and the sounds flow from the harmonic fingers of the Goddess like droplets of starlight.

The monster, torpid with slumber, was killed by the warriors of Enoshima, who gratefully consecrated to the Goddess a grotto paved with seashells, in which the azure of a perpetual evening was obstinate.

Hojo Tokimasa[2] sought the shade of the holy cavern in order to conciliate the protection of Benten for himself and his family. Knowing that the Goddess is propitious to cleverly organized poems, he composed artistically woven verses for her.

---

1 Author: "151 B.C." The legendary emperor nowadays known as Kaika is traditionally supposed to have reigned from 157-98 B.C.
2 The historical Hojo Tokimasa was a twelfth-century warrior, but that is incompatible with the chronology suggested in the previous note, so character is presumably a namesake.

Benten rose up over the waters like a maritime dawn. Her glaucous robe was hemmed with foam and spray, and her hair flowed like unfurling waves. In a limpid voice she promised Tokimasa the favor that he implored. She assured him that his descendants would triumph over the imperial throne, but that, if the hereditary power fell into unjust hands, it would not be prolonged beyond the seventh generation.

Benten, in her melancholy wisdom, foresaw the reigns devoid of clemency that would extinguish the radiance of that race.

When the murmur of the celestial words had died away, Tokimasa saw the aspect of the Goddess transform. She appeared half-woman and half-dragon. Her five long golden claws reflected the sunlight. She crouched on the sand, and three blue scales were detached from that monstrous and divine body.

Struck by a mystic stupor, Tokimasa picked up the three azure scales, which became the sacred blazon of his race.

And the Goddess, having spoken, disappeared into the sea.

The Nostalgic Conch

THE distant visage of Hikohohodemi is blurred by time.[1] Hohodemi belonged to a legendary dynasty of very ancient Mikados. History has not engraved his features, but fable has designed his undulating silhouette, surrounding it with a miraculous flora of tales and poems.

Hohodemi reigned piously about 580. His people gave him the nickname Yamasachihiko, the Very Adroit Mountain Hunter, for he was knowledgeable in the art of tracking and vanquishing. He invariable triumphed over all the ruses of foxes and all the revolts of wild beasts.

His younger brother, nicknamed the Very Skillful Sea Angler, Umisachihiko, was endowed with an incomparable skill in deceiving the fears of suspicious fish. Before the accession of Hohodemi to imperial power, both of them devoted themselves unreservedly to those rude sports, one of them wandering the mountains and the other leaning over the waves.

One day, Hohodemi, the Very Adroit Hunter, came to offer his brother, the Very Skillful Angler, his bow and ar-

---

1 Hohodemi is an alternative name for the legendary Hoori, one of the supposed ancestors of the emperors of Japan, also known, as in the story, as Yamasachihiko [The Prince of the Mountain of Good Fortune] or simply Yamasachi, the younger bother of the fisherman Umisachi in the story in *Kojiki* on which this one is based.

rows in exchange for his bamboo rod, line and hook. The Very skillful Angler consented to that, and they both went forth in the expectation of an unexperienced joy.

Hohodemi released the mooring of the junk and headed out to sea. For long blue hours he strove in vain to attract fish that were full of suspicion. Toward evening, he folded up the bamboo rod and line, with the humiliation of not bringing back the smallest prey. A new bitterness rose in his disappointed soul. He had lost his brother's hook.

The Very Skillful Angler was more terrible in his anger than the king of Dragons. Hohodemi dreaded his brother's fury when he returned to him. Beneath the declining rays of the setting sun, he searched among the rocks and in the deployed sand, and the distant melancholy of the moon saddened his laboriously fruitless search.

The Very Skillful Angler having returned empty-handed from the inhospitable mountains greeted Hohodemi's confession with criticism and threats. The latter, desolate at the reproaches of the Very Skillful Angler, took the triumphal blade of his first victories and broke it into five hundred and nine fragments, with which he forged five hundred and nine hooks. He offered them humbly to his brother, who refused them.

Hohodemi did not protest against the obstinate rancor of the Very Skilful Angler, for his duty as the older brother commanded him to be patient and gentle. Sadly, he wandered along the sea shore, searching for the lost hook, without hope, but with the tenacity of contrition.

Raising his eyes, he saw an old woman fishing for crabs, with hair whiter and smoother than flowers of ivory. Her footprints shone in the sand. In a cracked voice she asked him what he was looking for with such dolorous ardor.

On the response of the young prince she said to him:

"No longer search the shore; no longer scrutinize the violet shadow of the rocks; but descend into the sacred depths of the Sea and enter without dread the realm of Benten, the Goddess of the Waves. That realm is named Reyn-Gu-Jin. Benten, the changing Goddess, is both very cruel and very good. If you press her with your prayers, she will seek among the fish over which she reigns for the one that has carried away the lost hook in its throat."

The old woman gave the adolescent, who was mute with gratitude, her vast collecting basket. Hohodemi climbed into the wicker basket as if into a junk, and that strange boat sank under the water.

Miraculously, without terror and without suffering, Hohodemi traversed the sonorous penumbra. The din of the great tides buzzed within him and around him. His ears vibrated like two attentive conches. The limpid green consoled his eyelids, weary of not closing in slumber, and his eyes, troubled by tears.

A wave threw him into an orchard planted with coral trees. Anemones opened their living corollas there, and hippocampi darted between rocks carpeted with marine grass, their flight more hectic than a flock of butterflies.

Two Ningio[1] were babbling, sitting on the rim of a well whose fresh water surged forth miraculously under the ocean. Only dragons penetrated as far as those un-fathomable springs, for dragons, which take flight more audaciously than birds, plunge even more intrepidly than fish into the depths of the marine twilight.

One of the Ningio was deploying her coral-pink hair; the other was allowing her tresses, as violet as the algae that

---

1 Author: "Japanese sirens."

turn the waves purple, to float in the water of the evening, a darker green, as if saddened. Each of them carried a nacre amphora. As they leaned over the water of the well, they saw the reflected face of the adolescent through the red branches of the tree. Trembling, they wanted to flee, but fear mastered their motionless limbs.

Hohodemi, seeing that his presence was revealed, quit his refuge and approached the fearful Ningio. He asked them for something to drink. The Ningio with the coral hair handed him a large hollow pearl. Hohoemi rejoined in the freshness of the water; then, detaching with his dagger one of the seven magamata[1] that formed his royal necklace, he let it fall into the cup, which he returned to the extended hands.

Reassured by the stranger's gesture, the two Ningio thanked him with their voices, confounded in a single stream. Hohodemi, seeing them attentive, told them the story of his misfortune. They listened to him with compassion in their gazes and smiled. Then they named themselves.

The two Ningio were Tayotama and Tamayori, the two virginal princesses who serve the sovereign of the seas constantly. They took him to the palace of the Goddess.

On the walls, the seashells mingled their fluid gleams in a single radiation. A few concentrated their peacock greens and their intense sapphire blues. Others spiritualized their unreal mauves, intensified their saffrons and revealed their flesh pinks. They bristled their tenuous spines, rotated their designs, similar to the tormented structure of pagodas, or hollowed out their proffered cups. They were tangled like

---

1 Author: "Sacred jewels, of which Izanaghi, the God of the Air, made a present to his eldest daughter, Amaterasu, the Goddess of the Sun."

chrysanthemums and as thin as transparent paper. And from all those conches a music emanated that was both profound and distant, which was the entire murmurous soul of the sea.

Tayotama and Tamayori conducted the adolescent to the presence of the Goddess. Her kimono undulated in the flux and reflux of great tides. She smiled mysteriously under her veils of foam. Her hair was braided with algae, and her ungraspable gaze was like the furtive flash of waves. One divined that she was perfidious and benevolent, enigmatic and variable.

Benten welcomed the supplicant with favor and ordered, in response to his request, that the cortege of marine creatures should file before him.

There was a procession of monstrous or charming beings, which extended from the deformity of the whale, similar to some vast tenebrous architecture, to the minuscule grace of the hippocampus and the crayfish.

Hohodemi admired the humid rainbow of scales, the lightness of fins and the delicacy of gills. The lobster and the crab pleased him most of all because of the strangeness of their forms.

The marine creatures glided through the glaucous twilight. He contemplated the rhythm of their swimming. Starfish strewed the walls with living stars, and the phosphor of their pale lanterns illuminated the corridors of the palace.

Benten's brow remained anxious. "I haven't seen the bream pass by," she said.

The shrewd and wise octopus advanced to the foot of the throne and told her creator that the bream was afflicted by a bizarre illness.

"He seems to be suffering," she said, "and his fins are incessantly agitated by a convulsive effort."

The octopus added that he had doubtless swallowed the lost hook by mistake.

The Goddess sent an escort of dolphins with the order to bring the bream back, which appeared in the midst of a general attention. He was visibly prey to intolerable suffering.

On Benten's order, the octopus insinuated one of her long, thin tentacles into the bream's throat. She liberated him easily from the hook that was tormenting him. Triumphantly, Hohodemi took back the hook.

Then Benten, the Goddess of the Sea, turned to the grateful Mikado. She thanked him courteously for having descended to the depths of her mysterious realm. And, like a sovereign mortal with a sovereign, she concluded a pact with him that sealed the amity of the land and the sea. Thus was agreed the divine alliance between the wave and the coast. Benten promised the Mikado solemnly that the abundant tides would never submerge the shores that they assailed with their crests.

To confirm the alliance, Benten gave a sign to the two princesses who served her, Tayotama and Tamayori. They disappeared, and came back carrying two limpidly blue pearls. Benten took them from the hands of Tayotama and Tamayori and gave them to the Mikado. She told him that the two pearls were named Nanjiu and Kanjiu. The individual who possessed the pearl Nanjiu governed the flux of menacing tides; and the possessor of the pearl Kanjiu determined at his whim the reflux of weary tides.

The Mikado took his leave of the goddess, stammering his gratitude.

The two princesses, Tayotama and Tamayori, came in again leading an enormous crocodile.[1] The Mikado sat astride it as if it were a charger. More rapid than lightning, the crocodile brought Hohodemi back to Japan.

As soon as he disembarked, the Very Adroit Hunter hastened to return to his brother. He returned the lost hook to him, hoping finally to obtain the forgiveness of the vindictive Angler.

The latter, profiting from his brother's absence, had taken possession of the imperial throne. He had reigned over Japan during the three years that Hohodemi's sojourn in the realm of the sea had lasted. That day, the legitimate Mikado returned to claim his rights and recover his power.

The skillful and vindictive Angler shook with rage, but, no longer having any pretext to refuse forgiveness to his brother, he welcomed him with a feigned cordiality. With anger in his heart, he returned the scepter to Hohodemi and made him sit on the throne.

From that day on, he resolved to kill his brother.

One evening, Hohodemi was wandering through a rice-field, thinking about the realm of the waves. His eyes and his soul retained a regret for it. Lost in the dream, he did not hear his brother approach him. Alerted by a prescience, however, he turned round and saw frightful eyes, in which an inextinguishable hatred was burning, fixed on his own. That gaze of mortal enmity was his brother's gaze. Umisachihiko was holding a dagger in his hand.

Before the imminence of the peril, Hohodemi remembered Benten's words. He took the pearl Nanjiu and raised it as far as his forehead.

---

1 As in the tale of the white hare, the ambiguous reference in *Kojiki* probably intends to refer to a shark.

Immediately, the liberated tides bounded toward the shore. They reared up, magnificent and terrible, and rushed over the plains and forests. They invaded the rice-field tumultuously. One wave more powerful than the rest carried the perfidious brother away.

The vindictive Angler cried out, the terror of imminent death, to the brother for whom he had set cowardly ambushes. He implored his forgiveness with hiccups and gasps.

The merciful Hohodemi listened to the traitor's prayers. Having put Kanjiu, the Pearl of the Reflux, on his finger, he pacified the tides. Slack and weary, they withdrew.

The Very Skillful Angler, saved by the magical will of his brother, prostrated himself at his feet, for he venerated in him a supernatural power and he admired in him the generosity of forgiveness.

From that day on, peace reigned between the two brothers. Hohodemi governed Japan with justice and wisdom. Until the end of his existence, however, he took pleasure in wandering along the edge of the waves, contemplating the dawns, the fluid middays and the green nights in which the sea carried stars.

By way of memory, he entered for a second time the mysterious realm of the sea. His soul was akin to the nostalgic conch.

Illusory Sumptuousness

ROSEI was the son of one of the blind barbers who, in Japan, are surrounded by an atmosphere of esteem and benevolence. Rosei was cradled in the rude hands of poverty, but his soul was inflated by adventurous aspirations.

Having learned that the Mikado, deceived by infidel ministers, was searching the land, without concern for their birth or wealth, for honest and wise servants, he resolved to attract the imperial gaze. He departed one morning, at the hazard of the wind and the road.

On his road he met a bizarre stranger. The gaze of the unknown man was like the gaze of old priests accustomed to contemplating without terror the monstrous forms of the shadow.

The man told him his name: Rishi. And Rosei talked, as loquaciously as very young people do, to whom treasons have not yet taught the virtue of silence.

He made his companion party to his hopes and his triumphant visions. Without replying, Rishi smiled indulgently.

The fatigue of long marches in the sunlight overwhelmed the young man. While the innkeeper was grinding millet for the evening meal, Rosei became drowsy with an imperious slumber . . .

. . . A noise of horses and arms resounded clearly outside. There was the stir of a crowd, confused voices and appeals. A passer-by told Rosei that the imperial envoy had come to choose among the young men the one who, by virtue of his calm audacity, was worthy of being the Mikado's counselor.

Rosei presented himself before the man who incarnated his destiny. The boldness of his responses pleased the imperial envoy. The young man received the order to follow him to the Mikado's court.

The latter considered the newcomer with a radiance of smiling confidence.

Rosei was not astonished by the strangeness of the fate that realized in magnificence his most optimistic desires, for the rarest good fortune is less surprising than common and normal dolor.

The adolescent did not take long to recognize, however, that splendor bears within itself the punishment of its insolence and that glory is as bitter as agony.

The courtiers envenomed their envious words. He sensed, beneath the laudatory eloquence and the unctuous solicitations, the muted antagonism of intimacies.

One of his rivals, the minister Jiourozayemon, who was strong in all those accumulated petty hatreds, resolved to put an end to that odious presence. He invited Rosei to a sake feast. The young man, devoid of suspicion, chose the gift of his first visit and had himself transported to his rival's dwelling.

Jiourozayemon received him with a false cordiality and had a bath prepared, which, he said, would refresh his guest's lassitude, who was doubtless wearied by the summer midday heat. Rosei accepted and withdrew to the room reserved for ablutions, having left his garment outside, as was customary.

He entered the Goyemn-bouro and plunged into the limpid water.[1]

Suddenly, the water began to boil. And in a flash of intense horror, Rosei understood the execrable death that awaited him . . .

. . . The adolescent opened his eyes, still full of terror. A uniform noise broke the silence of the summer monotonously. The innkeeper was still grinding the millet for the evening meal . . .

The visions of sleep are sometimes mysterious messages from the divinities. Rosei understood the human grandeurs are more cruelly empty than a tormented dream.

He returned to the peaceful sunsets of his village and allowed himself to be cradled henceforth by the even flow of humble and serene days.

----

1 Author: "The Goyemon-bouro is a bath heated by an exterior fire, which takes its name from Goyemon, a famous bandit of the sixteenth century who, having attempted to assassinate the chief of the army, Taiko Sama, was boiled in oil."

The Angler's Symbol

GUANYIN sent to the Mikado Tchiuai one of those mysterious messengers known as dreams, and the messenger imposed on him, as a divine task, the conquest of Korea.

The cowardly Mikado, fond of happy peace, did not obey the order of the Goddesss.

Guanyin sent him another dream. Like a lotus leaf carried by the waves, the dream floated all the way to the Mikado.

For the second time, Tchiuai disdained the celestial order.

Guanyin, whose eyes consider terrestrial things from behind her eternally lowered eyelids, afflicted Tchiuai with a mortal fever . . .

But Jingo Kogo, Tchiuai's wife, meditated in her heroic soul, for the Mikado had communicated his dream to her.[1] She resolved to accomplish the task from which Tchiuai had recoiled. With that aim, she concealed the Mikado's death and took command of the expedition.

Almost amorously, the warriors followed that woman more valiant than a chief, wiser than a star-reader and more beautiful than a sacred dancer.

---

1 The legendary Empress Jingu, called Jingo Kogo in various nineteenth-century sources, was the consort of the Emperor now known as Chuai, and is said to have served as regent after his death for more than fifty years, perhaps in an era corresponding to the third century A.D. The story of her leading an army to invade Korea is included in *Kojiki*.

After a long day's march in the sun, the Empress stopped on the bank of the river Matsuragawa, which was rolling its indecipherable waves. The enigma of the water tempted the woman who was gambling her dream and her existence on the uncertainty of a dream. She listened to the splashing of the current as one listens to the obscure speech of a prophetess.

Leaning over the waves, she baited the line.

"If I am to triumph," she said, "I shall catch a fish. That will be the sign of the celestial will."

The imperious conviction of her voice imposed itself on the warriors who surrounded her. With an anxious gravity, they waited; and when the angler caught a carp, their faces brightened at that good omen.

On returning from her victorious expedition, Jingo Kogo solemnly engraved on a rock, with the tip of her bow, the word *Kokuo*, which signifies "governor of the realm."

The red sovereign of dragons, the king with five golden claws, marveled at the tenacious bravery of the woman who had confronted the fatigues and perils of such a hazardous expedition. He made her a present of the pearls that attract and dominate the tides, which the priests name Nanjiu and Kanjiu. Thus the imperial angler subjugated the waves as she had subjugated men.

After her death, the Empress was admitted into the assembly of the Gods. From then on she exchanged her terrestrial name of Jingo Kogo for the name of a Goddess, Kashii Sai Miojin. When she entered the splendor of the heavens, Amaterasu was the first to smile at her and equip her with her divine attributes: the Carp, the symbol of valiant patience, and Nanjiu and Kanjiu, the mysterious pearls that dominate the tides.

Seven Centuries in One Day

URASHIMA the crab-fisher lived in Ejima in the province of Tango.[1] He knew the violet rocks under which the heikegani lay in ambush: the crabs that once fed on the flesh of the samurai of Heike.

One evening, Urashima saw a marine turtle that had been cast up on the shore. The turtle is dear to the Goddesses, so Urashima returned it to the sea.

Three days later, at the same place where he had returned the turtle to the sea, Urashima perceived with astonishment a junk steered by a young woman as beautiful as the sacred lotus on which Guanyin traversed space when returning to the land.

The smile of the unknown woman was like the smile of the waves. Her eyes translated the appeal of very deep water. He followed her as one abandons oneself to a gentle current. What struck him about the stranger was the wisdom of her eyes, which reflected vanished times; they seemed to be perpetually looking backwards.

All day they drifted over the waves, and toward evening, the woman spoke.

---

1 In the version of this oft-retold tale that appears nowadays in a standard school textbook, the hero's name is given as Urashima Taro.

"I am," she told him, "the spirit who was incarnate yesterday in the turtle you saved and was returned by your aid to the sea; for, as the priests have informed you piously, unknowable spirits inhabit the bodies of animals. Benten, who watches over the obscure people of the waves, has sent me to you to recompense you for your benefit."

A shore darkened through the mists of the sunset. The junk stopped and Urashima followed his companion to a palace.

From then on, the months went by with the monotonous regularity of happiness. Time drifted, like the junk that had once brought the crab-fisher to that strange country.

One evening, however, the nostalgia of memory softened Urashima's soul. He wanted to see again the place that the ancient days had illuminated and darkened. He was haunted by past hours, less splendid and less tender than the present hours, but glorified nevertheless by the prismatic illusion of perspective and distance.

Urashima's companion read the mute desire in the depths of his eyes. She consented to the absence. When the crab-fisher departed she gave him a nacre casket with the moist gleams of the rainbow, enjoining him not to open it until they were reunited.

Urashima returned to his native land; but everything here was bizarrely metamorphosed. He thought he had gone astray in an unknown country, or rather in a star, or everything appeared to him to be incomprehensible and almost superhuman. The garments astonished him by their singular cut. He divined the modified speech confusedly, in which a memory of the language of long ago persisted nevertheless. He was a stranger, whom everyone considered with a vague alarm. Thus phantoms wander, plaintively obscure, in the midst of the living.

In despair, he broke the enigmatic casket.

Fumes of the heavy perfumes of incense rose up and flew away in the evening air. It was the seven centuries of his enchanted existence that were fleeing with the mysterious smoke. And when the last blue ring had vanished, Urashima fell into dust on the strange soil that had once been the soil of his childhood.

The Futile Wisdom of the Stars

IN the garden of the Mikado Toba grew the Four Most Beautiful Plants: the plum tree, the wisteria, the bamboo and the chrysanthemum. But the Mikado only contemplated his concubine, more odorous than the plum tree, suppler than the bamboo, more undulating than the wisteria and more sumptuous than the chrysanthemum.

Toba was declining in an inexplicable languor. His extinct eyes only lit up again in fixing upon his concubine Tamamo no Mae.

The beauty of that woman had something enigmatic and supernatural. When night came, she seemed to be surrounded by a halo of blue gold, like the Moon herself. That strange splendor disquieted the Mikado's courtiers and ministers considerably. They went to obtain the counsel of the star-reader Abi no Seimei, who possessed the wisdom of the worlds.

Abi no Seimei dreamed under the meditative gleam of the stars. The next day he asked the Mikado for an audience. Tamamo no Mae, gravely perspicacious, shivered on seeing him.

For a long time, Abi no Seimei contemplated the Mikado's concubine, trembling in her amber pallor; and, on a gesture of assent from Toba, turning toward the servants, he ordered that an altar be erected in the gardens of the palace.

The altar was decorated in the shade of black pines. An image of Guanyin smiled there mysteriously, her eyelids lowered.

The court assembled, with lamentations that seemed to challenge the insolent laughter of the sun.

The shade cast a pensive reflection over the faces of the young women. A nun, the issue of the house of the Emperors, offered a prayer for Toba's cure.

The Mikado listened through a dream. A starless void, like the distress of abandonment, oppressed him. He raised his eyes and saw that Tamamo no Mae was alone in not participating in the ceremonies.

He sent a messenger to her, who came back sobbing. Tamamo no Mae said that she was afflicted by a cruel fever.

The star-reader stood up and commanded warriors to bring the imperial concubine by force.

As beautiful and as tremulous as a wave, Tamamo no Mae appeared. Never had her gaze burst forth with so much splendor. A murmur of adoration and desire rose up from the attentive court.

She advanced hesitantly toward the image of Guanyin with the divine eyelids. The nun was praying in the midst of silence. The Mikado stood up, dazzled. Bewildered, he went toward the recovered lover. Already, his hands were reaching out to her when there was an exasperated clamor, like the howl of souls torn apart by oni . . .

The incomparable woman had disappeared, metamorphosed into a fox with nine tails, attempting in vain to go to earth beneath the altar . . .

The Mikado's concubine belonged to the race of fox-women.[1] Foxes, perfidious and maleficent animals, sometimes put on the appearance of a beautiful woman in order better to torment humans.

The Mikado was cured. But the star-reader, to whom the wisdom of the stars was revealed, was unable to appease the ardent languor that inclined the Mikado toward the memory or the nostalgia of the stranger that he had so vainly possessed . . .

---

1 Japanese folklore includes several other stories about the serially-incarnated fox-woman Tamamo no Mae. The astrologer called Abi no Seimei here is called Abe no Yasuchika in other versions.

Watanabe, Valiant and Joyful

AMONG all the rude heroes of old Japan, none was more simply valorous than Raiko.[1] His courage warmed the souls of those who followed him in his adventures. He was constantly escorted by five samurai, as joyful and valiant as their valiant and joyful chief.

Raiko carried on his robust shoulders a magnanimous renown. Alone among the samurai he had dared to lay siege to the mountain of Oeyama, the lair of a population of gaki, eaters of human flesh. At the feasts of those monsters, the guests drank human blood instead of sake. But Raiko had destroyed them one after another. Triumphant, he had thrown the bloody head of the king of the gaki at the feet of the Mikado.

Since that day, the race of gaki had disappeared from the face of Japan; and the victorious hero had come, disdaining pomp and glory, to live modestly in his native city, Kyoto.

One evening, the five samurai were sharing rice and tea. Released from perils and efforts, they were savoring raw

---

1 The great warrior Raiko is better known as Minamoto no Yorimitsu, as in the story translated herein as "The Threshold of Silence." The difference in nomenclature might signify that each of the two stories was written by a different author. Watanabe no Tsuna (953-1925) was his most celebrated sidekick.

fish and boiled fish, and singing while drinking generous sake. Only the foremost among the five samurai, Hojo, was displaying a clouded brow, and toward the end of the meal he said to his companions:

"My valiant and joyful companions, know that a gaki, the last of his race, is ravaging our city today. Terror is mistress of the city. The citizens, taking refuge behind screens, no longer risk leaving their houses after dusk, and no one, even in broad daylight, dares to cross the gate of Rashomon, where the gaki, the eater of human flesh, lies in wait for his prey."

Watanabe, the second samurai, interrupted Hojo. He laughed heartily as he emptied his cup of sake.

"Those are unreasonable words, my companion. The entire population of gaki was annihilated by our master Raiko. And if, by a miracle, a single one of the accursed race had escaped the massacre, how would he brave the destroyer of his race?"

Hojo, prompt to anger, said to Watanabe: "Until this day, no one has ever doubted my word. Why have you come, the first to accuse me of a lie?"

"I am not accusing you. But you have doubtless lent credence too quickly to the imaginations of old graybeards."

Hojo, prompt to anger, said: "Go out, my companion, and go to wander beyond the city gates. With your own eyes you will see that I have told the simple truth."

The incredulous Watanabe stood up. Having put on his helmet, on which a frightful visage grimaced, he handed a scroll of rice paper to his companions. "My companions," he said. "Take the brush and trace your names on this scroll of paper. At dawn you will see it fixed over the gate of Rashomon, the highest gate in the city."

As joyful and valiant as Raiko himself, Watanabe disappeared into the darkness.

The Moon was no longer gilding the extinct sky. All the stars seemed to be dead. A storm broke, magnificent and terrible. The thunder echoed like a resonance of gongs; the cold rain pierced the samurai's garments and dripped from his armor; and the wind howled like an unchained she-wolf.

The valorous Watanabe finally reached the Rashomon gate, where the eater of human flesh came to prowl every evening.

The black silence streamed around him. Only the wind threw its clamors into the night.

Smiling on observing that, as he had anticipated, no monster was troubling the calm of the dormant city, Watanabe used his dagger to pin the rice paper over the city gate. The scroll on which the names of the four valorous samurai remained fixed, irrefutable proof of the presence of the hero at the Rashomon gate.

Then Watanabe turned back. Scarcely had he turned his bridle, however, than heavy footfalls resounded behind him. In the darkness, Watanabe felt a hand seize the horns that decorated his helmet.

"Who are you, then, you who are stopping me in my route?" the valiant man demanded. And, groping in the dark, he touched the arm that retained him. The arm was as thick as a tree trunk and it was covered in long bushy hair.

Brandishing his sword forcefully, the samurai carved that invisible flesh furiously. A roar of anger rumbled in the nocturnal silence.

Ruddy moonlight having pierced the clouds, Watanabe saw the monstrous form of a gaki taller than the Rashomon gate itself. Its eyes were burning like the red moon, and its maw, wide open, resembled a gaping sepulcher. Valiant and joyful, Watanabe attacked the gaki, laughing aloud at its grotesque hideousness.

The struggle was arduous. It was bravery and skill against blind force.

In truth, it was a fine combat. Never had a more valorous samurai challenged a more terrible adversary. The struggle was arduous and was prolonged, implacably, until the first light of the morning.

Seeing that it could not fell its adversary, the gaki became fearful. The cold light of the nascent day dissipated its courage; and, thinking about Raiko, the destroyer of its race, it fled toward the mountains.

Watanabe, pressing his exhausted horse furiously, sought in vain to overtake the fugitive. The gaki fled more rapidly than Fujin, the God of Winds, himself. And the samurai had to renounce the pursuit. Disappointed, he returned to the Rashomon gate. The rays of dawn illuminated a bloody arm, as thick as a tree trunk and covered in bushy hair.

The samurai's joy was immense. The arm was a precious trophy. It established the proof of Watanabe's encounter with the gaki. No one henceforth would doubt his word, no one could deny the combat. The most incredulous would yield to the bloody evidence. The horse buckled under the burden of the monstrous arm. Triumphant, Watanabe returned to the dwelling where his companions were. They were all waiting anxiously. They welcomed him with transports of cordial amity, for they had feared that they might not see him again alive.

Watanabe told them the story of his combat and had the bloody arm brought before them. The four samurai rejoiced in their companion's triumph and praised his valor. Having called for the pourers of sake in order to celebrate the victory, they feasted until the dawn of the following day.

The news of the fine combat spread through the city of Kyoto and all the inhabitants of the region came in procession to contemplate the gaki's arm with a proud terror.

Watanabe ordered a bronze casket from the blacksmiths of the city, in which he placed the formidable trophy. He sealed the casket and placed it in his own bedroom, in order that no one would steal the prize of his victory from him.

Watanabe's glory resounded throughout Japan. His name resonated among the people like the echo of a sacred bell. The samurai remained indifferent to the noise of praise. Only the eulogies of those who were dear to him were precious and sweet.

One night, Watanabe's servants were woken up by the noise of blows struck on the door. A very old woman begged, vehemently, to be introduced to the presence of the hero. The servants tried to send her away, but she cried out obstinately, in quavering distress, for the samurai, whom she called her son.

Having heard the altercation, Watanabe appeared on the threshold of the dwelling. Having perceived the old woman, he embraced her for a long time, as children embrace their mothers, for the woman was Watanabe's nurse.

In his affectionate joy, the samurai did not think of being astonished by the strangeness of the hour that the old woman had chosen to knock on his door. He received the venerable visitor with great honors, and the latter stared at Watanabe with maternally amorous eyes.

She talked to him about the renown that, she said, had spread all the way to the most distant provinces. And the nurse had come to him, stirred in the depths of her tender heart by the rumor of the combat in which he had vanquished the gaki of Rashomon. Untiringly, she evoked all the twists and turns of the struggle, and finally talked about the severed arm that Watanabe had displayed to the marveling eyes of crowds for a short while.

"My son and my master," she begged, "grant the request of one who is both your mother and your servant. Permit my eyes to feast on the trophy of your victory."

Gently, Watanabe refused. He dared not lift the iron lid under which the arm of the vanquished gaki was imprisoned, he affirmed, for it must be prowling around the coffer jealously. It had doubtless resolved to recover its arm, and, as everyone knows, gakis possess the power to render themselves invisible.

The old woman became more insistent. Finally, as she collided with Watanabe's refusal, she wept abundant tears.

"My beloved son does not trust his mother. My master doubts the loyalty of his servant . . ."

Tears flowed between her wrinkles. Moved in his affection for the woman who had lavished solicitudes on his infancy, Watanabe yielded courteously to her plea. He opened before her the casket in which the gaki's arm reposed, jealously imprisoned.

The old woman contemplated the trophy with an avid gaze. A strange joy illuminated her face. And suddenly, with howls of delight, she threw herself upon the arm.

The tranquil face of the nurse was transformed into the sniggering visage of a gaki. The eyes dulled by age became flamboyant, and the monster, having resumed its veritable form, rose up into the air and disappeared before Watanabe, having recovered from his surprise, could hurl himself upon it.

Great was Watanabe's anger on seeing himself abused by the wily gaki, which, in order to recover its arm, had put on the familiar appearance of the old nurse. Great was, in truth, the wrath of the samurai on seeing himself robbed in that fashion.

For a long time, he lay in wait for the vanished gaki. Every night he went to wait for it at the Rashmon gate, but the gaki, rendered prudent by almost having lost its arm, never dared to return to confront Watanabe.

The city of Kyoto reposed then in happy peace, and the name of Watanabe, valiant and joyful, resounded, like the name of his chief Raiko, through the heroic songs of Japan.

The Moon's Tears

IZANAMI, the Goddess of Clouds, and Izanaghi, the God of the Air, were the generators of beings and things. They were the two First Causes.

After the monstrous and sacred act by means of which the world was procreated, after the nuptial embrace, Izanami purified herself in the immensity of the sea. For seven years she bathed among the waves. And during her long contemplation of space, her gazes were incarnated in two mysterious radiations, Amaterasu, Goddess of the Sun, the issue of her right eye, and Djoga, the Goddess of the Moon, the issue of her left eye. Izanami rejoiced in the birth of those two splendors. She gave the sky to Amaterasu and the ocean to Djoga.

Izanami then descended into the entrails of the earth, where she elaborated metals and gems.

In those times, there was no night. The monotonous whiteness of an incessant day illuminated space.

Djoga, the twin sister of Amaterasu, was a melancholy beauty. She wept relentlessly, sitting on the ocean. Her hair, woven with pearls, bathed in the waters, and her limpid tears mingled with the waves. She wept untiringly, for the memory of her divine generatrix persisted in her.

Amatserasu, who is infinite bounty, was moved by her frail sister's distress. She begged Izanaghi, the powerful God of the Air, to appease Djoga's anger.

The very wise Izanaghi meditated subtly. In order to accord Djoga the illusion of the obscure world where Izanami, the generatrix so dolorously beloved, reigned, he created the night, similar to the subterranean gloom. And Djoga, in the joy of the illusion, smiled palely . . .

Her bright smile traversed the beneficent darkness.

The One Who Enjoys the Moment[1]

THE MAPLES were reddening with all the ardors of autumn on the day when the crab who was the chief of the tribe of the Tatsugashira[2] encountered the perfidious monkey.

Strange crabs swarm on the shores of Dan-no-Ura with curiously modeled carapaces. A warrior mask has left its frightful and grotesque imprint hereon. Those crabs, moreover, carry within them the reincarnated souls of the samurai of Heike and Genji.

Nine centuries have passed since the supreme combat that the tribe of the Heike fought against the triumphant Genji. When the last Heike samurai had succumbed, the

---

1 Author: "This tale, which Madame Pimodan has given for the first time in French (*Contes et légendes du vieux Japon*, Plon, 1904) after the English translation by A. B. Mitford, is found, with variations, in several other collections, notably *The Japanese Fairy Book*." A. B. Mitford, the compiler of *Tales of Old Japan* (1871) was the first Baron Redesdale (1837-1916); *The Japanese Fairy Book* (1903) was compiled by Yei Theodora Ozaki.

2 Author: "A variety of crab only encountered on the beaches of Dan-no-Ura. Its name signifies 'Dragon's Helm.' The helmets of ancient samurai were ornamented with dragons with pointed and gilded horns. They are the largest crabs of the Heikegani species." The Battle of Dan-no-Ura, to which reference is made in the story, was fought in 1185.

nun Nii no Ama, who belonged to the sovereign family, composed a death song. The funeral poem resonated so dolorously and grimly through the cries of triumph that the samurai adversaries fell silent in order to listen, and dared not approach the nun. And, taking in her arms the imperial infant Antoku, Nii no Ama, the sacred poet, sank with him beneath the waves.

It is in memory of the samurai who fell in the noble defeat that the crabs swarming on the coast have received the name of Heikegani.

The crab who was the chief of the Tatsugashira tribe discovered a rice-cake under a rock. But the monkey, although he had searched all the corners of the beach untiringly, had only brought back a single persimmon seed, and, seeing the rice-cake in the crab's pincers, the monkey approached, envious and perfidious.

The crab rejoicing naively in his find, the monkey responded with disdain that hazard had made him a far superior present. He explained to the old crab that the persimmon seed, planted in fertile ground, would grow and become a powerful tree, green with emerald foliage and gilded with flavorsome fruits. He added that the future is infinitely more precious than the present hour. The crab was not able to respond that the future is quite illusory and that only the present hour is a real good; for the one who enjoys the moment is wiser than his neighbor who accumulates treasures for an old age he might never know.

The crab, therefore, listened to the persuasive words of the monkey; and when the monkey proposed to the crab to exchange the rice-cake for the persimmon seed, the crab consented to the bizarre bargain. He abandoned his rice-cake gladly to the perfidious monkey and went to plant the persimmon seed in a corner of fertile ground.

The seasons and the years passed. The maples caught fire and died. The willows leaned over streams languidly and subsequently shriveled, as if burned by red flames.

As soon as the first spring, a tender green shoot delighted the expectant crab. And gradually, the tree grew, splendidly, as the monkey had predicted, green with emerald foliage and gilded with flavorsome fruits.

The crab, who had watched anxiously over the growth of the tree, finally achieved the coronation of his long patience. He had grown old watching the superb elevation of the tree. There was a further disappointment: the beautiful ripe fruits were inaccessible to him.

He had to implore the aid of the monkey, who, climbing over the branches, could throw the coveted fruits down to him.

The monkey consented eagerly. Having scaled the tree, he sat down in the fork of the trunk. Hastily, he picked the finest fruit, the most flavorsome and the most gilded, and devoured them gluttonously.

The poor crab, who was waiting impotently under the foliage, was desolate in his little marine soul, for he saw another enjoying his work, while he had obtained no profit from it himself. In vain he implored and threatened by turns. The monkey continued to pillage the branches imperturbably.

Finally, carried away anger, the crab reproached the dishonest monkey violently for his cunning and his treason. Furious that his victim was criticizing him for his knavery, the monkey picked the greenest fruits and threw them at the crab.

The fruits, as hard as stones, broke the unfortunate crab's carapace, and the latter expired under the missiles launched by the monkey. He died, and his little marine soul was carried away by the wind charged with iodine and salt, which bore it into the distance.

Seized by fear after the murder of the overly confident and overly credulous crab, the monkey quit the tree and fled, jabbering.

All night long, anxious at not finding his father in the lodging hollowed out beneath a rock, the crab's son searched for the missing crab feverishly; at first light he came to the fatal tree at the foot of which the crab lay, his carapace broken.

The young crab, overwhelmed by grief, did not think at first of trying to penetrate the mystery of that end. Gradually, however, he pulled himself together and interrogated himself. Having seen his father lying at the foot of the persimmon, he remembered the bargain proposed by the monkey and accepted by the overly credulous and overly confident crab.

A certitude germinated in the mind of the young crab. The monkey, therefore, was the murderer of the old crab, his father. And the desolate son divined that greedy avarice had impelled the monkey to that unjust and cruel action.

At first, the young crab wanted to hasten toward the murderer and chastise him without delay. However, although, being young, he was ignorant of cunning, he understood that astuteness is only vanquished by astuteness and that ingenious weakness is a superior strength. The wily monkey was a redoubtable adversary for the inexperienced crab. Before the uncertainty of the result, the young crab went to ask the advice of three friends of his late father: the mortar, the water-chestnut and the bee.

Struck by amazement and anger on hearing the desolate son's story, the three friends of the deceased swore to avenge the murder of the crab. They consulted one another and deliberated for a long time.

The old crab was buried in the depths of the bay. The madrepores constructed a tomb of white and red coral. Algae flourished perpetually on his beautiful sepulcher, and wrack inclined, like long willow branches, over the little tomb.

The funeral procession unfurled majestically. The crab was honored by the entire marine population for his generosity and his stainless life. All the Tatsugashira of his race filed past, preceding the humbler Heikegani. The lobsters, the crayfish and the shrimps took their places, each according to their rank. Their forms, curiously graceful, outlined against the gray bed of the sea, darkened further the reflection of slate-gray skies.

Hypocritically, the monkey, with a great affectation of dolor, escorted the remains of his victim. And the young crab, in spite of his great sadness, never took his protruding eyes off him.

The days went by, undulating, and effaced one another as a wave effaces another wave. The winter passed, radiant with snow and frost. At the approach of summer, the young crab sent an agile messenger to the monkey: the bee, an old and faithful friend of his father. On behalf of the young crab, the bee invited the monkey to favor with his presence a feast given by the desolate son to commemorate his father. The relatives and allies of the crab were solemnly celebrating the anniversary of his death.

On hearing those amicable words, the monkey rejoiced, for he felt reassured, believing that no one knew that he was the crab's murderer. In courteous terms he promised to come to render the deceased the honors of memory. Weeping, he eulogized the departed to the messenger.

The prudent and sage bee, although not being duped by the abominable comedy, dissimulated her scorn and anger. She pretended to believe the sincerity of the lying monkey, and, prudent and sage, she took off again. The monkey followed the gilded flight of the bee with eyes bathed with hypocritical tears.

As she left, the bee buzzed aloud: "The lying and knavish monkey is weeping false tears today; tomorrow, he'll weep veritable ones."

The day of the funerary feast arrived, livid in a rainy sky. The friends and allies of the deceased had assembled around the young crab, whose dwelling was hollowed out between the marine rocks. Garlands and wreaths of algae were suspended from the walls, encrusted with seashells, and cushions of kelp strewed the floor, a mosaic of pebbles with moist hues.

The monkey, surrounded by the bee, the mortar and the water-chestnut, was crouched in the prime place. Devoid of suspicion, he was proud of the honors that were rendered to him. The cheerful sake was poured by shrimp into coral cups. Rejoiced by the sake, the monkey chatted cordially about the merits of the defunct crab. He praised him in florid terms and even composed, toward the end of the meal, a few stanzas consecrated to his memory. In the most profound meditation, the young crab listened to that funereal poem. Then, courteous in his mourning, he removed the nacre screens and had his guests pass into the hall where nautili were to serve tea in minuscule cups made from hollow pearls.

A cauldron formed by an immense seashell was allowing an odorant vapor to escape. The guests chatted while the tea murmured its light song before being poured into the fuming cups. Groups formed, mingled and dispersed. The crayfish and the lobsters fraternized.

Suddenly, in the middle of a complicated sentence—for he was a monkey of letters—the traitor and murderer found himself alone in front of the musical cauldron. The guests had inexplicably and silently vanished.

Perplexed, the monkey examined the corners where pools of turquoise water were turning blue. In vain he slid between the screens. Emptiness and silence were hollowed out around him.

A vague fear insinuated itself into his veins. In order to reanimate his courage, and also to staunch the devouring thirst ignited by excessively numerous cups of sake, he approached the cauldron. The tea was still murmuring its light song, green and gold through the diaphanous walls of the seashell. The monkey leaned over the cauldron in order to pour a few embalmed drops into the hollow pearl.

Suddenly, in an explosion, something struck his cheek and rebounded, leaving a burning imprint on his face.

It was the vengeful water-chestnut, which had been hiding in the hot brazier.

Howling with fright and pain, the monkey recoiled. But a sharp pain abruptly stung the back of his neck. It seemed to him that the thin blade of a dagger had been plunged into his flesh.

It was the vengeful bee, which had been hiding behind the coral screens.

The frightened monkey launched himself forth, in order to flee the dwelling where he had come to mourn his victim with lying tears. But as he crossed the threshold, a stone was detached from the wall.

It was the vengeful mortar, which had mingled with the rock velveted with algae and wrack.

The walls collapsed in their turn, shaken by the fall of the vengeful mortar; and the monkey, crushed beneath the mortal weight, uttered poignant cries.

Seeing his enemy, his father's murderer, struggling in futile efforts, the young crab approached him and ordered him to confess his crime and his treason.

In his last breath, the monkey lied again. Perfidious until death, he dared to calumniate the memory of the crab he had killed. He dared to declare that only the gluttony and the stupidity of his victim had caused that obscure death.

Outraged in his filial piety, the young crab advanced sideways toward his adversary, and, opening his formidable pincers wide, he patiently sawed through the monkey's neck. Having finally detached the head from the trunk, he let it fall, with a great eruption of bubbles, into a pool of blue and green water, which suddenly turned red.

In the distance, the feeble sigh of the declining tide rose up regularly.

CHINESE TALES

Victory is Uncertain

NU-KWA is the Primordial Goddess. She has the body of a serpent and the head of a woman, and possesses eternal prudence. The Goddess dwells in a forest whose shadowy foliage bears stars instead of flowers.

When the earth emerged from chaos, Nu-Kwa took some yellow clay, in which she molded the flesh of woman and man. But Kung-Kung, her brother, was jealous of the work of the Goddess. Kung-Kung built his palace above a torrent. He is the perfidious spirit of Water, as Nu-Kwa is the pacific spirit of Wood.

In order to annihilate the work of the Goddess, Kung-Kung ordered his waves to invade the earth. With his powerful forehead he bumped the imperfect mountain, the mountain of the universe, which Nu-Kwa has been trying in vain to round out since time immemorial, and the imperfect mountain collapsed. It broke the celestial columns and also undermined the supports sustaining the four corners of the earth.

Nu-Kwa, creative force, opposed her patience and her courage to Kung-Kung, destructive force. She melted, in a subtle crucible, the gems of the five colors: black, azure, red, yellow and white.

In order to replace the extinct sun, she caused the first spark to spring forth from two branches rubbed together, and the heat of metals in fusion warmed up the earth again, chilled by the death of the stars.

Nu-Kwa then cut off the feet of the sacred tortoise and consolidated the four corners of the earth with them. Having burned reeds, she spread the ashes over the devastating waters, which became submissive again.

Having saved the earth and pacified space, Nu-Kwa embarked on a lotus and, traveling through space, stopped on the pale shores of the moon. She planted the Eight Trees there, the fruits of which rendered the body of anyone who picked them as transparent as crystal.

Nu-Kwa returned to earth and elaborated jade. She decreed that anyone who ate that sacred stone would become similar to souls and would cleave the air with wings. The Goddess named jade "great and pure."

With reposing, the Goddess animated with her breath the mysterious people of the Lung, dragons. She created the blue dragon of the East, which bears spring in its golden claws, the dragon without horns, the guardian spirit of the waters, which traces the course of rivers, and the yellow dragon, which protects the sun.

She also created the dragon that watches over the celestial abodes. It carried her on the scales of its vast back. Nu-Kwa caused the dragon that commands the wind and the rain, and the black dragon that defends hidden treasures, to surge from the ether. She did not forget the four dragon kings of the four seas.

The Goddess embedded a magic pearl in the foreheads of the Lung. She gave them the power to reduce themselves to the dimensions of a silkworm and to reach the clouds, but she did not permit them to cross the azure beyond the clouds.

In compensation, she granted it to them to descend into the deepest wellsprings of the sea, where no fish has ever dared to venture. She also permitted them to render themselves invisible.

Nu-Kwa assembled around her the flock of red ewes that appear in dreams to the Sons of Heaven, presaging the disasters of the empire.

In those times, humans were ignorant of the art of materializing their thoughts and their dreams. They communicated their will distantly by means of knotted cords. Each knot represented a word. Nu-Kwa pitied that crude invention and sought a more ingenious way of linking souls.

She was wandering along the sea shore one orange evening, while she considered the bizarre imprints of the feet of storks in the sand. She admired the delicacy of those tangled tracks, in imitation of which she created signs and characters.

When Nu-Kwa had formed the first writing, the skies spread a rain of millet, disincarnate souls wept in the darkness and the dragons withdrew from the sight of humans.

Night fell and the Goddess came to sit down next to a red-hot fire. Suddenly, a branch crackled harmoniously. It was a branch of T'ung wood impregnated with savage odors. Surprised and charmed, the Goddess snatched the brand away and carved it into the form of a flute. It was thus that the first music sprang forth.

But she did not stop at that point in her labor. She diverted the course of the celestial river that links our globe to the heavens, the terrestrial current of which is named the Yellow Rover.

Nu-Kwa caused the clouds of five colors to surge from the azure. Those clouds are the sign of celestial wrath. Humans ought to fear her vengeance when these miracles are manifest:

The green clouds, which presage the swarming of crawling things;

The white clouds, which announce mournings;

The red clouds, messengers of battles;

The black clouds, which precede deluges;

The yellow clouds, which predict famine.

The implacable struggle between Nu-Kwa and Kung-Kung desolates space.

Kung-Kung hates Nu-Kwa as evil hates good, as ugliness hates beauty, and as stupidity hates intelligence. If Nu-Kwa eventually triumphs over Kung-Kung, humans will be happy and good, the equals of the immortal spirits. But she has not yet beaten her redoubtable adversary, and her victory is uncertain.

For good is as slow as the wings of evil are rapid. That is why the tortoise is the symbol of good, and that is why the fly is the symbol of evil.

The victory is uncertain . . .

The Dance of the Sunset

I will tell you about Pan-Fei, the imperial dancer whose steps caused lilies to surge forth. The Son of Heaven, Tcheng-Ti, chose her for his concubine.

Such was the scrupulous organization of her steps that she executed the most complex rhythms in the hollow of a hand, or a sake cup.

Pan-Fei composed her dances as sages compose a poem. She knew the infinite charm of the pause in the middle of the song, the attitude that succeeds the gestures. Her minuscule feet scintillated like frail living stars.

She first invented the narrow brodequins that imprison the feet of Chinese girls with a cruel grace, for she wanted all women to have magically small feet like hers.

One day, before the Son of Heaven, she danced the dance of the dawn. Seated, with her chin in her hand, she was sleeping a candid slumber. Then her amber eyelids were raised, and her astonished gaze wandered over the world. Gradually, the limbs were animated. A frisson of awakening ran slowly through them.

The dancer's kimono floated, as vague as the clouds. The pleats sketched their amplitudes. Lanterns stained Pan-Fei's garment with pink gleams.

With her wonderstruck eyes she greeted space. She offered herself to the indecisive and luminous light that was revealed to her. Her soul was born in her eyes. She hatched out all the ardor of daylight.

Then there was the dance of the sunset, a sumptuous agony in imperial gold. Lanterns bloodied with red light the expiring attitudes of Pan-Fei. The amber eyelids fell back. The lanterns bloodied her kimono, which opened over a mysterious wound.

In a final gesture of suffering and languor, she abandoned herself to the unknown darkness. It was death in imperial gold . . .

With the bound of a sly cat, Pan-Fei was upright again. She put on a marine kimono, embroidered with a design of coral and algae. The fluid pleats followed the soft curve of waves. Her green and white kimono sparkled, like glaucous water and swirling foam. Her attitudes evoked the harmonious flux and reflux of tides. Like the fortunate sea, she laughed at the sun. Like the feverish sea, she reared up against the implacable wind. She was enfevered in vain rebellion. And in the horror of anger, she lacerated her painful breasts with her fingernails. Then, like the consoled sea, she calmed down under the distant caress of the moonlight.

Then she incarnated Manju, the Goddess of Cascades. Her kimono streamed tumultuously. And, climbing impetuously the fall of the flood of fabrics, an embroidered carp, the symbol of struggle and perseverance, launched forth ardently . . .

The Son of Heaven took particular pleasure in the dance of the chrysanthemums, tangles of thrown-back silks, autumn defoliations, and a red rain of petals. Pan-Fei revealed to him then the dance of snow, the evocation of pale clarities, and the brightness of unreal whiteness . . .

She was winter perfumed by the breath of cherry trees asleep under the snowflakes. She was the spring-like winter that does not wither the flowers but envelops them warmly and velvets them with a protective frost.

Before the incomparable art of the dancer, Tcheng-Ti, smitten with reverential admiration, named her Fei-Yin, fleeting swallow. He said to her once, when she danced the dance of the willows sagging under the breeze: "Each of your steps, O Fei-Yin, causes a golden lily to spring from the ground that it brushes . . ."

That is why ingenious netsuke represent her detached from the lilies that her steps cause to spring from the earth . . .

But one evening, weary of the jealousies and vile rancor that do not spare beauty any more than glory, she transpierced her left breast while dancing the dance of the sword. Her gestures of agony and death were so melodious that the assembled courtiers believed them to be a graceful variation of the musical theme . . .

Shuttle on the Edge of Springs

CHANG K'IEN, a lover of adventure, departed one evening to discover the unknown sources of the Yellow River. A sunset of burning sulfur reverberated over the citrine waters.

For seven days and seven nights, Chang K'ien followed the current. The mysterious waves cradled the junk. Red nenuphars opened like ardent stars. Herons with orange wings pursued one another through the reeds. Tortoises delivered to the sky their shells, on which the Goddess Si Wang Mu once traced secret designs. And during the purple nights, the constellations reflected their uncertain gleams in the eddies.

For the first time, Chang K'ien saw a shrub unknown to the men of his homeland. It was like a liana laden with blue clusters. He stopped and collected the strange fruit. Chang K'ien was the first person in the Empire of the Sun to bring back the vine, from which the Persians extract a redoubtable beverage.

Chang K'ien followed the current. Terrible or charming creatures sometimes appeared on the banks. It was thus that Chang K'ien perceived the white tiger, lying in ambush behind a koku bush. The Tiger is the most perfect incarnation of the male principle. He is the sovereign of animals, for the character that signifies *king* was imprinted on his forehead by Kung-Kung himself. He measures seven feet in length, for the number seven is the fateful number of the male principle. In the same way, the gestation of the Tigress lasts seven months. The Tiger prolongs his existence for a thousand years. When he attains the age of five hundred years, his pelt becomes whiter than the spring snow, and the Gods then name him Peh-Hu.

The tiger's claws are a precious amulet, and his ashes, carried in an amulet, keep fever away.

Chang K'ien saw the white tiger, as beautiful as the sun. The two azure storks of Si Wang Mu brushed him with their wings. The Kwei, the tree of immortality, rose up before him to a height of ten thousand feet. Its foliage was motionless and shiny, like jade. It bore clouds of flowers and, simultaneously, fruits of flame that render anyone who eats them immortal. And Chang K'ien distinguished the Hare that lives in the Moon.

The seventh night fell. The blue banks drew away and widened bizarrely. And although the great nocturnal clarity whitened around the junk, Chang K'ien, for the first time, could not see the reflection of the stars in the river.

Around him, vast sonorous fires rose up. He was conscious of Space. Everything around him seemed unlimited. A wonder akin to fear fell silent within him.

Dawn gilded the immensity and finally revealed to Chang K'ien the mysterious sources of the River. Brighter than the pearls that are iridescent with a nocturnal gleam in the evening, they sprang, murmuring, from incalculable depths. Next to the sources, finally revealed, a melancholy woman was sitting, clad in a silver-gray kimono. She was laboriously tangling golden threads in a complex network similar to the tormented network of the zodiac.

Chang K'ien interrogated the weaver as to her name and the name of the country into which he had ventured. But without a single word breaking the suave line of her lips, the woman handed him her shuttle, which was subtly radiant, like nacre.

Chang K'ien returned to his homeland, following the curve of the river. The enigma of the voyage haunted his perplexed nights. He went to visit his friend, the star-reader.

The sage listened to him with all his attentive gravity. Then, standing up, he deployed a dilapidated scroll.

Solemnly, the star-reader told the adventurer that at the moment when the strange woman had appeared to him, a shooting star had crossed the Star Tchih-Nu.

Religiously pale, Chang K'ien understood that he had spoken to the Star Tchih-Nu herself, to the melancholy weaver who contrives a fabric of radiance in silence. Every seven years a bridge of red maple leaves permits her to wander the earth, where she was once a harmonious virgin venerated by poets. An assembly of singers once listened to her for a year without sleeping or taking any nourishment.

It is thus that Chang K'ien was the first to know that the Yellow River links the earth to the heavens, and that it flows through the empyrean. Since that time, virgins raise their eyes in the evening toward the Celestial River, whose current of stars flows through space.

At the Hour of the Goat

T'SAO AND WEI-HOW were two young Chinese women very simply and very fervently in love with one another. T'sao loved Wei-How because she was fragile and fearful. Wei-How loved T'sao because she was expert in the art of chosen words, rhythms and pauses.

They loved one another with candor. During indolent middays, Wei-How allowed herself to be lulled divinely into languor by her friend's singing; and T'sao, on moonlit nights when her tender companion was asleep in her arms, imagined naively complicated poems for her. The little sleeper's eyelids were amber in the light of a lantern, which allowed rose-red gleams to float over her slender body. Oh, how charming Wei-How was in her sleep! Her mysterious dreams enveloped her in an aura as indecisive as the one that surrounds the Daughters of the Moon.

T'sao got up at dawn in order to ornament Wei-How's awakening. She brought her red chrysanthemums heavy with dew, and wisterias, which resembled her more than any other flowers.

They did not think about the Future, which is cruel to women. Their virginity, devoid of dread and suspicion, was unconsciously happy. They rejoiced ingenuously in living. Their gaze did not belie their smile. It was the snow on the cherry trees in spring.

One evening, T'sao, having promised Wei-How to meet her at the Hour of the Goat[1] on a bridge near the radiant lake Lan Hiao, went there. The yellow heron with three feet that lives in the sun had folded up its luminous wings.

Clouds like red dragons seemed to be menacing other clouds like black dragons. The struggle was imminent . . .

T'sao was not alarmed by celestial menaces, her soul being brightened by the white thought of Wei-How. She waited with joyful patience, and she composed two poems for her that sang the fervor of her love.

I

When you were born.
  Wei-How,
Of unknown birds
Singing amid the bamboos,

  Similar birds
  Had never been seen
In all the empire of the sun.
Birdsong as beautiful
Had never been heard
In the realm of the dragons.
Your long tresses,
Expertly braided,
Are soft and fine
Like the fur of a hare.

---

1 Author: "The Chinese divide the day and the night into twelve hours designated by the following signs: the Rat, the Ox, the Tiger, the Hare, the Dragon, the Serpent, the Horse, the Goat, the Monkey, the Cock, the Dog and the Pig."

To what can I compare
My faithful love?
I will compare it
To the yellow heron
Which lives inconsolably
After the death
Of his companion,
And no longer chooses
A female in spring.

II

My beloved is like
A forest of flowering cherry-trees
That sways at the whim of the breeze.
My beloved is like
   A forest of cherry-trees.

My beloved is like
A limpid cascade
Enveloped by the mist of torrents,
And spangled by the sun.
My beloved is like
   A cascade.

My beloved is like
An opening violet
At the foot of the oak where the cuckoo sings.
Both are daughters of the dew.
My beloved is like
   A violet.

My beloved is like
A river whose waves roll gems,
A river scintillating in the sunlight
And palely iridescent under the moon.
My beloved is like
    A river.

My beloved is like
A little fir-tree
Curiously sculpted
By a laborious artist.
My beloved is like
    A fir-tree.

My beloved is like
A beautiful shore by the sea,
Odorant with the saline breeze
And melodious with the sound of waves.
My beloved is like
    A shore.

When she had finished those verses, the poet perceived that the water of Lake Lan Hiao, swollen by melted snow, was rising tumultuously. She saw immediate flight as the unique salvation.

Being truly a woman, however, she preferred death to the abandonment of her amorous post.

And the great waters caught her as she hung on with vain tenacity to the damp wood of broken supports. The great waters snatched her away, constant in her fervor. They carried her to the pale and tender regions of the Moon, where the consoled souls of amorous women smile.

Terrestrial Images of the Moon

YUEH, the Moon, is the visible radiance of the Feminine Principle, which the first Gods named Yenn. The Moon reigns over women, over darkness, over the earth, over female animals, over water, over pearls, over hares, frogs and grasshoppers.

She dominates the water, for the sage Pao P'uh Tse has said: "The vital essence of the Moon governs water. That is why, when the Moon is luminous, the tides rise irresistibly."

Pearls are the clarities that the Moon distils, the clarities that insinuate themselves through the thick oyster-shell and bloom in nacreous globes.

Pearls, being the emanation of the Feminine Principle, protect those who wear them against fire, which is the emanation of the Male Principle.

Certain pearls brighten at night with a gleam similar to the distant light of the stars. And pearls are hostile to spouses and courtesans. They only take pleasure in the fresh contact of the immaculate flesh of virgins.

The hare is the symbol of the Bounding Moon. The hare that lives in the Moon is called the gemmed hare. That is why Sanskrit inscriptions designate the Moon by the name of Sason, the leveret.

When the Son of Heaven is clement and sage, the Moon sends him the red hare in a dream, as a celestial assurance of glory and prosperity. Is not the Moon, in fact, the elder sister of the Son of Heaven?

Like tigers, hares have a thousand years of existence. When they have attained five hundred years, their pelt becomes whiter than the waves.

The sacred frog, Chan-Chu, also lives in the silver star, for the hia-mo is the symbol of the Pluvious Moon.

Chan-Chu was once a woman, Chang-ngo, the wife of How-I. As the Moon was imprisoned by the clouds during an eclipse, How-I liberated her by launching arrows against the sky. An incomparable archer, he also felled with his invincible arrows the ten suns that had appeared at the same time and had destroyed half the earth. In order to recompense him, the Goddess Si Wang Mu poured him, in a jade cup, the dew of the stars, which gives immortality to anyone who brings it to his lips. But Chang-ngo, the wife of How-I, stole the celestial dew and fled, carrying it to the Moon. The fugitive was transformed into a frog by Si Wang Mu, who named her Chan-Chu henceforth.

Grasshoppers and cicadas are emblems of the Moon, whose impetuous agility and disorderly leaps they have, for the ancients named the Moon: the One Who Bounds, and the Nocturnal Grasshopper.

In the Moon, a blackcurrant bush extends the shadow of its foliage. The untiring woodcutter Wu Kang fells it relentlessly, but relentlessly, the tree rises up again and flourishes again. The leaves of the lunar blackcurrant bush would accord anyone who could eat them the privilege of immortal life, and the person who could eat them would become as transparent as crystal.

The Moon links, with an invisible red cord, the feet of those who are predestined to love one another in the future. It is thus that the lunar cord leads those whose footsteps are wandering over distant roads toward one another, irresistibly.

The Jade Stone of the Emperor Shan

Open eyes do not always discern the
jade stone of the Emperor Shan.
(Chinese proverb.)

A MAN of the province of Tsen discovered a jade stone dormant in the side of a mountain. He thought he was seeing a glaucous reflection of the sea on freshly fallen snow. Mysterious gleams were imprisoned in the green dusk. The gem was simultaneously compact and diaphanous, cloudy and radiant; and the man contemplated it with an adoring anguish, for he understood that an incomparable treasure had been revealed to him.

He brought the jade to the Son of Heaven. He brought it without the hope of recompense, for the joy of that beauty, as the poets bring their patient labor to the insouciant universe.

He unveiled the stone before the Son of Heaven and the assembled court. The silence expanded. The man, exalted by amour and pride, contemplated with a renewed wonder the magnificence that he had extracted from the darkness.

But a murmur shriller than the hiss of vipers through the whisper of foliage awoke him from his ecstasy.

"The stone is false!"

The most renowned jeweler in the empire spoke thus before the treasure. And all the jewelers and lapidaries present repeated in chorus:

"The stone is false!"

The omnipotent minister, the favorite of the Son of Heaven, turned to the man, mute with hectic astonishment.

"For having lied to the Son of Heaven, the executioners will cut off your left foot."

The torturers obeyed the minister's order. Indifferent to his pain, however, the mutilated man persisted in proclaiming the pure splendor of the jade.

A year went by, mingling with eternity as a cloud is confounded with the azure. The Son of Heaven died and his son picked up the fallen scepter.

The man knocked on the door of the Sublime Palace again. He had dissimulated the terrestrial star under his rags and he held it out to the Son of Heaven.

Again the jewelers and the lapidaries hastened to deny the gem.

The executioners then cut off the man's right foot. He disdained the unjust punishment, but a great stupor drowned his soul.

Shortly thereafter, struck down by the fever, the Son of Heaven expired. The entire people dressed in white, as one does during mourning.

And Shan, the very glorious son of the sovereign, was resplendent in his turn on the throne.

The day after the coronation, the mutilated man had himself transported to the palace and requested an audience, which was refused to him. Then he began to sob for the first time.

The sound of his moans reached the Son of Heaven, who asked him why he was lamenting thus.

"I am not weeping for myself," replied the calumniated man, "I am weeping because an incomparable gem has been misunderstood. I am weeping for the blindness of those who have scorned a present from Guanyin."

These words resounded with so much dolorous fervor that the Son of Heaven considered the man for a long time. And Shan, Son of Heaven, summoned all the lapidaries and jewelers in the empire. The scales fell from their darkened eyes. They recognized the veritable glory of the gem. Before the assembled court, Shan placed it piously on his venerable forehead.

The man, impassive in felicity as in dolor, saw the triumph of his faith. But when the Son of Heaven offered him vast riches and the garment of a mandarin embroidered with golden dragons, he turned away, unshakable in his refusal.

Open eyes do not always discern the jade stone of the Emperor Shan.

IN THE JAPANESE MANNER

The Imperious Lips

YAMUNSA, daughter of Kotsuke, had flourished in isolation like a solitary camellia blooming in the snow.

She did not know the limpid past of happy childhoods. She mirrored herself in yesterday as in troubled and brackish water, for her mother, Oishia, had died of dolor after long years of a marriage more dolorous than a martyrdom . . .

. . . Oishia had felt growing within her the feminine rebellion against the base tyranny of the male. She hated unjust and libidinous men; she imposed her hatred on her child, who listened to her with an adoring faith.

When the sad Oishia went to take her place among the Dead crouching in their tall round coffins, Yamunsa wept for her inconsolably. Her youth withered in melancholy. The murmur of the koto importuned her exasperated ears. The sparkle of colors wearied her gaze. She no longer liked anything but the refuge of silence and the consolation of shadows. The saddened pleat of her eyelids rendered them similar to the lowered eyelids of nuns.

She cloistered herself in regret and in the interior dream, like convent-dwellers who have forgotten how to smile.

Kotsuke, who loved his daughter with all the bizarre tenderness of ferocious beings, was alarmed by that etiolation of a living flower. He resolved to seek advice from a magicienne renowned for her obscure wisdom.

She had the knowledge of invisible worlds. The dead woman had appeared to her in person, an infantile Sleeper sitting in the attitude of happy slumber with her cheek in the palm of her hand.

The magicienne informed her disciples of the doctrine of souls. For every human being has several souls. Anyone who only possesses a single soul is cursed by the Gods, for he remains irremediably stupid and miserable. The richer a man is in souls, the more he is favored by the heavens. Nevertheless, no man possesses more than nine souls. Only the Gods can surpass that number. Guanyin, the Supreme Perfection, has a thousand souls, which form a rainbow glory around her.

A man's souls are inseparable. When one soul is disconnected from the others, the man they inhabit becomes the prey of the most somber furies, and it is said that he is mad. And when a man dies, his souls go up together to the roof of his house, where they wait, for forty-one days, the moment to take flight toward the throne of the Buddha.

The magicienne also taught the pure doctrine of Guanyin, whose thirty-three different bodies incarnate all of feminine beauty, for she was the priestess of Guanyin, who looks down over the sound of prayers. She also served the Goddess that humans have called the Mist of Torrents, who was born of the pearl Tama, the adornment of the hair of Amaterasu. Piously, the magicienne called Amaterasu O-Hi-San, the Lady of the Sun. O-Hi-San is the One whom death and the oni fear.

Benten, the Goddess of Water and water bearers, also protected the prophetess. And Tchih-nu, the Virgin Star, allowed her tutelary light to fall upon her. Having the favor of immortals, being familiar with their splendor, the old magicienne was as good as she was powerful. She knew that mercy and benevolence are the beginning and the end of all wisdom.

The magicienne smiled with her habitual mildness when Kotsuke came to implore her advice on the subject of his mysteriously stricken daughter. When she had heard him out, she smiled again as she gave him a pink jade ring that, placed on the virgin's finger, would cure her miraculously.

Kotsuke returned home, his heart illuminated. He obeyed the magicienne's orders.

Yamunsa contemplated the pink jade ring on her finger with unseeing eyes. But when night fell she got up and, in the anger of her suffering, threw the magic ring into the depths of the pond that was shining beneath her windows. Then, exhausted by tears, she went to sleep with her chin in the palm of her hand, like the serene and infantile Dead.

Suddenly, a murmur of singing water slid toward her. It was an eddy that had just broken against the strand. Yamunsa raised her head in order to look through the window-panes, where a gilded green firefly was walking, the color of limpid tea.

The entire pond unfurled, florid with nenuphars, and resembled the Sacred River that streams whitely in the heavens. The entire pond unfurled, luminous with nenuphars.

And a woman appeared, lying on the water-lilies as beautiful as the Mist of Torrents born of the pearl Tama, with which Amaterasu, the Goddess of the Sun, adorns her hair. She attracted the charmed young woman with her gesture and her voice. In a glad stupor, Yamunsa parted the screens and went toward the fluid vision.

She no longer discerned anything, no longer understood anything. She sensed two arms cooler that the flesh of nenuphars envelop her with an undulating embrace. And, very weary, she fell asleep in the somnolent odor of nenuphars.

She slept thus until dawn on the bed of nenuphars. And when the sky was like an enormous block of pink jade, she woke up. She opened her eyes and smiled at the irises and the reeds. The pink jade ring was shining on her finger. It had the same hue as the matinal sky.

Yamunsa meditated, smiling vaguely, until dusk. When the vesperal breeze rippled the pool, she went to sleep, in a very calm slumber.

In a dream she saw before her the woman whose body was more coolly pale than the flesh of nenuphars, and she heard a fluid voice streaming, which murmured to her: "I am the one who loves you. I am Nanza, the sister of the nenuphars."

Nanza knelt down beside the trembling virgin and, with the sleeves of her kimono parted, she brushed the puerile arm with her lips. Her imperious lips became enfevered in the warm shadow of the armpit . . .

The virgin languished, strangely weak. Her hair veiled her dazzled eyes. An insidious torpor softened everything. She was intoxicated by disturbance and sweetness. She felt herself sliding with abandon over a bed of nuptial azure.

"This is the approach of death," she murmured. "Nanza . . ."

The imperious lips possessed her lips, and her breasts, ardent and fresh, espoused her young breasts. She heard the fluid voice streaming for the second time.

"It is not the approach of death, Yamunsa, but the approach of amour, more powerful and more fatal."

Yamunsa made the gesture of driving away the exquisite temptation.

"I ought not to know amour, Nanza. Toward what obscure peril do you want to draw me?"

She went on, feverishly imploring: "All my childhood was cradled in sobs. I never learned joy. I ought not to love and I ought not to be loved. I have given my inviolable promise to a dead woman. Leave me entirely to my dolor."

Nanza, inclined and suave, replied: "Ignorant child! The dead woman you are evoking in such a melancholy manner never knew amour. The woman whose ignorant flesh has only been subject to the ugly brutalities of the male has never savored tenderness in its plenitude and its expansion. It is necessary to pity the woman who does not know the virginal frisson of confounded flesh, equally pure, in a pure embrace; for the mutual amour of women is harmony expiring in harmony, perfume mingled with perfume, the flower inclined over the flower. I am the one who loves you. I have come to teach you the pure white amour of virgins. Benten has sent me to you, Benten the Goddess of Serpents and Waters, of Beauty and Music, Benten the Goddess of Love. In order to console you for all your bitter past, I will put on a human appearance and I will be your companion and your maidservant."

When she awoke, Yamunsa's lips were burning under two avid lips. She perceived beside her the form of her dream, undulating in a white kimono over which a design of nenuphars was quivering.

The felicity of the two Lovers was incomparable. They wandered in the garden respiring the same flowers. They leaned over the pond, where their two faces were confounded in the same reflection. In order to adorn Yamunsa's hair, Nanza picked two white nenuphars, which framed her puerile face.

But human ecstasy is like the smile of the Buddha.

Once, for all eternity, Buddha smiled divinely. And the infinite softness of that calm smile penetrated all the way to the most distant universes, all the way to the Three Frozen Hells, Atata, Ababa and Pundarika.

In the First Frozen Hell, lips, linked by eternal cold, can only proffer the long shiver: "A-ta-ta!" That is why the First Frozen Hell bears the name of Atata.

In the Second Frozen Hell, tongues, sealed in eternal cold, can only proffer the long shiver: "A-ba-ba!" That is why the Second Frozen Hell bears the name of Ababa.

And in the Pundarika, the Hell of White Lotuses, bones laid bare by the eternal cold resemble a florescence of white lotuses.

Now, the smile of Buddha warmed the Three Frozen Hells, which became suddenly verdant, like willows in spring. But as the smile of Buddha illuminated and warmed the worlds, a prophetic voice lamented in these terms:

"The smile of Buddha is not a reality.

"The smile of Buddha will not endure."

And the light disappeared.

In truth, human ecstasy is like the smile of the Buddha.

Kotsuke, Yamunsa's father, was infatuated with the sister of the nenuphars. He was infatuated with her with all his senile tenacity and all his male brutality. Being a violent man who knew no other law than the law of his desire, he resolved to bend the virgin to his caprice.

One day, when he tried to force her, blind with savage lust, Nanza ran away in an undulation of fleeing water and ran to the pond. She threw herself into its heavy glittering water . . .

A sob of amorous dolor rent the air. Yamunsa, in despair, sank in her turn beneath the waves.

The pond seemed to sparkle and shiver with light laughter. A sunbeam danced over the happy waters. And in the place where the two Lovers had disappeared, two pure white nenuphars flourished, their stems enlaced and their corollas leaning toward one another.

The Official Suicide of
Matsudaira Oki no Kami[1]

MATSUDAIRA OKI NO KAMI, one of the most valorous samurai of Japan, decided to put an end to his days. After having deliberated maturely, he finally concluded that the sum of joys promised by life did not equal the sum of certain dolors that it inflicts relentlessly.

Matsudaira Oki no Kami had passed through existence smiling, knowing that the smile is a form of courtesy toward men and of respect toward the Gods. When he announced the death of his mother to the host of his friends and servants, he maintained the heroic smile on his resolute lips. He smiled, not out of indifference or egotism, because he loved the maternal image with a religious love, but out of bravery and politeness. He knew that it is not equitable to trouble men with the spectacle of dolor.

Dolor is ugly in itself. It saddens vainly the indifferent soul to which it manifests itself inappropriately. It is an Intruder, and it is becoming to ignore it. It is necessary to dissimulate the baseness of life and only to reveal the best of oneself to friends and strangers one encounters on the terrestrial path. That is why, even amid the most somber

---

1 Author: "After A. B. Mitford, *Tales of Old Japan*, London: Macmillan, 1901."

anguish, a man ought to show his neighbors and relatives a smiling visage.

The smile is the noblest and most beautiful manifestation of the human soul. Guanyin smiles while lowering her divine eyelids over the sound of prayers. And Buddha smiles, for all eternity, with all of his radiant visage.

Matsudaira Oki no Kami never ceased smiling through all dolors. And while smiling, he announced the determination he had formed to die. He proclaimed it in all pomp and all solemnity, in accordance with custom; and, having announced his imminent death, he summoned the kaishaku who were to witness his suicide officially.

Matsudaira Oki no Kami, being one of the most courteous samurai in Japan, knew that, out of regard for his neighbors and relatives, the ceremony of the official suicide had to be prepared at length and knowledgably. He had criticized the conduct of Asano Takumi no Kami, a samurai who had opened his abdomen without warning anyone, in an unexpected and sudden fashion, in the palace of Tamura, a very powerful daimio. Asano Takumi no Kami had acted badly toward his relatives and toward the daimio, for spilled blood ought not to soil either the dwelling of a friend or the suicide's own dwelling.

Asano Takumi no Kami had therefore failed custom when he had soiled the daimio's house with his spilled young blood. He had also forgotten that a daimio ought to be treated with more deference than an ordinary samurai.

Thus, Matsudaira Oko no Kami, the most courteous samurai in the empire, not wanting to soil his house, had a bamboo palisade erected in his garden. Two doors opened on that palisade. He gave the northern door the name of Shugiyomon: the door for practicing the virtues; and he gave the southern door the name of Ubanmon: the door of the warm basin.

Afterwards, Matsudaira Oko no Kami had a white silk carpet bought, for white symbolizes mourning and funeral ceremonies. In the four corners of the enclosure, four panels were unrolled, also white, on which a brush traced four quotations taken from the holy books.

The location of the suicide was ready.

Darkness descended, odorous with camellias leaning over at the whim of nocturnal breezes. Fireflies shone in the grass and the foliage, like wandering stars. The branches of the willows were florid with flames. Over Matsudaira Oko no Kami's window, a single firefly trailed, as bright as a drop of fire on the paper panes.

Matsudaira Oko no Kami's four witnesses took their places at the four corners of the palisade, under the white panels on which the words of the holy books, traced by a brush, were shining. And Matsudaira Oko no Kami's servants extended on the woven mats two ample red carpets, which the blood would not tarnish. Four lanterns were lit at the corners of the palisade, where the witnesses were sitting. It was as if four pink moons had been miraculously illuminated at the four corners of the perfumed sky. The light was thus discreet and sufficient; for an excessive light is not decent on such occasions.

Everything was prepared appropriately. Matsudaira Oko no Kami came in. It was then the Hour of the Cock.

At the Hour of the Monkey, he had composed his funeral discourse; and, having composed it to his entire satisfaction, he had five red lacquer trays brought, charged with dried fish, crystallized algae and rice. Having eaten, he emptied two cups of limpid sake.

Matsudaira Oko no Kami then read his funeral discourse. It compared human destiny to that of an errant boat delivered to the hazards of the sea. It also praised the peace and splendor of the realm of the dead beyond the Celestial River, where souls slumber, enclosed in blue lotus calices. The maidservants of Guanyin water the dormant lotuses with closed leaves carefully, and when the hour of a new terrestrial incarnation has sounded, the lotuses open wide and reveal the souls, nourished on dew, in the depths of her moist cups.

After having read, Matsudaira Oko no Kami got up and went out, with grave slowness. He came back after having put on a kimono on which submarine landscapes had been embroidered delicately by patient feminine hands.

Obedient to a gesture from Matsudaira Oko no Kami, the servants brought two screens decorated with painted storks. Behind those two screens they deposited, on a red lacquer tray, a saber, a censer, a fan, a bowl of water and a basin to receive the entrails. These preparations having been accomplished, Matsudaira Oko no Kami had the witnesses presented with rice cakes and frail porcelain cups in which golden green tea was fuming.

The witnesses ate and drank. Matsudaira Oko no Kami went out again. He came back, having put on this time a kimono on which blue wisterias were ingeniously embroidered. And while the servants brought the witnesses gold lacquer plates charged with crystallized algae and cups of sake, he recited strophes composed by him in honor of a woman of his race, O Koyo, the daughter of Jih'ei. That valiant woman had killed with her own hand a courtesan of the Mikado who had addressed vile words to her. The Mikado, having condemned her to death, accorded her, out of respect for her courage, the honors of hara-kiri. But instead of handing her, as was done with the samurai, the saber with which they had to open their abdomen with the first wound, the signal of the execution, the executioners gave her a fan.

"That is why," said Matsudaira Oko no Kami, "I have had a fan brought with the funeral apparatus."

The witnesses, clad in white, bowed like courteous phantoms under the uncertain light of the four pink paper lanterns; and the servants, moving the screens aside, brought Matsudaira Oko no Kami a tray on which a wakiaszhi, a small dagger, was placed. Matsudaira Oko no Kami thanked them. Then he sat down ceremoniously on the red carpet. He sat with his knees and toes touching the ground, his body resting on his heels. And, having undone his kimono, he let it fall to the waist. His bare breast was as polished as ancient bronze. Smiling, he attached the long sleeves of the kimono around his knees in order not to fall backwards, for a samurai must die with his face to the ground.

The servants placed the paper screens before the man who was about to disappear, in order to hide the spectacle of the mortal act from the witnesses. One of them agitated the censer in order to dissipate the odor of blood.

And when the servants moved the two paper screens away again, Matsudaira Oko no Kami was lying motionless and stiff. He had died smiling, for he knew that the smile is a mark of courtesy toward men and of submission toward the Gods.

The Sea and Death

GREAT rejoicing illuminated the court of Keiko, the very august and very pacific Mikado, for his second son, Yamato, had just attained his sixteenth year. He was, therefore, the age of a man, the age of a samurai.

A double joy burst forth in those celebrations. Yamato was marrying, with great pomp, the tender Ototachibana, the daughter of a daimio renowned for his courage.

Soon, however, the brilliant festivities died away. A great disturbance was agitating Japan. Two redoubtable brothers, Kumaso and Takeru, were devastating the island of Kiushiu, one of the richest provinces in the land.

And Keiko, seeing that no one in his army was more valorous than his second son, ordered Yamato to go put down the rebellion and put the rebels to death.

Yamato accepted with a joyful heart, for he loved adventures and combats. But, knowing that he was very young and inexperienced in the art of war, he made a pilgrimage to the temple of Ise, consecrated to the Goddess of the Sun. The priestess of the temple of Ise, Keiko's own sister, was a very august nun, as beautiful as the Goddess she served.

The nun came out of the temple herself in order to greet the future hero. In nobly simple words she praised him for having obtained, while still so young, the confidence of the Mikado, his father. Having had one of her most magnificent kimonos, embroidered with sacred characters, brought by an inmate of the convent, she presented it to the young man.

"Do not forget," she said, "that every samurai must combine with the valor of a man the patience and subtlety of a woman. And may the gift of his kimono make you think of that eternal verity."

Yamato took the kimono from the pious hands of the nun. She had fallen silent, upright, in the presence of samurai and bonzes. She had fallen silent, and the radiation of the Goddess she served gilded her all over. Her flesh seemed kneaded with sunlight. She stood up, a living flame, in the midst of the splendors of the morning. And her holy blessing fell upon the young man as light falls upon spring trees.

Yamato, having bowed to the imperial priestess and having expressed his gratitude to her, returned to the Mikado's palace. He took with him the comfort accorded by the nun's holy blessing.

The same day, Yamato departed for the island of Kiushiu. The faithful and tender Ototachibana went with him. As mild as moonlight through bamboos, she was Yamato's luminous consolation during lassitudes and perils.

The task of administrator of imperial justice was heavy. Kumaso and Takeru took refuge behind a rampart in the mountains. The route was cut by torrents and obstructed by rocks and tree-trunks that the winds had felled. Neither the courage nor the endurance of the troops could triumph over obstacles beyond their strength, and Yamato, seeing that the land itself was their enemy, meditated. He had only one weapon against nature and men: cunning.

Yamato remembered then the words of the imperial priestess, is father's sister: "Do not forget that every samurai must combine with the valor of a man the patience and subtlety of a woman."

Laughing at the project that he had just conceived, Yamato went into Ototachibana's tent.

The nun's kimono was shining like magically woven radiance. Warm gemstones sparkled over the weft of light.

Still laughing at his unknown project, Yamato, aided by the tender and faithful Ototachibana, put on the kimono of the imperial priestess; and the kimono emitted such a bright light that it glorified the flat masculine face of Yamato and transfigured it with an almost feminine splendor. Thus enveloped by an illusion of beauty and grace, Yamato, coiffed in the manner of women, quit his young wife and went on his own to the enemy's lair.

Toward the end of the day, the two rebel brothers were reposing in the shadow of their tent. They were talking about the second son of the Mikado, renowned for his bravery and his wisdom, who had just battled with them all the way to their fortress of mountains and rocks.

While they were talking they saw a woman advancing, surging from the shadow, a woman as radiant as a blossom of sunlight. Her features seemed vague through blinding flames.

Dazzled by the sudden illumination, they greeted the stranger, and both rejoiced in her coming, for they had not seen the delicate face or slender body of a woman for many days. Kumaso and Takeru, marveling, asked the unknown woman her name.

"I'm a seller of sake," replied her voice, which was too harsh and too deep. "My smile gives feasts a sharper savor. Hold out your cups, O warriors, and I will pour you amour, with strength and courage."

Kumaso and Takeru held out their empty cups to the stranger. She poured them a sake in which reflections of topaz and gold sparkled. Avidly, the two brothers drank by turns. A subtle warmth slid into their veins. It was like a softening fever running through their blood, and their souls were filled with a deceptive languor.

Suddenly, there was a flash of steel. The woman, stripped of her illusory beauty, stood up, menacing. The dagger shone and reddened. Kumaso, the elder of the two brothers and the more redoubtable, fell dead at Yamato's feet. The second brother, surprised through intoxication, attempted in vain to flee. An implacable hand gripped him by the throat. He gasped in a spasm of agony.

Straightening up in a weakening effort, the dying man seized the hand that had just struck him.

"Won't you suspend your vengeance for a moment?" he sighed.

"Why should I suspend it even for an instant?" interrogated the avenger.

"Before dying, I want to know the name of the man who has triumphed over me," replied the dying man.

And the victor said to the vanquished: "I am the second son of the Mikado, my father's administrator of justice and the avenger of your victims. I am the young Yamato."

"I will give you another name as I die," gasped the expiring Takeru. "I name you Yamato Take, in memory of your first victory. I bequeath you that name with pride, for you are the most valorous samurai in the realm."

And having said that, he died.

The young hero returned to his father's court. The entire people saluted him with splendid rejoicing. Ototachibana, tender and faithful, reflected the joy of the crowds and the triumph of her husband. She was beautiful and utterly delighted on the other's behalf. And because she was tender and faithful, her husband Yamato did not love her.

In that epoch, the province of Idzumo was ravaged by a third brother of the two brigands, Idzumo Takeru. Yamato, remembering that cunning is more powerful than force, took another name than his own and went to the devastated province.

Under his borrowed name he became the guest of the redoubtable Takeru, and, having slid into his enemy's favor, Yamato carved and fashioned a wooden saber. Then he invited the redoubtable Takeru to an open-air feast on the bank of the river Hinokawa

The sun was burning implacably in an implacable sky. Yamato, turning to his guests, proposed that they bathe in the limpid water.

Overwhelmed by the heat of the day, they all consented joyfully. And having undressed, Yamato succeeded in exchanging his wooden saber for Takeru's saber without anyone noticing.

Having bathed in the river the guests put on their kimonos again. As if in play, Yamato proposed a sword fight to the redoubtable Takeru.

Unaware of the cunning exchange, and confident in his strength, Takeru accepted the challenge, but it was in vain that he tried to unsheathe his saber. While he persisted in futile efforts, Yamato, brandishing his adversary's saber, ran the redoubtable Takeru through.

When he returned to his father, the people received him with a redoubled delight. The Mikado felt his paternal love increasing in regard to the hero. Ototachibana, tender and faithful, admired him in silence, but because she was tender and faithful, Yamato did not love her.

In that distant time, the Japanese, a wandering people newly disembarked in the radiant island, were completing the subjugating of the original inhabitants, named the Ainu, and had already driven them back into the eastern provinces. While the rejoicing of the people saluted Yamato's second victory, a great rebellion burst forth among the vanquished Ainu, "the Eastern barbarians," as the Japanese called them, disdainfully.

For a third time, Yamato Take took command of his father's troops.

Before departing for the accomplishment of that arduous task, Yamato made a second pilgrimage to the temple of Ise, whose priestess was the Mikado's own sister.

As before, the nun came to meet him, as splendid as the Goddess she served. A living flame among flames, she was radiant with an ardent beauty. Yamato told her the story of his adventures. He told the priestess, with a tender gratitude, how the present of the kimono had inspired him with the project to which he owed his first victory, and he implored the nun's benediction.

Having granted him her holy benediction, she went back into the temple of the Goddess of the Sun. She reappeared carrying the saber Murakumo, which had never quit the altar of Amaterasu. That venerable saber was the symbol of the power and courage of the imperial race. The strength of Japan was attached to the possession of the heroic sword.

Before that new present, magnificent and sacred, Yamato felt a great humility curb his head. In a tremulous voice he expressed his gratitude to the imperial priestess, and the imperial priestess, smiling like the Goddess she served, also gave the young hero a sack fashioned by the pious hands of bonzesses, filled with sharp stones from which sparks sprang.

The radiance was concentrated on the face of the priestess, and surrounded her with a flamboyant aureole. Standing in the sunlight, she predicted a further triumph for Yamato.

At the head of his troops, Yamato traversed Owari and Suruga. The chief of the rebel Ainu made propositions of peace to the Mikado's son and welcomed him sumptuously.

Yamato concluded an amicable pact with the chief of the Ainu, and the hospitable chief invited the Mikado's son to a sumptuous hunt.

Yamato, who liked hunting almost as much as war, consented gladly. Bolder than the other guests, he drew away from them in the ardor of the pursuit, and went astray in a plain of long grass.

The long grass undulated like waves in the breeze. It piled up and calmed down by turns. Suddenly, blue smoke rolled toward Yamato, who was amazed at first and then incredulous and revolted. In order to cause his death, his perfidious adversary had set fire to the long grass. The entire plain was ablaze.

Seeing that he was close to an abominable death, Yamato evoked the radiant face of the priestess. Again he heard the prophecy that assured him of victory, and, determined not to die without a struggle and an effort, he brandished the saber Murakumo, of which the nun had made him a present. With a broad gesture he used the saber like a scythe and cut down all the surrounding grass. Opening thereafter the sack that the imperial priestess had given him, Yamato, rubbing the sharp stones against one another, lit a small fire . . . and the small fire ran to encounter the immense fire; it is thus that hunters fight flame with flame.

Having contrived a clear area by means of the saber and the protective fire, Yamato waited.

The flames, stopping in front of the cleared area, did not cross that barrier. They recoiled on themselves. A wind that suddenly blew up rejected them to the other side of the plain, and, driven by the unexpected wind, they fell upon the perfidious chief and his escort, who were burned in the flamboyant whirlwind.

Having been saved by his ingenious idea and the force of the wind, Yamato rendered thanks to Amterasu, the Goddess of the Sun, for she reigns over the winds and the tides, and all the elements are submissive to her. He divined that she alone had ordered the winds to turn against the Ainu chief and bury him under the flames that he had lit in order to make his confident guest perish.

Having rendered thanks to the omnipotent Amaterasu, Yamato raised the saber Murakumo toward her and gave it the name Kusa-naghi-no-Surughi, the saber that scythes grass. To the open space where he had taken refuge, Yamato gave the name Yaidzu.

Ototachibana followed her husband through the lassitude and perils. Gently, she enveloped him with a warm tenderness. But the hero, infatuated with combats and adventures, no longer thought about the woman who loved him with such a patient fervor. He had a free soul similar to great birds of prey, avid for space and carnage.

Lassitude had faded Ototachibana's grace, and perils had hollowed out precocious wrinkles in her face. Because she was less splendid for having loved him too patiently and too magnanimously, her spouse separated from her.

The hazards of a new campaign forced Yamato to traverse Idzu in order to reach Oari. There, in a pagoda ornamented with bizarre bell-towers and surrounded with beautiful attentive pines, reigned Princess Miyadzu. She was as splendid as flowers in the rain, for she had known neither lassitude nor perils; and above all, she was ignorant of amour.

The hero submitted, for the first time to the gaze of a woman. Similar in that to other men, he loved a woman who did not love. His charmed hours went by in Miyadzu's gardens, under the beautiful attentive pines. Radiant among the musciennes, she listened to the vehement appeals of the samisen, wedded to the perfidious prayer of the koto. The music attracted, retreated and betrayed by turns. As insinuating as the music itself, and similarly fugitive and perverse, Miyadzu slid eternally through the arms that tried to retain her. Her lover never possessed her soul. Abandonments left him still thirsty, and all the more dolorously infatuated with the woman who did not give herself, and never had.

Ototachibana saw, with anguish, the amour that had never been granted to her lavished foolishly on another; and in the bitterness of her regrets, an obscure joy slid into the depths of her soul, a joy that remained incomprehensible to her: the joy of knowing that the insouciant hero had buckled, like the disdained woman herself, under universal amour.

In spite of the languor of days and the sensuality of nights, Yamato had to depart toward new adventures.

Before quitting the land where he had loved for the first time, however, he wanted to bid a sumptuous and public adieu to Princess Miyadzu.

Scorning the tender Ototachibana, whose sole fault had been not to be able to make herself loved, he commanded her to mingle with the servants, dressed without adornment and stripped of all imperial pomp.

Because she loved her husband with a subservient tenderness, Ototachibana obeyed that cruel order. Dressed without adornment, she placed herself in the last rank, behind the servants. Patiently, she dissimulated the tears that burned her cheeks; for never, amid her long suffering, had she addressed the mildest reproach to her husband.

Stripped of all imperial pomp, she saw Miyadzu approach among the musiciennes. Seeing her rival so gloriously beautiful, the humble amorous woman understood and kept quiet. Before such beauty, only submission and silence were possible.

Placed in the last rank of the servants, Ototachibana heard the oath that the young hero made to Mitadzu to love her with an inexhaustible amour and to make her, when he returned, his unique and legitimate wife.

Having made, in the name of Amaterasu herself, the oath to take Miyadzu as his unique and legitimate wife, Yamato turned round. He saw the eyes of the faithful Ototachibana, the disdained wife, fixed on his own and filled with an inexpressible sadness and astonishment. But no remorse pricked the lover's heart.

After quitting the splendid princess with regret, he took the road to Idzu, a city situated by the sea. When they reached the port of Idzu, the samurai serving Yamato searched in vain for junks numerous enough to transport them as far as the shore of Kadzusa.

While he tried to gather a sufficient number of boats to cross the strait, Yamato, standing on the shore, sensed impatience consuming him, for the dear and deceptive image of Miyadzu was shining before his eyes. In his amorous impatience, he mocked the samurai engaged in the vain search bitterly.

"Why," he jeered, "so much effort and so much worry to traverse a little stream? This trickle of water truly doesn't merit the name of sea."

Trembling, Ototachibana listened to that blasphemy. She knew that Rin Jin, the Dragon to whom Benten has confided the guard of the sea, the dragon that governs the waves, is also vigilant and implacable. And the tender Ototachibana feared that Rin Jin might have heard the impatient hero's sacrilegious words.

Finally, the ships were chartered. With a sigh of contentment, Yamato embarked, surrounded by samurai.

But as the army was sailing in the middle of the strait, a contrary wind blew up. The fuming waves bounded around the fleet. They collided and tore one another apart in feverish anger. Impetuously, they launched the assault, and the boats were tossed around, more derisory than porcelain cups, at the whim of the wind and the eddies. Death enveloped the samurai, who felt viscous bonds tightening around them.

When hope had disappeared from the depths of pupils obstinately fixed on imminent death, Ototachibana stood up and spoke in these terms to the sea:

"Only the jeers of my husband have unleashed your pitiless wrath O sea, I know that. When I heard his blasphemy I was chilled by fear and thinking about your sure vengeance. But if the sacrifice of a consenting victim can appease your just anger, accept my life, freely offered in exchange for that of my husband."

Having implored the angry sea in those terms, Ototachibana, a consenting victim, plunged into the waves.

Immediately, the waves calmed down. The sea had accepted the amorous immolation. The tender and faithful Ototachibana had given her life in exchange for that of her husband. For, in spite of his disdain and coldness, Yamato alone had possessed the fervor of his wife.

Before the beauty of that heroic death, the son of the Mikado sobbed his futile remorse. For the first time, he sensed how unworthy his fickle heart was of that unshakable heart. For the first time, he recognized himself as disloyal and cowardly, in spite of his splendid exploits and his boldness in perils.

But the sun was shining on the sea again. The waves sparkled with dancing reflections. The waters were laughing in happy indolence. And Yamato, rendered to ardent and luminous life, no matter how sincere his dolor might have been, sailed on toward unknown desires.

Ototachibana, however, did not die in vain, for lovers learned of her beautiful death from the mouth of poets.

Let Us Go All the Way to the Sea

NADESHIKO,[1] as sad as the dusk that was falling, reread a scroll on which characters were delicately traced with a brush on a piece of silk. Darkness entered through the windows. Nadeshiko respired without disturbance the faint odor of wisteria. Her dreams went, with a desolate tenderness, toward her preferred friend, Tsuyu-no-inochi.[2]

She repented of having made the creature that she loved suffer, and she glimpsed obscurely, in her little Japanese soul, the cruel truth that we always cause the being dearest to us to suffer. Consciously or unconsciously, we are the torturers of the beloved individual.

Nadeshiko divined other verities just as dolorous as that one. Melancholy, she listened to the sighs of the evening breeze in the bamboos.

Tsuyu-no-inochi is sad, by my fault, she reflected, *and yet I love her passionately*.

---

1 Author: "Pink" [the flower]. Yamato Nadeshiko is the Japanese name for *Dianthus superbus*, the Large Pink, the term also being used to signify unadorned female beauty.

2 Author: "Dewdrop." The literal meaning of the phrase is "the life of dew." According to Lafcadio Hearn, it is usually used metaphorically to refer to the evanescence of the human lifespan.

She reread the poem that her friend, after having composed it for her, had traced with a brush:

> I am sad for loving you,
> And the song of the cuckoo
> Makes me shed tears.
>
> It saddens me
> To see the camellias
> Swaying in the wind.
>
> It saddens me
> To see the bamboos
> Florid with fireflies,
> And my existence resembles
> The obscure dream of a long night,
>
> I am so sad
> That I would like to repose
> Under the shade of grass.

Nadeshiko's oblique eyes darkened . . .
I have made the woman I love suffer, she thought, *and I am not happy myself.*
She evoked the entire ardent story.
Hina[1] alone, as thin and puerile as her gracious name, was dominant in the soul of Nadeshiko when she entered the temple of Guanyin. She came to implore the one whose gaze floats above the sound of prayers.

---

1 Author: "Doll." Hinamatsuri is an annual Japanese festival involving elaborate displays of ornamental dolls.

Tsuyu-no-inochi was kneeling, pious and dreaming. She was a flower of felicity, a song of water and the cuckoo. She was as splendid as golden Guanyin.

Thoughtfully, Nadeshiko considered her. When they came out of the temple, the eyes of the two young women met. And, as if obedient to an intimate order, the unknown woman held out to Nadeshiko the chrysanthemums that she had bought to the altar of Guanyin.

Every day, Nadeshiko returned to the temple of Guanyin in order to contemplate the young devotee. One morning, she was sweetly moved to receive a bunch of wild chrysanthemums. A few words were traced by a brush on the thin rice paper that enveloped the gift:

The dreams of spring are brief,
Dolor wears the mask of joy,
And everything that flowers must perish.

Nadeshiko sensed a vast sadness through those words. She loved the unknown woman for her melancholy.

And since that moment, the dawn of tenderness had risen in the two souls. But an anguish oppressed Nadeshiko. Her new friend implored, almost demanded, the rupture with Hina, as thin and puerile as her gracious name.

How could she find the strength to make Hina suffer, that overly delicate and overly frail being? Hina asked so little of her—the alms of a rare caress, the humblest place in her shadow. How could she withdraw that meager happiness and plunge her into the night of a complete absence?

Nadeshiko was indecisive. Like all tender souls, she had the cult of the past. The amour of old was dear to her for being distant. And yet, was it not necessary to come toward Tsuyu-no-inochi, the heart pure of any other image than her own?

Her meditation was suspended. A little hand parted the partition and Hina appeared, thin and puerile.

"Nadeshiko," she said—and dolor rendered her voice more harmonious—"I have come to bid you a long farewell. You no longer love me. You love the woman who sent you the chrysanthemums. With what an expression of regret you watched them shed all their petals! And I am, for you, more vain and forgotten than fireflies whose light is extinct. Adieu, you who were as sweet to me as the smile of Guanyin herself!"

And, in the flutter of her blue kimono, on which, magically embroidered, was the pallor of moonlight on snow, Hina disappeared.

The former amour elevated its tenacious plaint in Nadeshiko. The past made her forget the present. As a sign of mourning, she dressed in funereal white. During long nights she wept, while listening to the melancholy song of the cicada.

Mortally saddened by the sadness of her companion, Tsuyu-no-inochi went to consult the magician Kusa-Hibari, for the magician was celebrated throughout Japan for his knowledge of things present and to come.

Not without apprehension, Tsuyu-no-inochi entered Kusa-Hibari's dwelling.

It was an almost royal dwelling. Unreal pagodas and lakes were silvery on the screens. Pink jade ornaments cast auroral gleams. All the splendors of art dazzled the eyes. They translated nobly the patience of infinite labor, the strength and the faith of infinite amour.

And among that magnificence crouched a man clad in miserable rags. He lived poorly in the midst of all that sumptuousness. He seemed the living reproach of all that precious beauty.

"Why do you live so miserably in the midst of your wealth?" the young woman asked, astonished and curious.

"I know the manner of joys and riches while retaining the virtues of the poor," the magician replied. "Thus I am both venerated by men and cherished by the Gods."

When Tsuyu-no-inochi had revealed to the magician the cause of her suffering he smiled with a sad indulgence.

"Neither felicity nor dolor can be durable," he said. "Only ennui and peace are unchanging. Neither peace nor ennui perish beneath their immutable wrinkles. Their old age is immortal. But joy lasts longer than dolor. Of all ephemeral things, dolor is the most fleeting and the briefest. It reenters oblivion as the river into the sea."

He stopped before repeating, very slowly: "As the river into the sea."

He went on: "The sea is the great symbol. It is the commencement and the end of the world. It is the infinity in which dolors are lost. It is life and death. It harbors landscapes in its depths more beautiful that terrestrial landscapes. Its horizons are unlimited. It possesses abysms and stars. The sea is the commencement and the end of the world. Being uncertain and unchanging, it is eternal."

Tsuyu-no-inochi did not understand those words. And because she did not understand them, she disdained them.

She went back to the fragile dwelling of screens and paper partitions. Nadeshiko was asleep, lying on cushions.

She was asleep . . . Two tears filtered slowly between her gilded eyelids, running along her cheeks.

Tsuyu-no-inochi contemplated her, so near and so distant, and above all mysterious. Tsuyu-no-inochi thought gravely about the enigma of sleep, as incomprehensible and as fatal as the enigma of death. She knew that those who sleep allow their souls to voyage in strange regions. She knew that, during their absence from the body, the souls of sleepers can encounter evil thoughts that become harmful to them, and sometimes mortal. And Tsuyu-no-inochi trembled in thinking about all the perils that lie in wait for the vagabond soul of a sleeper.

Nadeshiko woke up, as beautiful under her tears as a chrysanthemum under the dew. And Nadeshiko said to her friend: "If you loved me, Tsuyu-no-inochi, you would go with me, in order to search with me for the trace of the vanished fugitive. I love you, but I cannot forget that I once loved Hina. I loved Hina, the little doll, for her fragility and her plaintive softness. And I am sad knowing that she is wandering and afflicted. Even in my joy, I am sad for the little absentee. For one never abolishes what one loved. One always keeps, in the darkness of the heart, the memory of what was once poignant joy and sweet dolor. Memories are the only Gods that never break."

She stopped, her eyes in Tsuyu-no-inochi's eyes.

"I cannot forget, dearest of all. I do not know the cruel art of becoming a stranger and hostile to my past. It flows obscurely in the circulation of my veins. It sleeps in the depth of my slumber. It resuscitates with my dawns. I cherish it for being as impalpable as the future. I cannot forget, in the joys of the present, the anguish of the past."

Tsuyu-no-inochi leaned, dolorously, over the dolorous soul of her friend. And they both shared the search for the wandering, vanished Hina.

In vain they traversed forests, mountains and torrents, the mist and the rainbows of which caused them to marvel by their immaterial beauty.

In vain they traversed cities and villages. Nadeshiko finally sat down under a bamboo and wept.

Tsuyu-no-inochi recalled the strange words of the magician. She said to Nadeshiko: "Let us go as far as the shores of the sea."

They both went toward the shores of Ejima. The moonlight blanched the strand, and the nocturnal waves were as radiant as the sky intoxicated by stars. The night reposed, simultaneously voluptuous and serene. It was collecting itself in the calm strength of felicity.

Seashells glittered magically in the moonlight. Their nacre seemed a more fluid iridescence. They seemed rare and more delicate. Chidori[1] were no longer fluttering. The sea was in love with silence.

Suddenly, Nadeshiko uttered an exclamation of ecstasy and amazement; for, mingled with the currents and eddies, Hina was undulating at the whim of the changing breezes, an alga among algae, a wave moving among the waves . . .

Nadeshiko put into her appeal to the Lover of past hours all the regret and all the memory of her tenacious soul. And Hina, obedient to that imperious evocation of what was, allowed herself to be drawn by the tide toward her companion of old . . .

---

1 Author: "Little birds that fly over beaches." Literally, "many birds," it usually refers to plovers.

The One was who Hina, the little doll, undulated, an alga among algae . . .

She responded to Nadeshiko's astonishment: "Benten has smiled upon me, Benten, the Goddess of the sea, in whom humans admire beauty and music, Benten, the sovereign of servants and dragons. Seeing my distress, she smiled upon me. For, being amour, she is as compassionate as she is perfidious.

"Benten, who deigned to lower her gaze as far as me, took pity on my human dolor. She granted me the mercy of another existence under a new aspect. And, uniting me with herself, she made me an eddy of the sea, a wave among waves. My fluid body is like the fugitive substance of the water; that is why she named me Konami."[1]

By the light of the indecisive moon, Nadeshiko saw her past vanish, a frisson of the waves in the glimmer of starlight . . .

The two Lovers, Tsuyu-no-inochi and Nadeshiko, being, like most mortals, unskillful in separating dream from reality, believed that, thanks to compassionate Benten, Hina had become a wave among the waves of the sea. They believed that Benten, the Goddess propitious to amours had united Hina with herself, in the depths of the waters . . .

And in the immense ignorance in which we are all groping with an equal uncertainty, who would dare to affirm that the two Lovers perceived the truth clearly, or whether they were the dupes of a chimera?

---

1 Author: "Little wave."

The Stranger in the Mirror

O KOYO was born amorous. But as no desired being had yet crossed her path, she fell in love with her reflection in the mirror of polished silver.

O Koyo was not rich in memories. Only a few happy days shone in her recollections. There was the Festival of the Dolls that happened every year. Every year, friends of her father and mother came to bring her, in great pomp, kimonos, lacquer boxes and fans for her dolls. Sitting solemnly on silk cushions, the dolls contemplated the visitors and their offerings with an immutable gaze. There was also the day when she had put an obi round her waist for the first time as a sign of her passage from puerility to adolescence.

When the little girl had attained the age of seven months, her mother died. In her last hour she had bequeathed her silver mirror to her.

"The soul of a samurai is like a sword, and the soul of a woman is like a mirror," says the ancient proverb.

The dead woman's mirror was strangely bright. Everything was reflected there in beauty. It was simultaneously illusory and veridical. O Koyo contemplated her oblique eyes under amber pupils therein, ardently. Sometimes, she believed that she saw a stranger smiling at her. Her own gaze penetrated her with a singular disturbance. In contemplating herself she was smitten with another, a stranger, an unknown person. Having placed her lips on the unreal face, so close to her real face, she wept bitterly at only loving herself while desiring an unknown person, a stranger.

The years went by thus, both similar and alike; as in a pine forest, one tree is different from another, but all of them resemble it. O Koyo fell ill with a mysterious languor. She felt that she was dying very gently, almost amorously. She rejoiced in becoming weaker every day, more distant from the earth, closer to being united with her dreams.

But that increasing weakness alarmed the virgin's father. Divining that only the scant appetite she had for living was causing the young woman to languish, he wanted to reattach her to existence by the bonds of carnal affection. A husband and children would retain her on earth, he thought. But he attempted in vain to convince her of the amorous mystique. In vain he brought before her the most highly reputed young men in the region. O Koyo was scornful of their faces and their rude voices, which collided with the idleness of her dream. All of them she disdained, all of them she sent away with a firm refusal.

The determination of the old father exasperated her. From threats he passed on to violence, and the desolate O Koyo, heartbroken and weeping like someone forsaken, was obliged to serve the nuptial tea in porcelain cups. The husband was a young man who resembled all the other young men. O Koyo turned her eyes away from his face, which was too different from her dream. She hated him for his masculine ugliness.

After the anguished wait came the horror of the wedding night. Darkness enveloped everything with its merciful veil. Frightened and hostile, O Koyo had to abandon her grimly folded little body to the will of the husband . . .

But instead of the brutal embrace, instead of the dolorous bruising, there was the brush of a light caress. There was the kiss of lips like hers, freshly tenacious lips. There was the contact of a body as smooth and soft as her own body. There was the tremor of anxious breasts against her own breasts.

O Koyo delivered herself entirely to the incomprehensible ecstasy. She yielded herself, simultaneously feverish and appeased. It seemed to her that her young blood was humming like an incomprehensible music. She died, like a chord, and was reborn, as a song is reborn, with ardor. She had never felt alive with so much youth.

The night went by like a flood of obscure flames carried through space. O Koyo, divinely weary, went to sleep before dawn. Divinely weary, she became somnolent in the arms of her weary companion.

Benten, the Goddess compassionate to the amorous, appeared to O Koyo, sleeping in the arms of her companion. Benten was sparkling in all her glaucous scales, for she was half woman and half dragon. Seashells decorated her hair, the color of algae. And Benten said to the wonderstruck O Koyo:

"See, I am the Goddess compassionate to lovers and the protectress of those whom the chimera torments. Seeing you smitten with your dream reflected in the mirror, I resolved to incarnate for you the most ardent of your dreams. In order to please you I metamorphosed the male who had imposed his laws upon you into a companion as beautiful as yourself, and such, in sum, as you had seen, loved and desired yourself in the mirror. You shall know neither the profanation nor the pollution of virile desire, for your fortunate lot is passionate feminine tenderness."

And Benten, inclining toward the sleeper, also said: "Ornament my altar with the mirror that was once so dear to you, for I have granted to you what you loved in your reflection: the other, the unknown person, the stranger who has become for you the companion, the lover and the friend . . ."

Benten disappeared. Dawn had broken, the dawn of a night of amour. O Koyo, waking up in the arms of the beloved, saw her long smile poised languidly over her.

A PARTIAL LIST OF SNUGGLY BOOKS

LÉON BLOY *The Tarantulas' Parlor and Other Unkind Tales*

S. HENRY BERTHOUD *Misanthropic Tales*

JAMES CHAMPAGNE *Harlem Smoke*

FÉLICIEN CHAMPSAUR *The Latin Orgy*

FÉLICIEN CHAMPSAUR
The Emerald Princess and Other Decadent Fantasies

BRENDAN CONNELL *Clark*

BRENDAN CONNELL *Unofficial History of Pi Wei*

ADOLFO COUVE *When I Think of My Missing Head*

QUENTIN S. CRISP *Aiaigasa*

QUENTIN S. CRISP *Graves*

QUENTIN S. CRISP *Rule Dementia!*

LADY DILKE *The Outcast Spirit and Other Stories*

CATHERINE DOUSTEYSSIER-KHOZE *The Beauty of the Death Cap*

BERIT ELLINGSEN *Now We Can See the Moon*

BERIT ELLINGSEN *Vessel and Solsvart*

EDMOND AND JULES DE GONCOURT *Manette Salomon*

GUIDO GOZZANO *Alcina and Other Stories*

RHYS HUGHES *Cloud Farming in Wales*

J.-K. HUYSMANS *Knapsacks*

COLIN INSOLE *Valerie and Other Stories*

JUSTIN ISIS *Pleasant Tales II*

JUSTIN ISIS (editor) *Marked to Die: A Tribute to Mark Samuels*

JUSTIN ISIS AND DANIEL CORRICK (editors)
Drowning in Beauty: The Neo-Decadent Anthology

VICTOR JOLY *The Unknown Collaborator and Other Legendary Tales*

BERNARD LAZARE *The Mirror of Legends*

BERNARD LAZARE *The Torch-Bearers*

MAURICE LEVEL *The Shadow*

JEAN LORRAIN *Errant Vice*

JEAN LORRAIN *Masks in the Tapestry*

JEAN LORRAIN *Nightmares of an Ether-Drinker*

JEAN LORRAIN *The Soul-Drinker and Other Decadent Fantasies*